Wings:
A Voyage

Wings: A Voyage

A HIMALAYAN LOVE STORY

Ramesh Patel

Translators:
Dipika Kevlani
Shilpa Parmar

PARTRIDGE
A Penguin Random House Company

To order additional copies of this book, contact
Partridge India
000 800 10062 62
orders.india@partridgepublishing.com

www.partridgepublishing.com/india

This Book is dedicated to my Master Osho & my beloved wife Daxa who are the main source of my inspiration.

I am thankful to my staff Hussain Chauhan, Rajesh Panchal, Manoj Patel & Mahesh Mujumdar—without their support I could not have written this book. Because of their innate hold in my business, I could get space to write this novel.

About the Book . . .

In the contemporary times, when the knowledge and education has crossed all the boundaries of language, state, culture and nation as well, translation as a discipline has emerged as the most significant area to facilitate the crossings of these dimensions. It is through translation only that the culture, lifestyle and literature of one region can be known by the readers of other region. So is the attempt of Mr. Ramesh Patel, the author of this novel Pankh who asked us to translate the present novel from Gujarati to English. The given work was a pleasure to both of us.

We have passed through the translation work not only as a project but as thorough readers as well. And on the basis of our reception, we would like to offer a critical glimpse of the book:

The novel deals with the main theme of love. A character called Aakash has been passing through an interesting life journey coming in the contact of family, friendship, college life, nature and society. In the beginning, he has been portrayed as an average human being who wants to live his life at its fullest just like any other average human being. In the beginning, we are informed that he is a great lover of nature. And his very love towards nature leads the interest of the novel showing Aakash's paradoxical life journey which is torn between nature and society. As the novel progresses, reader becomes firm that Aakash no matter how much is confused among society, nature, women, friends, family, job, and career, he is basically a man of nature who has been searching for his 'Raison de etre.' And this reason for his existence is achieved in the attainment of pure love through Kajal in the lap of nature only.

To reach to the final attainment of love, Aakash has to pass through many psychological conflicts. And he becomes able to identify his reason for existence through the sermons of Osho. Meditation performed by him leads him successfully to the attainment of pure love. Thus, the novel is a conflicting journey of Aakash from corporeal to immortal love. And it is not possible to reach to the final stage of immortality unless one has undergone the process of corporeal experience.

The author of this novel has really given an interesting account of Aakash's life journey.

We are thankful to him for giving us an opportunity to restate the whole story through the medium of translation.

—**Dipika Kevlani**
—**Shilpa Parmar**

SANDHYA

1

Sky means (is) sky! The firmament! It is as mystifying and magnanimous as can never so well expressed in any definition. It is void and still full of accomplishment. And sky means Aakash Patel too. The second offspring of Sureshbhai and Sushilaben.

In the majority, only a small number of people signify their names in real sense of the term. The name may be Shantinath but the one may be full of uproaring—the nature, the behavior may comprise of incessant bustle. The name may be prafull but consisting of displease in his appearance and behavior. The one naming Kuber may be begging taking a bowl in his hands. Whatever it may be in others, but, Aakash although could never be or imply the sky, had tremendous affection towards the sky. His fondness for sky was up to the extremity of obsession. Along with the sky, he had deep warmth for nature and its numerous appearances.

Shades of the sky diverge each and every moment. One may love the milky sky of moon night; the other may feel affection for a profound sky of dark moon night full of twinkling stars. One may be keen on the monsoon sky covered with clouds or the running clouds in the sky or may be in love with the sky where disintegrated clouds may be in search for someone. Someone might be the devotee of winter blue sky. Someone may adore the dawny sky of the pre-rising sun with the dim-ray shining of the sun. The other may be devoted to the splendid sky of the setting sun. Someone may be the great fan of seashore sky, and the other may be the beloved of the veiled sky under the mountains. But Aakash had desirability for each and every flash of sky, whether it was of midnight, of dawn, of scorching noon, of torrential rain or of wintry weather. He would love intensifying his eyes into the sky at his leisure. And Aakash was also privileged as neither he nor his family were the inhabitants of metro cities like Delhi, Mumbai, Kolkata or Chennai; otherwise he would have to be discontented witnessing the polluted sky consisting of air and environmental pollution. Perhaps he would not have been gifted to experience the profundity or splendor of the sky.

Aakash used to reside with his family in Kalka populated with 30-40 thousand people, located in the Himalayan valley. And that also in the corner of Ishaan direction, the last house located in small Nisarg Society among the 100 houses. The house number was 33 to which he considered his lucky number. His house was the most forlorn. His society was at the end line of his house. After his house, there was a tall, wired fencing society's compound wall followed by the sloppy down hills of Himalayas.

Even builder may have lost the hope for the trade of this end house. But it was Sureshbhai, Aakash's father who had gone on his own free will to acquire this residence. The nature devotee Sureshbhai expressed his desire to purchase that domicile facing a trivial disagreement from Sushilaben, Aakash's mother. Considering the customer crazy and rare to get again, the builder inflicted that house upon Sureshbhai and this is how he derived a gorgeous dwelling.

Sureshbhai, Aakash's father, was an officer in the nationalized bank. He was a nature follower. Perhaps this nature affection was in heredity to Aakash from his father. Sushilaben, Aakash's mother was a housemaker. Though she didn't do any job but was active in all the activities. She was fond of being involved into social work and therefore was either a member of or an administrator of city's women cell, bhajan cell, societal women cell, women development organization, women awareness organization etc. and was in the role of a leader at occasional moments. Aakash's elder sister Dhara was four years older than him whose marriage was held just last year, soon in the vacation just after her B.com being over. And she had got settled in Chandigarh with her husband.

It was a small residence with a sitting surface, a kind of society. There were two bedrooms, a hall and a kitchen on the ground floor. There were narrow stairs outside the house to go on the terrace. The benefit of the residence being at the end was that it was an autonomous one. When Aakash was in 10th standard, his father had facilitated him with an independent room on the first floor, to avail him with a reading convenience for 12th science. It was the only room whether a study room or a bedroom. There was a bath-toilet at the outskirts of the room attached to it. Wash basin was situated between the end (entrance) of the room and the lavatory over which there was a small mirror attached with.

Aakash had derived his most preferred situation. To sit on a chair in the open terrace, reading and if exhausted watching the sky, enjoying the mounts of Himalaya, watching the nurtured trees of the Himalayan hills, listening to the birds' chirping, observing the pebbles jumbling down and getting placed randomly. He witnessed the natural prospects daily but would never get satiated for its being full of mystery—this was his real nature worship.

Just today, the exams of 12th science had been over. This was the first night of leisure after the strong hard work of two years. As the papers were good, therefore also there was too much of relaxation. It was an effort to convert the two years' hard work into amusing moments as quickly as possible. And therefore, Aakash was laying asleep half naked with Barmuda on the double bed. The wind was cold flowing inside the open window in the moon night; hence Aakash had switched off the ceiling fan during late night.

There was a complete silence all around, with the only sounds of crickets. It was 2–3 at night. Aakash was sleeping, his lashes being down. Still from the movements of the lashes, it seemed that a dream was going on inside Aakash.

6-7 years old Aakash has been playing in his terrace. The stones were put on the two sides of the bed sheet at the parapet of terrace. The other two sides of the bed sheet were tied with two supports distancing from a parapet so that there could be a so called shadow under the bed sheet. It was midday of scorching noon. The sun was blistering at its fullest. There was a complete stillness in the society. Aakash, sitting under the shadow of the bed sheet, was reading his favourite cartoon book of Tom and Jerry, enjoying the sky. All of a sudden, a noise of something falling down, of getting tumbled caught the attention. He wondered. Raising his face from the book, he saw that a bird had slipped down, was injured at a distance. He felt amazed glancing at the bird. He had never witnessed such a bird ever before. It was a bird with golden appearance, violet wings and red beak resembling a sparrow. It appeared totally unusual from others. Aakash thought: 'It is a small bird, the poor one, may have got departed from his parents and wandering into the sky here and there. Considering it an unknown one, any native bird may have attacked over it and so is laid here getting injured.'

Aakash went to it running and took it into his lap soon. Shifting its wings, he saw that it was little wounded and was bleeding. He brought it in the shadow and went downstairs into the house swiftly, took cotton, bandage and soframicine tube along with edible seeds, biscuits in the tray and a little water in the bowl. Coming upstairs, he sat beside the bird, took it into his lap, slowly lifted its wing and cleaned the wound with cotton. He thought of rubbing tube on the cotton and tying bandage then after. Since it appeared impossible, he left the idea. Slowly he put down the bird on the floor so that it can munch grain seeds, biscuit and water. But a bird which had done nothing upto now and was in full co-ordination, it gave a strong bite on Aakash's hand. He shouted loudly. It was obvious not to be expected such a retaliation in turn of kind service shown. Still he didn't become angry upon the bird and was compassionate. The bird was constantly looking flipping its small eyes. Aakash slowly offered seeds, biscuit and water to it. He wandered observing the behavior of a bird. As soon as he came out of surprise, he felt a kind of hot liquid running through his body, surpassing under the skin. The body began to turn into red. He got fearful.

His eyes were suddenly opened. He sat in the bed getting awaken. He thought of having watched a dream. He felt scared. Surprisingly, the boiling liquid was still flowing through his skin. The body was converting into red colour even then. Whatever he faced whether it was a dream or a childhood memory! The low memory was flowing out with much clarity now. But the childhood experience . . .

and the burning liquid moving through the skin even now? How come was it possible? And why was it being experienced even then? The hand where that small bird had bitten in the childhood was completely all right. But, all of a sudden, he felt itching at two sides of his waist. He began itching at two sides of his waist with his two hands. And as soon as he continued itching, the size began to increase. The itching enhanced with the growth of the size. It grew upto an extent that it started bleeding with drops of blood at the sides of his waist. He couldn't stop himself after the drops of blood flowing out. After some time, he witnessed feeling something was coming out or growing out from both the sides. Slowly and gradually that growing thing continued coming out in an increase. Aakash felt something was budding up. Two big wings had fully grown sides of the waist. He got anxious and got down from the bed. While getting down, his foot was put on the floor forcibly due to his apprehensiveness. He was lifted higher into an air as a result of a floor jerk on the foot as if there was no effect of gravitation on his body. Once again, he jumped down slowly, this time with a purpose, and he was sprung extremely upper than his leap. It was good that he had switched off the fan because of the cold wind coming inside at late night otherwise his head would have collided in the fan wing for sure. He came out in the open terrace slithering his two legs slowly. Now there was no fear to get smashed in the ceiling. He was filled with wonder, awe, excitement, pleasure and newness to such an extent that he began jumping. And he was raised into an air than his hops. The two grown up wings at the two sides of the waist began extensively fluttering. All of a sudden he was carried into an air, wings broadened and slowly and gradually he began flying in the air.

While flying into the air, he took a long round turn of his society. Small houses, roads and street lights became visible. He flew a bit higher and began strolling in the city. Some vehicle lights were visible on the way from Chandigarh to Shimla. Railway station appeared complete lonesome. City roads and streets were utterly quiet. Flying into the air, he saw his school. He forgot the pre-felt fear now. He started enjoying. He went upto the Himalayan valley which used to be a focus of attention for him. Raising his neck, he saw the sky and stars and he was utterly pleased.

He, now, returned on his terrace after flying for two three hours continuously. He witnessed that his wings began disappearing into his body slowly and gradually. He was experiencing as well as observing this event out of astonishment and blissfulness.

Going inside the house, he laid asleep in his bed. He couldn't sleep due to gladness, eagerness and surprise. But this exhaustion of his exams being over which was too much than his happiness, curiosity and wonder and therefore he slept very fast in no time.

2

The sun heat from the outside window began spreading on the bed of Aakash getting raised from the floor as the Sun went higher. Slipping from the bed and body of Aakash, it began to glide over his face. As the day was increasing, the sun heat was getting utterly blazing. For some time, he didn't care for the heat and ignored it due to his dear sleep. But when it started scorching his skin, he couldn't tolerate and he had to wake up out of his bed.

Aakash stirred his head as an effort to get fresh from his sleep. He viewed the time in the clock attached to the wall. It was 11 in the morning. For a moment he got scared thinking that it was late but later reminded that exams were over now and it was vacation time. Then there is no matter to worry about. If it was an exam time, then his mom also would not have allowed him to sleep so late, and would have waken him up again and again. She would have satiated only after waking him up. Only to allow him to take rest, she would not have asked him to get up. Thinking all these, Aakash began to brush his teeth.

He recalled the last night happening; 6 years old Aakash. To save the weird bird, bird's bite, the hot liquid running through the body and suddenly being 18 years old. The same boiling liquid being experienced inside the skin, itching at two sides of the waist, wings growing out and flying into the air, coming back after an exciting air flight of society, city and Himalayan valley—air voyage! Aakash wondered whether it was a dream or reality! He used to read lots of fantasy books in his childhood. Even after being adolescent, superman, spiderman and Harry porter were his most favourites. But for the past two years, he could not have found any chance to read either a novel or watching a movie or television because of the 12th science fear. And after the exam being over, he had slept in a way as if he was tired for the long two years. Perhaps he would have watched the dream. He got confused. Became puzzled for the solution and started looking here and there with a view to searching the evidences of last night fly. But he couldn't find anything. He remembered that wings had grown up near his waist last night as a result of which he had been able to fly. He thought, "No matter wings were not there but any mark would surely be there". He checked at both the sides of his waist but there were neither the marks of itching nor of wings. He doubted—May be his constant study oriented mind would have taken help of his favourite subject fantasy as a symbol to get relaxation from the awakening nights of his 12th exams, preparation of his exams, continuous busy schedules of his schools and tuitions. Without scratching his mind much and scattering the night recalls, he brushed and took a bath and then got busy in planning the whole holiday of how to make use of it.

Aakash reminded that he had decided to go to Sunil's house today at 12 after the lunch. They had thought of enjoying, playing cricket or go to watch a movie together. Aakash came downstairs getting ready to go outside. His mom had already made the food as she had to go in one of the meetings of women cell. Aakash finished his dinner listening to the routine counsels of his mother. Aakash went out taking the bike, informing her about his getting late that day.

Aakash was just outside the entrance of his society gate, he saw Sandhya Yadav going somewhere from behind. Punjabi tight kurta, loose trousers, and her loose hair half-tied with long clip ... expressively graceful walk. Sandhya was looking sexy. Especially Aakash found her attractive today. Generally Sandhya used to reside in the same society and that is why it was obvious that he might be familiar to her. But the main cause for being more acquainted with her was his sister Dhara. Dhara was one year elder than Sandhya. They had done their B.Com from the same college. Sandhya often used to come to meet Dhara. She used to come to get the information of earlier year, to discuss the matter regarding study or to get the old books. When she came at home, she also used to do Hi-Hello to Aakash but they were in no more deep relation or communication with each other beyond these greets. In all these, Sandhya had lessened her arrival at Aakash's home from when Dhara had got married. Dhara had got married just before a year. Sandhya's father was a bank employee just like Aakash's father.

Today Aakash had a severe desire to communicate with Sandhya. Today, glancing from the back side, Sandhya appeared completely striking. Her height was not much but the stature was fair. Aakash slowed down his bike, fetched it near Sandhya and asked "Where are you going? Means where do you want to go? If I am going that side, I can give a lift to you and drop you down at your place." Aakash spoke with some panic as if she might misinterpret him and get annoyed. Sandhya's eyes became widespread out of a surprise. She continued staring Aakash. As if she was thinking "a boy, who had never crossed the boundary of Hi-Hello, even though she had gone his home often and had voluntarily spoken to him, was approaching her on his own. Miraculous!" But Aakash was completely infatuated as Sandhya stared into his eyes for a few moments with the playful expression of her hair on her cheek. It was fascinating, little awful as well as she may reprimand him. Aakash spoke with a little terror "it was sizzling noon and going on foot! If I could be of some help . . ."

Sandhya laughed with a mischievous expression in her eyes and said, "It is completely alright. Thanks for the offer. And many thanks to plunge me upto the bazaar as well!" "But I have not informed you yet about my going to bazaar and you decided where should I go? And where should I drop you?" Aakash felt relaxed with the warmly behavior of Sandhya. With her naughtiness and light words, he calmed down and derived his mood. "Who else would be helpful to the society girls in such a hot summer if not the boys of this society? And why should I let the benefit of your company go? Uttering these words, Sandhya got settled at the rear seat of Aakash's bike.

Today, Sandhya's dark complexion appeared charming to Aakash. Her hair moving through her cheek looked more treacherous than the knife. What was it—the sensation of leisure or of age!

Actually Aakash was to go at Sunil's house from Chandigarh highway to south but now he had to go to railway station through city. It was to be notably a long route. The childhood friend Sunil would be waiting for him. Aakash himself was punctual about his schedule yet he liked it. He didn't feel sad in making someone wait for him. After Sandhya's sitting at backside, he glanced slightly at his clothes before bringing the bike into gear. Blue Jeans and green t-shirt were alright. He viewed his face and hair in the side-mirror of his bike. He moved his hand on his hair smoothly. He started the bike after getting contented of everything.

Road was good. As it was noon time, the rush was very low. Therefore there was no fear to fall down from the bike. Still Sandhya had pressed his one hand on the shoulder of Aakash as if being frightful. The conversation began on the moving bike. Aakash understood well where she had to go exactly. They had to go in a multi-stored building situated beside hotel lotus. Going near that building, Aakash stopped his bike going under a tree. Sandhya got down from the bike and stood there coming beside Aakash. Perhaps they wanted to speak on a lot of things, wished to communicate but their tongue and mouth seemed small to express the words. They kept quiet for a few moments. Those silent moments gave the impression of hours to Aakash. He felt perturbed. As he could not tolerate the trouble more, he initiated as all the common men do and asked, "Why had she come there?" "I come here up in Mona Beauty Care" uttering this she pointed her finger at the board of Mona Beauty Care attached on the second floor.

"What is the need of it to you as you are already beautiful!" Aakash suddenly spoke out, and hesitated when reminded of covered beauty care apart from the perceptible splendor.

"Thanks for complimenting me as good looking. But I come here to do the classes of how to keep and make one and others beautiful.

"Then you will have to come here daily, don't you? In such a hot summer!"

"Yes ... five days in a week except Monday and Tuesday."

Aakash nodded in affirmation. He wanted to stay, but there was no gossip to continue. As there was no subject, he put his leg on the kick looking into his wrist watch and thinking that she might be getting late in case.

"Today I have reached 10 minutes early due to your bike. I am in no more hurry. If you are in hurry . . ." Sandhya left the sentence half completed.

The prompt attitude of Aakash to reach at any place in time, the remembrance of Sunil's waiting pulsed him inside but Aakash said "No . . . no . . . I am also free. There is a vacation from today. Thus, completely liberated. I was just going to meet one of my friends."

They dispersed after communicating on some irrelevant topics. But in the very first meeting Sandhya was completely privileged upon Aakash.

In their communication, he had known the arrival and departure time of Sandhya. Therefore, initially it was easy for him to find out any excuse to give a lift to her and then to drop her back at her home. As there was no reason of denial, Sandhya also used to accept his offer gladly. No one could know about how did Sandhya's hand which used to be on the shoulder of Aakash in the initial stage reached his thighs. From thighs, it reached at naval one day and it pressed it hard even due to the fear of falling down. A kind of romantic jingling passed through the body of Aakash. His centre of masculinity had been vigorous now. Sandhya would have known about the sexual passion of Aakash if her hand had slipped down a bit lower. Sandhya was three years elder than Aakash. She was his elder sister's friend and yet this happened.

But what could Aakash have done? Actually Sandhya's chitchat, her amorous signs and her coquetries were responsible for such a situation of Aakash. It was not that

Aakash had to hesitate looking at the attitude of Sandhya but entering into his adolescence, Sandhya was the first woman to perturb him in his life.

Aakash could not sleep that night when Sandhya had encircled her hand around his naval and had yelled lightly fetching her mouth near his shoulder as if got frightened. Even after changing the sides here and there, he did not feel to sleep. And finally when he slept, Sandhya emerged in his dream even.

Aakash is driving his motor cycle at a full speed towards the ways of jungle. Sandhya is sitting behind him. It is dusty around them due to the dusty way. Sandhya is saying something in his ears but he is not able to listen to it due to the reverberation of wind and his motorcycle. So he asks her the same matter three to four times. Therefore Sandhya gets annoyed and bites his ear and laughs loudly. Aakash becomes furious at this. Aakash stops his bike and flings her down in the heap of grass lifting her from the shoulders. Sandhya continues laughing even in the heap of grass. Her hair has covered her forehead now. Sandhya's figure looks completely gorgeous. She is dressed like a rural women. A tight blouse which focuses her breast. They look attractive from the cuts of her blouse collar. She has worn a sarong upto the knees.

Aakash's anger is converted into his sexual obsession now. Aakash jumps upon her and showers kisses on her cheek and lips. His chest plays hardly with her breast. His excitement increases even more. He wears her clothes off and enjoys physical pleasure at last. Sandhya's laughter continues during this process too.

Aakash got awaken from his sleep. It is midnight. The next bed is vacant. He had reached to the peak of sexual pleasure in his dream due to the satisfaction of physical playfulness. He was still huffing. He became sweaty and felt guilty as if he had deceived someone.

Suddenly, burning liquid began to move under his skin. The color of his body turned red. He recalled the night when his 12th exam had been over. He was conscious and aware tonight. He observed that it was not a dream seen by him but was a reality. He examined his waist; wings were growing out from there. The weight of his body was getting lessened. He came out in the open terrace from his room. Wings had come out in full bloom. He jumped his leg slightly on the terrace and began flying into the air. He became so excited with this experience that he could not think about where to go. But his wings were guiding him the directions. He went higher and higher. He flew towards Himalaya.

3

Aakash was flying into the air. It was a marvelous occurrence flying into the sky. Aakash had never been into plane. This was his first experience of flying so higher into the air. It was really special as the travellers sitting inside the plane may get higher into the air but are surely deprived of the external feel to enjoy the atmosphere. They may view the upper sights from the window but are not able to sense it. But Aakash was experiencing it. He was feeling it from all the four directions. He was feeling the intoxicating touch of the chilly fascinating breeze, twinkling lamps visible beneath, and the luminary stars able to be seen above. The more he went higher into the air, the more small houses, the less brightened lamps, and the whole Kalka city were engrossed in his entire sight. Slowly and gradually, the city became distant and he flew from the mounts of Himalaya.

Due to the reflection of the street light radiance and polluted environment, there was a gigantic discrepancy between the two skies, one visible from the city, the other from the Himalayas. The sky was in its entirety. The stars were twinkling, it was chock-full and the Milky Way was visible somewhere. Today there was neither no moon night nor full moon night. Perhaps it was eighth day of half lunar fortnight. Therefore, the sky was looking like the enlightening dark blue colour. Looking beneath, the sloppy Himalayan valleys were visible. The distant valleys were appearing soft light while the nearer were appearing of dark grey colour. Wherever he passed through in the moon light, there appeared the upper portion of the crowded tress or somewhere valleys. It was a mesmerizing panorama. Aakash got lost in the vista to such an extent that he couldn't realize of where he was going. There occurred even no single thought in his mind of where he was going. He was dumbstruck. He was getting pulled through an unknown force into some direction. He didn't even doubt who was dragging him away. He could not even think that if this unknown force would drop him down anywhere then how it would be possible for him to return at home. He didn't think that the wings which were carrying him away whether they would bring him home or not. If his mind had been active, he would have shivered out of fear but he was stunned. He was amazed. His mind had also been hushed.

For how long did Aakash fly in the air and on the mounts of Himalaya, he could not recall it. But after sometime, He began to get down slowly and gradually. The speed of flight also began to be slow. The more he got down, the more clearly the sights began to be visible. Various kinds of trees were apparent now. In majority, there were pine trees. Tall cedars. Although the land was sloppy, they were straightly grown on the poised land from 90 degree angle. There were apple, plum and fig trees somewhere. There were rocks either or there were flat, big stones somewhere. In the process of getting down, Aakash began to come down on the tall valley of Himalaya. The landscape became more noticeable while getting down. A few sparkling lamps became visible on the slope of the mountain. He began to go that way and his mind became cognizant a bit now. Coming across the lamp, he thought it might be a small town, population or a small campsite situated on the mount of Himalaya. He went more close to those lamps. The scene became full now. Going near, he witnessed that a small ground was created on the slope due to one rock where 50-60 strength of people were dancing lightening the torch lights. Ten elderly men were enjoying the dance sitting at one side. Nothing appeared like cottage or village looking here and there. Aakash got scared and became uncomfortable. He thought and worried where he had come. Before he thought more, his wings dropped him down near that ground on one side of the slope beside one tree. From the close of the tree, he was able to view the sight clearly. This outlook was magnificent visible at midnight. The chorus sounds were fully enthralling. Lyrics were incomprehensible but it seemed as if it was a love or a prayer song. Aakash himself had learnt music and art but what to say about this music! It was divine. As if it was unworldly. It was as supernatural as was heard in the descriptions of mythical stories of gods. The celestial music notes were in the godly accompaniment of the Himalayas. The serenity of Himalaya, the seclusion of night, the festoon of stars in the sky, the half circular moon, the stillness of the trees, the tranquility of the atmosphere were adding their harmony to this music. In place of artificial light, here it was natural bright flown out from torch lights, the light which was in action with the movement of human beings and was as if vibrating with dance and music.

When Aakash observed this minutely, his surprise reached at its extremity. The men playing on the instruments did not have the instruments possessed by the maestros. They had assembled the wood, stones, bamboos, pieces of metal and plants from the surroundings and made the musical organs out of them and yet the music coming out from these organs was startling. Some organ was made through carving from the trunk of the tree while the other was covered with any fur. Somewhere laid the multi-sized sand vessels over which music was being created through bamboo stick, while somewhere else music was being crafted in the bamboo holes blowing the air into it. Somewhere different sized stones were being smashed creating melody. Lyrics of the song were heart touching although inconceivable. Aakash was so engrossed in the harmonious tranquility of the music that his sense of fear and terror ran away. He even could not become conscious unless was caught by two men through his arms. He could not scrutinize when those two men came, from where did they come and how they caught him.

The music session stopped. All came on one side. Aakash was presented before a head like man. Aakash looked here and there. Men had worn lower garment upto the knee. Rest of the body was naked, while the ladies had wrapped only one sari kind of cloth on their bodies which was covered from the waist upto the knee and was fixed into the waist passing from the back, shoulder and breast. He looked at himself. He had worn only night Bermuda. There was no cloth on his body except it. Bermuda was upto the knee. It was of red and white colour design with the background of blue colour. He hesitated.

There was a sense of strictness and wonder on the face of that head like man who was sitting on the stone. He asked with a sharpened and rough voice

"Who are you? Where have you come from? How have you reached here?"

Aakash understood everything of what that camp's head asked in his own language living in an unknown place situated at the mountainous area of north India. It appeared like a dream. He had never listened to that language. He understood the stern questions of the very first time spoken language. This was not a dream ... but reality. Perhaps, shouts, expressions, eyes, half-pronounced words ... perhaps dread ... That is why Aakash ... understood the sense and meaning of the words.

"I am Aakash", Aakash frightened. Now terror had encircled him extremely.

"Where have you come from?"

"Kalka" realizing that they might not know about Kalka said "from the valley of Himalaya"

"How have you reached here?" The leader asked the last question harshly widening his eyes.

"Through flying" saying this when he looked at his waist, the wings were vanished. He got terrified and thought the answer given may look half and rumorous, therefore said "I had wings grown at my waist and they brought me here."

"Do you consider us foolish?" The head roared. Aakash became frozen observing the fearful face of that man. He horrified. One girl from the dancing troop standing beside came running and begin discussing something with that man. The girl had also worn one cloth on her body like all other women. But her eyes were big and profound. She had made one side parting in her hair and tied it from the bottom. She had a square kind of oval face. Forehead was large. Colour was brown.

Suddenly, there came modesty in the leader's eyes. Moving that girl softly away asked Aakash: "You are making us fool. How can a man fly? And that also the shrewd men like you! Impossible! You do not seem to reply correctly without punishment." He uttered angrily. He indicated something to two men. These natural people used to speak through eyes more compared to words. They used to make use of essential words only when it was impossible to communicate through eyes.

Everybody was quiet except the main leader. There was a sense of wonder in their eyes towards the arrival of an outsider. Their eyes were reflecting contempt. Only that girl standing slightly away from the leader was deprived of any such sense of disrespect or hatred. Aakash was in dilemma. Two men were coming near him with big knives. Now Aakash was ascertained about his death. There was no way which could save him. That girl tried once again uttering "papa" and nodding her head in negation. But the leader like father was out of any influence. Still he looked at the girl and spoke as lovingly as he could:

"Dear, you are still younger. You are not completely aware about the selfishness of this man's world. These men destroy any kind of being invading in this way and that is very clear to them."

"But papa, this is a young guy. He is without any weapon. He seems innocent and appears as if have reached here in his slumber.

"You won't understand. Stay away from this matter. There is a danger for our world to let the outsider go alive in his world."

"Not everyman is dangerous. There is a difference in every man. The way in our world not all are same, some are dangerous too. In the same way, there are also good natured men in outside world. Thorough investigation is needed before any punishment." A loud and powerful voice came from behind Aakash. That girl went there calling him "Baba". That powerful voiced man hugged the girl and came near slowly and gradually. Witnessing him coming, many of them began bowing down courteously to him. The leader also bent down addressing him as "baba".

"Baba" was a tall and stout man. He had long hair upto his neck parting from middle. He had worn a long, brown colour robe gown from neck to legs.

Now there was a sense of delight and assurance on girl's face. She looked at the boy.

Looking into the girl's eyes, Aakash lost all his fear immediately. He became quiet at all. He became free of trembling. He even lost the concern of going back. It was as if something had gone inside him just looking into the eyes of that girl. There was a special magic in her eyes.

'Tell me the truth now, boy.' Baba asked Aakash.

Aakash mentioned everything in detail except the description of his dream. His wings had brought him there. He clarified that he had not come here on his own wish.

'But how will you go back?

'Perhaps . . . through flying, if wings come back, and help me out." Aakash told. "But if any outsider comes here and goes alive, it is not good for our lives. If you would allow him to let live, it would happen for the first time. It would be disastrous! Baba! The leader again repeated.

"Not for the first time, it would happen for the second time. Why? Have you people not accepted me? Have I done any harm to you? Baba laughed saying this. The girl also laughed.

The laughter of that girl was innocent. Her teeth had sense of balance and were beautiful.

"No . . . But you are with us. You are honorable." Father said. "But this boy belongs to the external world. How can he be allowed to go? We are not even acquainted to him. If he aspires to live, he would have to stay here only."

Baba got engrossed in thoughts. That girl came near to Baba and began whispering something in his ears.

Baba uttered: "If he is true and has brought by his existence here, who are we to prevent him? The way existence has brought him here, would carry him away. In my perception, he does not appear to be a spy who has come here to detect something with the help of scientific instruments. Still for the sake of our safety and confirmation, we can have an oath from him that he would never bring anyone here nor would do anything which harms us" Baba told.

"But is that enough?" Father told.

"If not . . . so what? He is even not familiar with the way. If he brings anybody, how would it be possible? He is even not sure about whether he would be able to fly. Baba turned towards him and said, "Is that correct young man?"

"Aakash nodded in affirmation and said, "I promise that I would do nothing which serves the intention to hurt you. I would not bring anybody here. Even I am in confusion how to go home back?

The leader like father and Baba discussed something for some time and decided to let Aakash go.

Father said "We put trust in you. You can go. If your wings bring you back here, you are welcome."

Aakash felt relaxed. He thought internally: "Leave about coming back, how should I go now that is the question. When came, I had wings. But now how to go in the absence of wings? He looked at Baba; he had created faith in Baba's thoughts.

Baba spoke as if had perceived the problem of Aakash "Aakash, you have come here with the desire of existence. Therefore, close your eyes and pray to existence joining hands in the sky. If it aspires, you will be able to go back home through flying.

Aakash did accordingly. He had no option otherwise. To his surprise ... the wings grew out from the waist and he was lifted. He looked with a sense of gratitude towards everybody, he greeted through his hands to Baba especially, to that girl and the father.

Once again the same splendor of Himalayas, beautiful slopes, mountains, stones, forests and rocks. Leaving all these behind, he reached near his city. It had begun to be dawny now. It was the beginning of sweet chirping of birds. There were some movements in the city now. Everybody was busy in their works on the roads, still what if Aakash was seen by someone! Aakash got scared. But it was not in the hands of Aakash to prohibit them looking at him. It was not even possible for him to hide somewhere in the sky. Slowly he began to get down on the terrace of his house near wash basin in his own society. Remembering about the mirror which was attached on wash basin, Aakash had a desire to look his own image with the wings in the mirror. He became stagnant. He continued staring in the mirror. But unless his legs touch the floor-terrace, his reflection was not visible in the mirror. The moment his legs stroke the terrace, his reflection became clear. Slowly wings shrank and disappeared. He calmed down thinking that flying Aakash would not be noticeable to anybody.

Having awakened for the whole night, he felt asleep. Whole night exhaustion covered his body. He slept in the bed. The wonderful experience of the whole night and tiredness became stronger and he slept fast in the bed within no time.

4

Due to the late night awakening, Aakash was awakened by his mother at the time of lunch and was fed reluctantly. After taking lunch, Aakash slept again. His half a through sleep got completed upto 3 in the noon. But he lay in the bed due to the laziness of getting up and scrutinized the last night happening. He hesitated reminding the lovely dream of Sandhya. He reminded everything including that innocent girl, Baba, father, amazing Himalaya, mysterious night, the supernaturally disconnect residence from this world, their natural dance, the mesmerized music. Suddenly he regretted for not being able to know the name of that girl, although the names of Baba and father were not known by him. The eyes of that girl, significant smile had touched his heart. Still that sight was lively in his eyes. His flight, experience of flying, going at unknown places, facing difficulties, coming out of the difficulties through an unknown help and coming back was now not a dream but a real experience to him. He thought whether the wings would be active again? If yes where would they lead him? Into new desirous experiences or in sorrowful occurrence? What do these puzzling wings want him to do? Are they playing a game with him? When unanswered questions were harassing him into his drowsiness, he heard a sound in his house coming from his compound gate.

"Hey Aunt" Surely it was Sandhya's voice. From her sound of foot and voice, it seemed that she was entering inside opening the compound gate and ringing the doorbell of the house. The house door got opened from inside and Aakash heard his mother's voice.

"Hey Sandhya, how long you have seen . . . Please come inside."

The door closed. Certainly Sandhya had come inside. Now the voice coming had stopped. Aakash wondered. Why Sandhya would have come? Aakash got up with curiosity. Getting up, he came near the steps very slowly where there was a ventilator to let the hot air come out from the kitchen, he put his ears there and listened what was being communicated. It was easy to listen to the conversation going on in the kitchen and the attached drawing room with it. There was no door between the kitchen and the living room. There was only an empty partition of the wall and there was a big portion open for coming and going.

"I had a wish to meet all of you for a long time. But keeping Aakash's 12 science exam into consideration, I thought not to disturb you."

"Aakash does exam preparation on his own, I remain always free."

"You also remain mostly busy in women cell . . . therefore I did not come."

"That is true. But it does not mean that I have no time at all. Most of the meetings are in the afternoon. In the morning and evening, I stay at home."

"But at that time you might be involved in Aakash, due to his 12th science."

"Oh not at all . . . but now we have been free even from that. There have been many days after his exam being over."

"Ok. How were the papers?"

"He is saying well."

"And what about Dhara?"

"She is settled in her marital life, enjoying."

"I am happy to know that Dhara is well settled." Looking here and there she asked, "Where is Aakash? Has he been with his friends?"

"Oh no, he is still sleeping up in the room. I hardly woke him up in the noon for lunch. After having it, again slept. He may get up in the evening now."

"Yes . . . might be enjoying the vacation relieving his exam tiredness."

"What about you? When are you going to marry?"

"I am doing the course of beauty parlour. Parents have been searching for a groom. Everyone opine to make me marry this year." Sandhya said while standing, "If I have come here, let me go and meet Aakash to let know how his papers were and what his further plan is."

Aakash thought Sandhya might have stood to come upstairs. So quickly raising, slowly going back in his room, closed the door of his room slowly and slept in the bed as if was fast asleeping.

Aakash was listening to the sound of main door getting opened and stepping on the stairs. He thought Sandhya would knock the door. Instead of knocking, Sandhya came inside thrashing the door. She slowly closed the door coming inside. She went near the bed of Aakash without making noise and carrying her mouth near his ear spoke little loudly "Aakash".

Everyone can act in the time of need. Listening to the voice, Aakash got awakened from sleep as if was startled. Noticing Sandhya beside him, he turned his two hands drowsily round her body.

He pushed her face near him through the weight of his hands and put his lips on hers. Sandhya also responded through her lips without any opposition. Aakash derived some more daring. Carrying and lifting Sandhya from her waist, he placed her in the bed. Sandhya kept smiling lying there. Aakash lay upon her excitingly and started kissing quickly upon her lips, cheek, neck and breast. He recalled the last night dream. Dream was coming true. He got excited to snatch the chance of completing his dream. But at that time, his mom's voice came from downstairs, "Come downstairs Sandhya—Aakash. Tea and snacks is ready." Thank god Sushilaben did not come upstairs to call them otherwise the door was only turned. Aakash left Sandhya. He got down from the bed. Sandhya lied smiling there for some time. Then they came down adjusting their clothes.

"Aunty, it would have been ok if you had not made snacks. I have just had it." Sandhya laughed wittingly and looked at Aakash uttering this. Sushilaben was filtering tea. She asked raising her face.

"Snacks, where did you have it?"

"I had it from home" Sandhya said. Acting is easiest for women. "Leave snacks, someday I would have full-fledged lunch" Sandhya finished her sentence looking at Aakash purposively.

"No problem, have snacks today. You can have lunch any other day." Aakash said.

"Sandhya, Aakash is right. Do it same." Sushilaben uttered. Aakash nodded his head. Sandhya laughed.

There was no matter of laughing yet observing Sandhya in the state of laughing Sushilaben felt strange. She looked at Sandhya with a question mark in her eyes. Sandhya realized her mistake and changed her behavior.

"I would definitely have lunch some day but I am laughing looking Aakash's tactfulness. He has grown up now, hasn't he?"

As Sandhya left, Sushilaben commented "she seems whimsical". To mom Sandhya was whimsical but Aakash found her smart.

Having experienced the last noon happening with Sandhya, Aakash began to feel himself the proprietor of Sandhya. Now he used to drop Sandhya righteously and proudly on his bike. He used to meet her without hesitation. He did not stop only upto dropping her in the class but also used to reach at the finishing time of her class and took her for long rides and in the small temples situated into Himalaya valleys. Sandhya also accompanied him without any complaint. Both used to enjoy the moments of each other's touch, smooth kisses, body play and humour. Aakash was flying into the seventh sky. Aakash lost with Sandhya upto that extent that he also forgot the vacation plan made with his friends after 12 science exam ... for instance, trekking on Himalaya, playing cricket, watching movies, having fun etc. He used to give excuses even to his friends sometime of health, sometime social or sometime of mood and laziness. He only used to accompany a little time to Sunil. As a friend, Sunil had lot of rights on Aakash. Sunil and Aakash studied together in the same school from the very first standard. They had also thought of taking admission into mechanical engineering in the same college. They also read together in 12th science mostly. They were close to each other to that extent that they used to share all their secrets with each other. But this was for the first time that Aakash had not informed Sunil about Sandhya and the mystery of flying into the air. Once Sunil had even reproached him "You are not seen nowadays. You had made so many plans of vacation and you yourself have forgotten them."

"No dear, it is not like that. It does not always happen as per the plan. I feel lazy in the vacation. I am keeping all my tiredness out of 11 and 12." Aakash said.

"I don't believe from your answer that you are speaking true. Are playing any other game all alone?" Aakash could not decide whether Sunil spoke this just for saying or he had really had some idea. But he finished the matter there without stretching more.

One day Aakash dropped Sandhya at "Mona Beauty Care". They talked for some time and as Sandhya turned towards classroom and disappeared, Aakash started his bike and was about to go. At that time, a stout, straight faced, Gogals worn young man, elder than Aakash came on his Bike and stood before Aakash's bike. Adjusting bike on the stand, that young man came before Aakash.

"Hey, what is your name?" asked very strictly.

"Aa . . . Aakash" Aakash got scared.

"Why have you come here?"

"To drop Sandhya"

"How do you know Sandhya?"

"Friend . . . only friend"

"Don't try to serve Sandhya being her close friend. If you are found again with Sandhya, you will have to go to hospital to get served, understand?"

Aakash was terrified. His head was nodded in affirmation. After threatening this way, that young man went near his bike, started it and went away. Aakash had no such experience of dread. He had even no experience of such bulliness. He started perspiring.

Keeping the handkerchief out from his pants' pocket, he wiped his face. For the first time, he was under this situation due to hiding the secret of his love story. He got shivered with the fear of fight. He decided to sacrifice the love and attachment of Sandhya. He firmly made up his mind not to meet Sandhya ever again and went home quietly.

It was a sudden autumn out of spring in the love story of Sandhya and Aakash. Villain had arrived to take love test. Now there were only two ways. Either to be a hero and face the villain as happened in the common movies or to let love go. Aakash chose second option.

Three four days passed but Aakash did not go either to drop Sandhya or to take her back. He spent these days more and more with his friends. He considered it appropriate in terms of safety and psychologically as well. Friends wondered and he felt well. Sunil commented "How come this gratitude upon friends! What is the reason? What is the reason of laziness going away suddenly? Whether this lethargy gone on its own or by someone else? Aakash had no answer, "C'mon guys ... it is nothing like that" he stopped the matter saying this.

One day Mummy had gone Chandigarh to meet Dhara early in the morning. Papa had gone Bank. Aakash was resting in his room after taking the food early whatever was made by her mother. He was reading a story book and his door thrashed. Aakash saw that Sandhya came inside from behind the door. Aakash asked looking at her,

"You? Here? Right now? Have you no class?

"Yes, I have but I bunked it today."

"Why? Any reason?"

"You were not found for the last four five days so I have come to meet you."

"Yes, I was busy. I was with friends. They were complaining that I did not meet them. Therefore ..."

Aakash's words weakened as he spoke. It was clearly visible from his face that he was speaking lie.

"I know you are lying. The matter is different."

"No no, it's nothing. Why would I lie to you?" Aakash enough tried to save himself.

"Because . . . someone has threatened you not to meet me, therefore you don't meet me and lying." Aakash was caught and therefore he had nothing to say anymore. He nodded in affirmation.

"When you have loved, don't be afraid of anyone. Why are you scared of? Don't worry. I have talked to that Bhupat and now he won't harass you." Sandhya said confidently.

Aakash chilled out and felt surprise too. How Sandhya would have been able to convince that bully? He was in the confusion and Sandhya said, "come on now, honour me with hospitality."

"What should I do?"

"Have you forgotten that you had invited me for the lunch someday?" Sandhya looked with the sense of naughtiness and laughter towards Aakash. And Aakash got excited. He lifted Sandhya and placed her in the bed. He pressed his body upon hers. Keeping his lips upon hers, he began to suck the juice of her lips. It began from the lips and went ahead upto the cheek, neck, and breast and further. Clothes were worn out and they returned back after enjoying the corporeal pinnacle. Sandhya kept sitting there in the bed with open and dispersed hair and Aakash adjusted in the chair. After some time, his unconscious mind became active.

"Why did you bunk your class today?"

"Because, I wanted to know the reason of sudden disappearance for the last 5-6 days."

"But if Mummy would have been at home . . ." Aakash glanced at both the bodies turn by turn saying this.

"I knew that your mom is not at home. She has been out of town."

"Really ... how did you know?" Aakash understood Sandhya's game.

"I had seen her going somewhere with a bag in the morning."

"You are so smart. But tell me how did you convince that Bhupat?"

"Have fruits only. There is no need to count the trees." Sandhya said raising her neck and closed the topic.

After sometime she left from Aakash's home.

Aakash felt corporeal fulfillment. In some corner of his heart, he enjoyed it a lot and in some other corner he felt discomfort. He felt discomfort not because he had had bodily pleasure with a girl secretly also not because he had done socially immoral behaviour nor even because he had had the pleasure with her three years elder sister's friend. Aakash did not believe in such social rituals or forcefully imposed traditions but he was continuously sensing in one corner of his heart that he had cheated someone. But this amoral was only possible if he was married or had been in someone's love or if he had made a commitment to remain loyal to somebody. Actually this was for the first time Aakash had been into a corporeal companion with any woman after entering into his adolescence. From when then this deception came? Then why is he getting hurt inside? Aakash could not understand this. He scratched his head. He tried to forget everything into which the pleasure of having bodily relationship became cool; his excitement was lessened but that sense of deceiving someone remained the same.

Aakash suddenly reminded the mounts of Himalaya where he had been once at night. He started sensing the sights of those mounts, that camp, that Baba, father and that innocent girl from his internal eyes. Aakash felt slight itching and romance in his body the moment he recalled them. He understood that this was the indication of wings grow up. He did not want to go in his Bermudas just like that day and therefore before wings grow out, he wore his jeans, T-shirt and was in sport shoes if he needs to walk!

Aakash felt that wings would come out and he would fly. He would fly and reach at the same place. But it was not necessary that his wings would carry him at the same destination. These were the wings given by nature; they may lead at any place on the whole earth. In place of Himalaya, they may lead him into any city or any sea. But Aakash got scared. He was strongly feeling that he would reach at the same place where he had reached last time. What a strong conviction! To which he was also unfamiliar. Aakash wondered.

His imagination of growing the wings out came true. With a slight itching and romance, the wings grew out and Aakash came out from the room in the open terrace and stood there.

5

Wings came out and he again began flying in the same way. Going high into the sky, he saw his Kalka city. He went higher watching the movement of crowd, Railway station, Kalka temple and his school. He slipped near Himalaya. He was fearless as he had no concern that he would be seen by someone flying. This was his first experience of flying in the light of the sun and watching Himalaya from this height. He was excited. He was having a sense from inside that he would reach at the same place where he had been that night. On the other hand, his conscious mind was skeptical thinking whether these wings might not carry him at an unknown and risky place. On that night, he had only flown unaware of the fact that where and into which direction would he reach. Today he was having a faith that he is going at the same place of a camp although was flying towards Himalaya. Today he was realizing his speed. Although the mind being cynical, he had no fear and therefore was enjoying the journey, Himalaya and the sky. Due to the height and swift pace, roaring wind was smashing to the body. The wind was flittering to his hair and clothes although his body was unaffected by it. His eyes were not getting enfolded in the enormous wind. He was able to savor the sight easily.

The sky was totally diverse while flying through Himalayas compared to the visibility of Kalka. It appeared more cavernous, clean, azure, and in huge vicinity. While the sky perceptible from Kalka appeared bluish grey colored due to the environmental dust, smoke, and chemical debris. Its profundity was immeasurable due to the pollution stratum. Its horizon was not clearly visible due to the obstacles coming in between the eyes. The splendor of the sky was lessening as he went near the metro cities due to wreckage and blockage increase into it. The sun heat, although being rigorous compared to the land, was not scorching him as it was breezing cold. Due to the polluted environment layer, it felt too much sweat although the sunlight searing less. Whereas, it was too much sunlight here still appearing pleasing due to the absence of pollution.

Initially when Aakash saw beneath, the Himalaya was arid, including small—big valleys, pebbles and sand. Somewhere trees were spread. Slowly as he began to go higher, the strength of trees increased and Himalaya also became huge having rocks and big mounts. The rivers and streams also enhanced. The more he went higher and deep, the more clearly the beautiful valleys from between the mounts appeared. A river was passing through the valley. It was being wide and rushing when the streams were mingling to the river somewhere. Snowy peaks were appearing at a distance. The number of pine trees increased. With height, the pine trees appeared dark, vivacious, and plump. Slowly, Aakash entered into another hill crossing a huge mountain. Where the mounts seemed close, the slops of Mountains were flatly balanced, and the whole hill was covered with pine trees. It appeared as if a river was passing by where the mountains were meeting deep beneath. Slowly, he got down and the river appeared energetic. There were apple, cherry, fig and plum trees apart from pine. The space between the two mounts emerged more expansive. Going more underneath, a small and flat space on the slope came into view. Aakash began to realize that he had come on the same place that night. But the ground seemed small and different compared to that day. Slowly he got down in the small ground. His wings slowly got vanished into his body. As he saw there, it was Baba sitting on the stone to whom he saw that night.

Seeing Aakash, Baba did not feel any wonder. He said smirking, "Came again, son?"

"I have not come but have been brought. Who brings me here? Why? I don't know. Everything appears mysterious."

"Existence is mystifying. Perhaps you owe an obligation to this land for what you are brought here."

"Your belief of existence and debt is completely alright but growing wings is inexplicably unscientific."

"Why only that is considered truth which is comprehensible, which fits into our logic and science. It may happen that Science might be the part of existence. Therefore, something which is inconceivable, not get fit into science and logic, it is not be unaccepted. Whatever happens is truth, therefore believing and accepting it is appropriate."

"You speak like Osho and wear the attire just like his believers."

"Yes ... because I am also the disciple of Osho, a believer. I love my mentor and am trying to search myself at his indicative way."

"I have also read one or two Gujarati books by Osho."

"Which of them?"

"'Search your Conscience' and 'Woman.'"

"Did you find them interesting?"

"I enjoy them reading but most of the things go beyond my head." After some time, Aakash asked further, "But how did you become the follower of Osho coming at a long distance in this Jungle, Baba? How did you make contact with him, his books' and CDs'?"

"Why? If you can come here from the external world, can't I come here the same way? Although I have no facility of wings the way you have, but there might be some walking path."

Aakash recalled that night when he was caught by the camp people and there had been a conversation between father and Baba where he had mentioned about the outsiders' coming there for the second time. Baba's language and apparel was just like an outside world. His language was understandable. While the language of the people residing in that area was of eyes, gestures and expressions. They used to make use of words in very rare condition and that also incomprehensive.

Aakash became curious to know more about Baba. He wanted to ask him, "How did you come here Baba? From where? When did you come? How long are you here?" but before he asked, a girl entered there to whom he had seen that night whose eyes were innocent and profound, face blameless, laughter childlike and charming from the path of ravine. She wondered finding Aakash there but immediately greeted him with smile. Looking at Baba she told, "Baba, I have brought the snacks and fruit juice. Both of you have it." Baba laughed at the wisdom of that girl. He took her into his arms and kissed on her forehead. He brought her near Aakash and said, "Son . . . he is . . ." He realized that he did not know the name of that boy.

"Aakash" Aakash uttered.

"I know . . . Father had asked him his name that night before you came." Girl said.

"And Aakash this is my Kajal, a darling daughter of the whole camp including me. Kajal takes care of me a lot."

If there is a girl of city, a conversation can begin with Hi—Hello, but how to speak with a camp's girl? How to start? Aakash puzzled, he could not decide therefore only gave a smile. Kajal also laughed in response.

"Aakash has come here once again being helpless through his wings. And he is with us until he gets his wings back for flight. The only difference is that he will not have to be threatened by us today, but will get fruit juice and snacks to eat, right?" Uttering this Baba called Aakash through his gesture and the three of them sat together to have snacks. Aakash had relished the juice made from juicer machine and chapattis made by her mother, but this was a delicious taste. He could not decide whether it was excellence of the splendor of Jungle, of the atmosphere or of the naturally grown fruits or meals or of Kajal's hands? Aakash relished the snacks a lot. After the snacks getting over, Baba said, "Dear, please show the places to Aakash, introduce him with father, show him mountains, jungles, rivers—may he get the intention of existence." Baba laughed loudly saying this. He patted Aakash hard and raised his hands as if wanted to convey the mystery of existence was the greatest.

"But how would it be possible to show everything in one day, Baba?" Kajal said.

"Show him as you can. And Aakash will have to continue coming here until the purpose of existence gets over. And always people are in hurry, but existence not. It has more and more time."

Kajal and Aakash proceeded to meet the camp.

The path was beautiful but dangerous. There was a track like way on the mountain slope. Above and beneath were the rocks and jungle only. If any mistake had occurred, then there were full chances to fall down thousand feet down the jungle way, thrashing with the trunks of the trees.

There was no hope of savior. Death was definite. To walk on this way was more dangerous than the adventure show "Khatro ke Khiladi" telecast on Bindaas channel. It was good that Aakash had worn sport shoes. He was able to have grip on the stone and land. He was walking taking utmost care. He was putting his foot carefully taking the support of the rock through both his hands. While Kajal was putting foot normally, bravely and confidently as if was playing while walking. Aakash felt sorry observing that Kajal was walking without shoes and felt "the pebbles and stones might hurt Kajal's foot; I would bring shoes for her next time."

"Aakash why do you afraid inspite of having boot?" Kajal was walking slowly taking Aakash into consideration. She turned and glanced at him again and again. She waited for him until he came near and then walked again.

"How did you come to know that these are called boot?" Aakash wondered on this note that she listened to his heart and acquainted the boot.

"Feeling surprise, Aakash? Although we don't wear boot, but are familiar with few things of the city." This was a second stroke of surprise for Aakash. His continuously thoughtful, confused and astonished mind got lost in more and more thoughts. And his leg slipped, his body twisted downside the slope. Aakash would have surely tumbled down, if Kajal had not reached in time and caught his hand. Kajal pulled him up grabbing his hand. Aakash's heart beats became fast due to the fear of falling down and he sat there being scared.

"Kajal, don't you get afraid of falling down coming this way daily?"

"No, I pass through this track even in the dark of night."

This was a third stroke of shock to the scientific minded Aakash.

"Are you comfortable walking bare foot? Aren't you hurt through pebbles and stones?"

"No, in fact I enjoy it. Pebbles and stone create tickling in my legs, therefore I enjoy a lot. Goddess Dharti clutch my bare foot and therefore I don't fall down. If you also begin walking bare foot, you will also derive the contentment of Goddess Dharti's touch."

Kajal's idea was filled with knowledgeable self-assurance. Aakash decided to walk without boot but not now as he had still not learnt walking on that track in boot. They took one long hour crossing the track which took 20 minutes only due to Aakash. When they reached on the place seen that night, it was almost night. It was an open place having small ground. There was a big stone supported from land to rocks on both the sides beside that open ground behind the partition of a stone. And that naturally carved stone craft was a place where 100 people could stay. There resided Kajal's community. Aakash observed that father sat on a small stone. Some kids were playing naked on one side. A few women were making food. A number of men were working in the corner. Aakash wondered thinking that there were many men that night, where they could have been.

Aakash greeted father. Father again got surprised seeing Aakash once again. Kajal went running to him and explained everything in detail. Father gestured Aakash to sit on the small stone situated beside. He gave a welcoming smile to him. Aakash felt easy knowing that father was not angry today.

Aakash sat there watching the phenomenon of nature. He continued looking the reddish sky and red light. He thought why Baba or father did not ask him much about himself. They didn't ask about his parents' name, not about his village's name, not about his study nor even about his family background. He really found these men backward in social customs and rituals. He got irritated in this silence and just sitting the same way. The moment Kajal came near, he said, 'May I go now, Kajal?"

"Go after having food. It is ready."

"No—I will have it at home."

"But how will you go? Only if you wings come up again? If you go taking food, then we will also pray for you. Otherwise you will have to stay here only," Kajal said smiling. Aakash worried realizing the uncertainty of wings growing out. Still he said, "I have just had snacks with Baba, therefore not feeling hungry."

"If you are not hungry, then eat less.

Mummy had gone Chandigarh to see Dhara who was to come tomorrow. So he would have to eat either the morning remains or in any restaurant. Compared to that, if he gets refreshment kind delicious food, he should have it. Thinking this Aakash convinced.

There was only sabji-roti in food, but the 32 varieties of food were nothing compared to its taste. All the food items made in the restaurant, the various creations of food were tasteless before this. Aakash thought that people invent multiple food products to get taste; instead they should learn to create taste in the food items.

Aakash thought, "one day I would explore the mystery of this taste."

It was sunset and dark was about to spread now except usual trivial light. Other men had also begun to come back; perhaps they had been to work in the forest. They were noticing his presence, but spoke nothing. There was not a sense of rejection in their eyes. At that time, a strong and weighty hand was put on his shoulder. Aakash turned and saw that stout man. Kajal came quickly and said, "Aakash, he is Bheemo."

Aakash hailed him with a smile. Bheemo went away without uttering anything. Aakash sought permission to go. He closed his eyes, prayed with his hands looking at the sky in the same way as he was taught by Baba and wings grew out. He greeted everybody and waving his hands started flying. Everyone responded his greetings with a smile. Kids were waving their hands and looking at him. Kajal's eyes continued staring him, the same innocence and depth. Aakash's heart was moved like anything.

Aakash continued thinking during the flight. His thoughts were wandering sometimes in one direction, sometimes in other and sometimes collectively in many directions.

The way Kajal had accepted him normally and offered him snacks, food and introduced with others; he should also do something for her. He should offer her a gift. He aspired to bring a present next time. But which gift should he offer? In attire, these people wrap only one cloth. They don't make use of make-up kits and all. Here, the food also lacks multiplicity. Their food is luscious compared to outside world. What if they don't like the artificial things of outside? Something is to be brought, but what? The worldly people always find scarcity of things. If there is no light for some time, it becomes tough to survive. And here, how happily these people live without any sources in limited things.

These people have limited requirements, simple food and simple living. These people live cheerfully even in the deprivation of modern luxuries and comforts. Would my friends believe this? They will laugh at me. They would not admit that this kind of world also exists in the advanced and modern times. They would doubt on my information. They would consider me mad if I say that I reach there through flying.

Sunil is my best and childhood friend. I have never hidden any minor thing from him upto now. But I have not told him about Sandhya and my flying. I regret for hiding this. But how should I tell him that I fly. If I tell him, he would ask me to fly. And how would it be possible to show him that I can really fly as wings do not grow when I desire. He would mock listening that being a science student I grow up wings and fly. If I tell him about Sandhya, I would lose respect from him. Sandhya is Dhara's friend and three years elder than me. He would outrage knowing that I have had corporeal pleasure with her. Sunil is a man of morality and society and simplicity. He would get shocked listening all this. I would lose love and respect from him. So Aakash thought, "I should keep this matter limited upto me."

But why does this existence make me fly in the opposition of science? What can be its purpose? I love nature, sky and Himalaya but watching all these, I am not able to write any poem, essay or a story. I can fly but can go at only one place; in that sight, to community, to Baba, to Kajal. What would be the purpose of existence? Does it carry me there to derive existential essence from Baba? Or I will have to search out a mystery resided in the Himalayan hills. Will have I to help Kajal? Will have I to bring her in the city? Or will have I to help the members of that community from the modern world?

Thoughts exhausted Aakash. He did not realize when he reached and got down on the terrace. It was late evening reaching there. He had had the food there. He had got tired and so changed his clothes and slept in the bed. Within no time, he slept fast.

6

Aakash got up early in the morning. 12th science result was nearby. The more close the result time arrived, the more tension for results increased. He began doubting even in those papers which seemed to go very well after the exam being over. The more the intensity of thoughts grew, the more fear induced. He got afraid thinking that he would fail in those papers which had gone great. He was worried thinking whether examiner would find it correct or not. He was fearful of examiner's mood. He frightened thinking that he would not be able to get admission into engineering college. And if he get into it; it might not be in the desired branch. And if he gets into desired branch, it may happen that he does not get it into Chandigarh situated nearby his town.

Aakash wished to take admission into Chandigarh and into his favourite mechanical engineering branch. This time it seemed that everybody wanted to go in mechanical engineering. It seemed as if there was lot of competition in mechanical. How many numbers of students would be in 12th science only in Haryana? How many seats of mechanical would be there? How many girls and boys can score more marks than him? What about reservation seats? What about management quota? The more he thought, the more he scared. If weak students understand the importance of 12th science and under the pressure of their parents score more doing tuition classes and apply for mechanical, then his chance would surely go, perhaps even from engineering. Then he would have to be a teacher or a clerk in the bank. His stress increased in the last three days. He talked to Sunil to release his tension.

"Hey pal, I am really nervous thinking whether I would get into engineering or not."

"If you are under this condition, then what would happen to me? I always score 2-3 % less than you."

"It was happening upto now, but everything may go wrong in 12th science."

"It may happen. But it is not possible in our case. You are clever and fortunate both." Sunil laughed saying this.

"It is alright with clever, but how could you credit me with fortunate? I have not got admission yet and you are talking about good fate."

"Ask your own self. Luck plays a great role in many things in life apart from study." Sunil spoke straightforward.

Sandhya—her companionship, Kajal—gorgeous Himalaya, Baba—His divinity, everything passed through the eyesight of Aakash.

Then they dispersed after discussing many irrelevant issues. Although he asked to Sunil about the fate issue again and again yet he changed the topic smartly.

The results were declared. Sunil was proven right. Aakash had scored 84% and Sunil 82%. No matter how much a man possesses, whether it is money, achievement or marks, he/she always finds it less. Aakash also found 3-4% less. "If he had derived 3-4% more, it would have been definite to get admission into Mechanical Engineering College at Chandigarh. But now he would have to wait." Aakash accepted his result with this regret. His parents, friend circle, Dhara were happy. This was a celebrating happiness. They distributed sweets to everybody. Friends and relatives called to congratulate or came at home to offer their good wishes. Dhara had also come with her husband from Chandigarh.

Everybody were discussing about further studies after having lunch. At that time Sandhya came. She became happy seeing Dhara. She hugged her happily.

"Dhara . . . when did you come?"

"I came in the morning. My brother had a 12th science result today.

"I have also come to know about 12th science result." Saying this, she looked at Aakash and asked, "What is it?"

"84%" Aakash replied sadly, he was still feeling lack of 3-4%.

"Congratulations" Sandhya stretched her hand saying this. Aakash also shook hand. Sandhya tickled with her finger while shaking hand.

"So, let us celebrate, Aakash!" At the same time, Aakash's mother Sushilaben came out bringing sweets. She offered it to Sandhya.

"It's an amazing news and only a piece of sweets? Aakash this is not fair, I need full feast." Sandhya uttered this stylistically and with stress on the word 'feast'. As Sandhya put stress on the word 'feast', Aakash became conscious and came in mood. "Done, today we will offer a full feast. Come in the evening."

"Today it's not possible. Mummy—papa are out of station. I am all alone at home, so will have to stay at home." She again stressed the word 'alone' and stared at Aakash. Aakash got the sign. Sandhya went back after talking for a while. After her departure, Sushilaben said, "she seems foolish; it is good to stay away from her." Sushilaben said in that way addressing to Aakash as if was skeptical about him. But his mind was not present in the home. He was in the sweet imagination waiting for tonight.

Aakash was missing Sandhya strongly in the corner of his heart even though he was busy in the tension of admission, among the friends who were coming to wish and among the rush of relatives. It was a fiery remembrance as there was a desire of physical pleasure involved into it. It was harassing him. He was eagerly waiting for tonight. Aakash said after having dinner in the evening at nine.

"I am exhausted meeting everybody the whole day, I go for strolling." He left saying this on his bike without asking for the permission of anybody.

The society was not that small. There were total 200 houses. Aakash carefully reached near Sandhya's house. Nobody seemed in the society. Assuming everybody busy on the television, he parked his bike opposite to Sandhya's house under the gulmahor tree and came near her house acting as if doesn't know anything. He opened the compound gate, stepped on the stairs quickly and knocked the door reaching near the main gate. He preferred to knock the door presuming that the door bell may sound loud. Sandhya opened the door within few moments as if was stuck on the door. The moment Aakash went inside, she hugged him hard after closing the door immediately. She strongly kissed on his lips and said, 'heartily congratulations on my behalf now.'

Aakash also hugged him hard and said 'thank you' placing his lips on hers. They sat on the sofa set.

Sandhya was in a pink night gown which was open from upper side, low cut, tight from the waist and sleeveless. The curves of the breast were visible due to low cut. Hair was open. She was sitting on the sofa raising her one leg up.

The other leg looked open upto knee due to the gown being up. This was an invitation of wild magnificence. Aakash was impressed with this style, but this time he was not in hurry to reach the peak of bodily pleasure. He wanted to play fully with Sandhya's body. Aakash began playing with her hair, lips, breast, waist and inner parts. He began savoring her through lips and hands. Sandhya was also co-operative. She was also playing with Aakash's body parts with hands and lips. After playing for some time, Aakash lifted her naked and carried her in the bedroom. After going in the bedroom, they reached the zenith of physical ecstasy.

'Happy now ... you have derived full feast.' Aakash said laughing.

'Hunger is such which increases the next day' Sandhya also said in intoxication. After gossiping for a while, Aakash walked out. Investigating there is nobody outside; he reached his home on his bike.

Today Aakash did not feel any fear or hesitation compared to last time. But still a sense of repent or deceiving somebody was hurting him. Aakash could not understand why does this happen? To who have I deceived? Still ... this pain! Aakash tried to come out from this pain. He hardly involved his mind in the thoughts of admission, admission procedure, and in the thoughts of college life.

The admission procedure began in the engineering colleges. All the students of the state were called out at one place as per their merit on different days. And they were given admission in the college as per the availability of branch and seats. Aakash's turn came after 5-6 rounds being over. He had fear of going away from the city or what if he did not get admission into his favourite branch. Although he had fear of all these, he got into Leet College of Engineering, Chandigarh. There was a last seat and his admission was ascertained. He was happy that he would not have to go anywhere leaving his house. He would be able to get everything now: Mummy's handmade food, the lonely room of the terrace, meeting with Kajal on Himalaya and Sandhya's companionship. Sunil also got admission in the next two rounds. He got in the same college into which Aakash had got but in the Electrical branch. Sunil was compromising in his choice. For him, to be an engineer was of more importance than the desired branch. To live with Aakash and commuting from the house near the city was much important for him.

Now it was relaxation. The burden of mind was released. Now they had to go in the college directly after two months. There was a facility of college buses as well, from which one or two buses also fetched the students from Kalka. Of course, its charge was separate. Although Aakash and Sunil wished to commute on bike turn by turn, as their parents did not get convinced, they had to pay bus expenses.

Now the subject of discussion was changed among the friends. Which branch has more successful future? Which college is apt? What is the syllabus? What should be done after studies? Whether to pursue job, personal business, further studies or further studies in USA? Such subjects were discussed. Discussions were there, but stress was no more, it was full leisure. In this way, after meeting friends, Aakash was returning home and Sandhya met on the way. Aakash could not see her, but she stopped him raising her hand. She had a bag in her hand. So Aakash asked, 'Are you coming from the market?'

'Yes' Sandhya who was able to stretch the topic desirously from a simple question replied in one word only which disturbed Aakash.

'Do you want to go home?'

'No ... turn the bike; I want to talk to you on an urgent topic.' She sat on the rear seat of the bike after saying this.

'Tell me!' Aakash doubted a bit. Sandhya who was ever smiling and expressive was serious today.

'The topic is long. Take it near the river bank of Shiva temple.'

Aakash could not deny. Aakash started the bike and Sandhya placed her hand crossing his waist. Although Sandhya had told Aakash with full confirmation and self confidence that she has talked to Bhupat, Aakash got scared. He looked carefully around whether 'Bhupat was there or not?' Today Sandhya had sat a bit away from him catching softly. Her face was also away from his shoulder.

They reached near the temple. Today there was neither Monday nor any festival of Shiva ... There was a low rush of the worshippers at the temple. Both sat lifting their legs. Aakash was finding moments as hours. Immediately after sitting he asked, 'Tell me what you want to say?'

Sandhya uttered slowly lowering her eyes down, 'The matter is that there has been a problem about the day when you had come that night at home.'

Aakash got scared. Would anyone have found it out? Will Sandhya's parents have come to know? All such thoughts came together, still he remained silent.

'After that day, although the date has gone, I have not got my periods. It seems that I am going to be the mother, of your child!'

Aakash was dumbstruck. He was flying in the seventh sky out of happiness for getting admission, and fell down on the land very harshly. The darkness spread before his eyesight in place of successful career. He could also see and realize that he is not ready to marry Sandhya. He could say forcefully, 'so what now?'

'What do you mean by this? Now there is only one solution, we should marry and that also at once.'

'Any other solution?'

'What is the need of other solution? Do you have any problem to marry me?' Sandhya said strictly. Aakash did have a problem, yet he said, 'I have no problem, but our age, caste, society! Would everybody accept us?'

'You do not worry about them, do you want to accept me or not?' Sandhya was trapping Aakash tactfully and strongly.

'No . . . but I have to learn yet, make career. I don't even earn. Don't you think it is too early?' Aakash said hesitating.

'Without diverting the topic, why don't you tell me directly that you don't want to marry me?' Sandhya said laughing, 'I was just joking, I am smart in taking all precautions, don't worry.'

Aakash was relieved now. The numb mind again became active. 'How it could be possible for Sandhya to learn a lot just within two times experience? She might have other experiences as well.' Aakash was relaxed now. He said, 'so you had brought me here to joke, to frighten and to discuss this matter here?

'No . . . I just wanted to check you. The fact is that my marriage has been decided. It may get arranged within one or two months.' Saying this she became a bit weak.

Aakash slowly went near him and moved his hand on her shoulder and started kissing her hands. He was younger, yet budged his hand on her head. Actually he was not hurt knowing the news of her marriage, he was feeling relaxed from inside, perhaps it was a relaxation of not being her pregnant. It was Sandhya who had given the thought of pregnancy therefore he was frightened of maintaining physical relationship.

'Is marriage settled against your wish? Are you hurt therefore? Aakash was not hurt but he couldn't understand the reason of Sandhya's pain, so asked.'

'No ... I am hurt because I would be separated from you, stupid.'

'Yes, I would also get hurt, but this was supposed to be sooner or later.' Aakash also felt bad a bit; still he was saved from a problem therefore lectured philosophy.

Both hugged each other. They left for home after kissing each other. Aakash left for home after dropping Sandhya her home.

Sandhya got busy in marriage preparation. Still they could manage time to meet each other at Aakash's room and built physical relationship. It was possible for Aakash to meet there in the noon time as Sushilaben rarely stayed at home due to women cell meetings.

There were ten days left in the opening of colleges and Sandhya's marriage was arranged. Sandhya personally came to invite Aakash's family at his home. She invited the whole family and demanded courteously to attend.

Before the three days of Sandhya's marriage, Aakash began to grow his beard and began wearing robe gown and trousers in place of pants and shirt or T-shirt. He stopped going out anywhere and used to remain in his room for the whole day. He used to dine, breakfast and sleep in time. He performed all the routine activities in time and behaved normally with everybody in the house. Therefore nobody doubted that Aakash was in pain. He heard sad songs for the whole day in his mobile plugging ear phones in the ears sitting in the chair. Aakash thought, 'Sandhya is his first love. So he should have pain for her marriage as she is his first love and he won't be able to enjoy much with her.' Aakash had to create pain with efforts. He was upset thinking that nobody sympathized with him on his suffering. The family members thought, 'he is a boy, so may act as per his mood. It is alright that he completes all his routine in time.'

The marriage day arrived. Sandhya was Dhara's friend. Sushilaben believed that they used to reside in the same society and socially also they should go with family. Asking Aakash to get ready, his parents got ready for the marriage. As Sushilaben went upstairs to meet Aakash in his room, she saw him staring the sky sitting in the terrace in his long beard, wearing robe gown and trousers, plugging ear phone in his ears and switching off the lights.

Everybody in the house knew that Aakash was moody. He may have not listened to her shout due to the ear phone in his ears, thinking this she asked once again, 'Get ready now . . . we have to go to Sandhya's marriage.'

'I don't want to come.'

'OK. What would you have in food then?' Sushilaben found the question of making food in the house more disturbing than his denial for coming in the marriage.

'I don't want to eat anything. If I wish, I would manage on my own.'

This is how half an hour passed. Aakash was just sitting after stopping to listen to the songs, at that time he heard the sound of someone coming upstairs. Assuming that the sad person should not get involved in other activity, he sat there without looking around.

'Hey . . . why don't you come in Sandhya's marriage?' It was Sunil's voice.

'I have no mood to come.'

'Now don't be smart. Tell me directly that you were in love with her therefore hurt for her getting married.' Aakash was surprised, 'How could Sunil come to know about this?

Although he comes often at my home, but how does he know Sandhya and about her marriage?

'How do you know Sandhya?'

'Leave about knowing her, but I know her full horoscope and your being with her for the last few days too. You need not feel bad for Sandhya.'

Aakash continued staring before Sunil as if wanted to say why?

'The reason is she was playing with two boys like you. In school, she was in love of a boy named Vikram. In college, she was in love with Bhupat and you are third.'

'But how did you come to know all these things?'

'My father is the manager of that bank into which Sandhya's father also works and therefore I have also come in the marriage.'

'Sunil, if you connect others name with Sandhya, that is OK but connecting my name is not proper. We were only friends. And there is a difference between our ages . . .' he left the discussion half a through saying this. 'Don't consider age in love. Love is not restricted through age. I have seen you many times gossiping for long with her and Sandhya adjusting her hand crossing your waist.'

'So observing this, you scripted the whole story, Sunil?' Aakash said with a sense of anger.

'C'mon brother, I know more than this. I have seen your bike near her house when I was coming to meet you on the day of result at nine during night time.'

Actually Aakash was regretting to hide the matter from Sunil. Now as Sunil disclosed the whole matter, there was no meaning to hide. Still he accepted only love and not physical relationship. The matter of physical relationship was also new for their relation.

Both the friends began gossiping there avoiding to go in the marriage. Aakash forgot to remain sad in the gossip. And after knowing more about Sandhya, there was no meaning to regret now.

Aakash was thinking after Sunil left.

'Is Sandhya really flirtatious? Is she wrong for being in love with many boys? She may have made the physical relation with others too. The way she has been precautious during sex, it seems she has been into physical relation with others. But how can Aakash credit her wrong because of this? He has also enjoyed with her. And Sandhya has also not misused him. She has never demanded anything from him. She has also given pleasure for deriving it. In fact, she saved him from a bully like boy, no matter she was in love with him in past. Sandhya has never taken any advantage of situation. She might be bad for others, but she is very good for me. She was a pleasure giver. How can I curse her? I should wish her all happiness in life. May God fulfill all her desires!'

Aakash did not know when he slept with these thoughts.

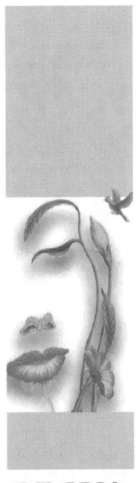

PRIYA

7

Next day, Aakash got up; there was still time for the sun to rise. There was little lightness. Cold breezing. The Himalaya appeared coated in grey vein from a long distance. It was intoxication in atmosphere. Suddenly he thought that before the college starts once I will go at beautiful hills of Himalaya and will meet to Baba, Kajal, Bapu and family members. It was just his wish but he frightened that if wings would be grown? If the wings will grow, and it will start to fly then . . . . Even I'm not ready. I am in night dress only. I thought I will get some gift for Kajal but I have not still purchased. I must give gift to Kajal but what shall I get? Some new things, gadgets or some food item but it is not useful or not wished. Even it is not necessary. Last time Kajal walked on the stone paved road without footwear. When I saw it at that time, it was shameful to my sports shoes. Then how I can think for Kajal's sport shoes? No, but I want to take something for her that is sure. In his thoughts and with his feelings, by raising hands he told, "Dear God, Keep awaiting of flying for 24 hours so that I can find out the gift for Kajal. There were no wings with the surprise. So he relaxed.

After getting ready again he started to think about the gift. But didn't get anything. So he went in market. Aakash's father was not rich person even Aakash himself was not the earning member. He has only the pocket money which he saved. He thought that he will purchase something from his savings. He wandered in the market but he didn't get anything as per the situation and as per the life style of people over there at last. He got tired and while returning back one native girl in a traditional dress requested him to purchase something. She had a beautiful necklace of multi-coloured stones to sell. The shapes of stones were not equal even though it was looking beautiful. Aakash found it totally suitable for Kajal as she was associated with nature. Sure she will like it. He was remembering that Kajal has not worn any ornaments on her body. So after "wearing this necklace she will look more beautiful". After deciding like this, without any argument he purchased that necklace. He satisfied and now he is mentally prepared to go next day.

He informed his mother in the evening only that, "tomorrow early morning I will go out with my friend. We will take breakfast at my friend's house and then after we will go. I will return in evening, don't worry". His father was simple man. Does the job, and when he gets the salary he gives to Sushilaben. His nature was never about inquiring and discussions of others. While Sushilaben was very clever. She asked more like, "where do you go? With whom are you going? Why do you go?" Before she began any such discussion, Aakash has finished his dinner and went in his room. As he reached in his room his mind was bewildered. He had enjoyed physical pleasure with Sandhya before going to Himalaya's Valleys. In fact is it there any association with fly? If it is related then how I will fly tomorrow? I thought like that. Still I was well prepared for tomorrow. He kept the stone's necklace in his pants' pocket at night. He kept the clothes separately which he is going to wear for tomorrow. Somewhere he has a deep faith that he can fly tomorrow and for that his wings will support him.

Aakash got up early in the morning. He took bath and got ready to fly and prayed for the flight. Before the prayer being over, his body felt a change. The hot fluid was moving inside in the skin, wings grown. He started to fly, that Himalaya, that beauty, those rocks, that mountain, that majesty, that rivers spring.

Even though one should glimpse again and again he/she should not satisfy. The scenes are so gorgeous that one should not be satisfied. On that morning at 7 o'clock Aakash reached into the valleys. He thought that he will reach towards the flat portion of small family but he was being gone as per his expectation with surprise... he himself felt that he was gone very much downhill. He couldn't stop himself and as he reached it was forest. Slowly he got down with the help of tree. He was scared what he saw behind the tree.

One leopard was lying on the ground. In front of leopard, Kajal was sitting with the back side from Aakash. Leopard was staring each and every side. The scene was look like that Kajal is sitting by holding the legs of leopard. Even sometimes it looks like that Kajal is pampering by another hands to leopard. Aakash has seen into the circus that players played with undomesticated animals but he has observed first time into real life that one young lady—Kajal set so silently with the wild animal. Something was going wrong, he scared and something was perplexing in his mind. How to abscond Kajal from the leopard? How can save her? He was puzzling into his mind at that time Kajal said.

"Aakash, please bring the vines lying here and there on the floor, I need to make a string." Aakash was surprised, "he came down so slowly and silently even though how can

Kajal comes to know that I reached?" Kajal was asking for the creep to make the string so surely to tie up the leopard. Kajal sat on the leopard if she will stand up then the leopard will attack on her. She must be waiting for someone that somebody come and give her the creeper and can make the string" He was thinking like this and started searching the creepers. He collected very fast many creepers and went to the Kajal. He was afraid of the Leopard but he develops into a courageous to save Kajal's life. He went near to Kajal. When he reached near to the leopard he saw that the leopard was injured with one leg. May be he got hurt by the jagged stone. It was continuously bleeding. Kajal was trying to stop that bleeding by applying the ayurvedic medicine, she has hard-pressed her hand into that injury to stop the bleeding. She has taken the creepers from Aakash and directly she put the leaves on the injured part and started covering it. After that she made the string and tied up leg of leopard. As the bleeding stopped she pampered on his face and slowly she got up from there.

"let's go" slowly she shake off all the dust from the hand and she pointed out to Aakash to go with her.

Aakash was eagerly waiting to share that he got 84% in 12th science. He got the admission in Mechanical branch at Engineering college of Chandigharh. He wants to do something in future etc." but if Kajal will ask then he can share! Kajal was never interested in his past or future because she has never asked about this. Not only Kajal but even Baba has not asked any detail then how it can be shared? To share about himself he could ask to Kajal but what he should ask?

There are no such awards, no recognitions, no competitions, no best, no education, whatever Kajal is she is, infront of him, what can be asked? When he got 84% in

12th Science every lay man wished him at Kalka because they know about the 12th science result. While Kajal is illiterate girl how can she know about the education and about the 12th science?

By thinking a lot he was climbing rocks up and up. He started to walk with Kajal with the speed but he was tired. Kajal was also taking care of him and she was looking back. If she goes ahead little bit then she stops and she waits for Aakash. If there will be any difficulty in some rocks then she catches the Aakash's hands and helped him. How to climb, how to maintain the balance, she explains all such points. Aakash was tired. He felt to take a rest. He sat on the Rock. He was wheezing. Kajal looked back. She saw he was tired. Aakash called her and told her to sit. Kajal sat with him and Aaksh said.

"Kajal I brought something for you" he said slowly.

"what" Kajal Asked.

"this" said and he showed the colorful stones necklace.

After looking at this necklace she started laughing. Aakash was surprised. He didn't understand that what was there in that necklace for laughing?

"Why are you laughing? What is there for laughing in this ? Aaksh became silent and stopped his wheezing.

"You show this necklace to Baba and tell him that I brought it for Kajal. So he will explain." Said Kajal and again she started laughing. After some time they started to climb again. And after sometime they reached at the place of Baba.

He was sitting on the slab. Baba was impressive in the maroon (Burgundy) color clothing. He appeared with the leisurely smile. Kajal ran and reached to him. Baba hugged her and kissed on her head. He called Aaksh where he was standing very far.

"Baba, Aakash gave me a gift of this necklace." She said like this and started laughing again. She showed the necklace to the Baba. Baba also started laughing. Aakash was nervous and he couldn't understand that why these people are laughing? After looking at him Baba told to Aakash "do you know why we are laughing?"

He nodded his head and said 'no'.

"Because, since many years there is custom in this family that the person who is proposing to a woman to marry before that time he gives the gift of stone made necklace."

Aakash got the point now. By chance … he has proposed Kajal, that he has understood. "Sorry" he pleased.

"No problem my son, sometimes by mistake the God reveals some intentions to human!" after saying like this Baba was staring at Aakash.

"What in this what is the intentions (symbol) of God or nature ? It is just a co-incidence. It is just an accident." Said Aakash.

"What happened?" asked Baba.

"I wished I will bring something for Kajal. I thought a lot but I couldn't find any thing, I went in market but even though I couldn't find any thing, so I was roaming. I met one small native girl who was selling these type of necklaces and I purchased."

"You thought about the gift should be for Kajal, did you think anything about me? my son," he exclaimed and laughed.

"Again Aakash thought why this idea didn't come into his mind?" truly I can say Baba apart from Kajal I didn't think about anybody." Replied Aakash.

"I was just joking" said Baba and he gone into meditation.

Kajal brought the food and they all three sat for food. During food Kajal and Baba was sitting silently and Aakash also remain silent. Kajal and Baba was enjoying the food while Aakash was eating fast. He didn't like the silence. As he was uncomfortable this was observed in his behavior. Baba has pragmatic all this into him. After food, Baba sat on one slab and Kajal and Aakash was sitting on floor even though they didn't sit properly, at that time Aakash said, "Baba today kajal was helping one dangerous and injured leopard."

"yes, I know." Aakash was shocked. "As Baba knows this even though he has allowed to play this dangerous game to kajal?" further Baba said, "As she had taken the breakfast she heared groan of some animal. Truly I say, I didn't hear anything but only she proclaimed that Baba, the leopard is injured, I will go and cure it, and she gone."

"but how did you allow her in this dangerous condition?" Aakash said.

"you have seen the dangerous part of this treatment because you are from modern world. Where there is the importance of safety and selfishness, while the world of these people is full of love and sympathy. Modern world belongs to mind where the self means 'I' and here the self means 'all', there is only importance of self pain while here the others' pain is self pain."

"Yes, that's right, but there is no need to take risk for life? Kajal might die in saving leopard's life. The philosophy in which you believe, that should be known by leopard! Then and then one can be saved?"

"even though Kajal saved, and look at her, she is just standing alive in front of you? Do you know why? Because they live life with hearts and among them Kajal is the nearest and dearest of all. She is the nearest to all hearts so she understands the language of hearts and silence. She understands the language of silence and hearts she understands the language of animals, birds, trees, rocks and understands the language of rivers. She came to know the soreness of leopard and the same way leopard also understands the love of Kajal. That is why it was not possible that the leopard would attack on Kajal. Even here there is no chance that any native families interrupt to animals or birds and animals do not interrupt to families."

Aakash was surprised, he asked "how it can be possible? In our world the snake bites us whom we never know and we never harassed any dog even though it bites."

"for that you need to maintain and make the strong feelings and attachment. The person who stays in himself is always confused and he can never listen and never understand himself. Where the human being never knows his heart can never approach the others, it is not tough but it's impossible and that's why the snake and the dog bites."

"but what can you do for that. How can one prevents the thinking as it works continuously?"

"it was observed as you were taking breakfast and the way you asked questions, and it is also observed how do you live your life i.e in your own self. Even though there is something in you something would like to come out"

"What can I do?" Aakash remembered his life in which he was always being in intellect and mind only. He was anxious by his mind and he was happy with intellect.

"My son, I can show you the way where I can get the happiness on which I can trust and whom I love, and that is the way of Sadguru Osho's vision. You read and listen his preaching. You engage yourself in the prescribed meditation then you can approach towards your inner strength of your heart."

"I have read only two books but now I'll read and listen more but tell me more about meditation."

"Meditation is the most important. Without meditation only reading will satisfy only your mind—make you strong. So the meditation is very important. Start yourself actively for meditation. Get up early in morning or attend the meditation center whichever is nearest center of Osho and do the meditation. That will remove the contaminated thoughts from your mind. That will make alive your lungs. Your inner strength will be stimulated."

"For that what shall I do Baba, How can I do the meditation please explain me"

"move towards the ladder of Dynamic meditation, do as per the instructions, in that there are five steps explained, do as per that. First do the ten minutes exhalation into the air. After ten minutes without any hesitations start inhalation. It will be difficult and surprising you in the beginning but gradually it will be habituated to you. In the third step, leave your hands into the air and shout hu . . . hu . . . and jump. Your inner strength will be activated. After that in your fourth step stop yourself and stand and feel the changes whichever have been found by that movement in yourself. In the last step, last 15 minutes, enjoy the dance on light music and make yourself free."

Aakash found it interesting. And he decided that he will do the meditation. He couldn't identify the wish that whether this influence from the heart or to impress Baba.

"Baba, one more question, the Dynamic meditatation must be possible when there should be accurate situation. But show me the simple one which can be easily done?"

Baba Laughed, "It means shortcut! You have to do the Dynamic meditation but whenever you are free like you getting up in the morning, sleeping time, or while travelling you can do the Baudh's meditation (Vipshyana). In that you have to concentrate on the breathing like from where inhalation is coming in and going out." Like this it was explained by Baba.

Aakash was interested; at least he was ready to do the meditation (Vipshyana). Because it was easy for him and he can do it wherever. But he didn't know that it was difficult because his ever wandering mind. It was going to be an evening and after permission of Baba, Aakash departed towards home.

8

oday it was the first day of college. Aakash has spent the whole night into excitement. He was thinking like new college, new friends, new atmosphere etc. even though he got up early in the morning. He has taken bath but still it was only 7:00 o'clock. He has to catch the college bus from the gate of Nisarg Society at 9 o'clock. So he went on terrace for the meditation (Vipshyana) instead of getting ready for college. It was difficult to do the Dynamic meditation for him at home. But meditation (Vipshyana) was easy to do. He sat for 10 minutes but he felt that it was for one hour, still the breakfast is remaining, clothes need to be changed and have to reach at the gate even if the bus will come early. He could not concentrate his mind and stood up from the meditation. As he saw it was only for ten minutes. Again he tried but he was chaotic into thoughts. Thoughts derived from different areas whatever and however. His attention was derived from the meditation and got up. He started reading the book which he brought yesterday, "You become as you think" of Osho. It was o k. Now it was the time of college.

He opened the cupboard to change the clothes, he saw that the gray pent and half sleeves white shirts and blue tie was hanging at one side. It was his school dress of 11th and 12th standard. Till standard 10th he was wearing gray colour half pant. As he was in school he has to wear this school dress every day. But today he is a collegian. He is young man. Today he can wear anything but it should be proper, it should not be vulgar. He wore the blue jeans and gray T-shirt and sports Shoes. He applied gel in his hair. He kept his hair little rough, if he had done like this in his school then he must had been banged by his teacher. But this is college so one should be stylish.

He took his breakfast and left his house. There is only 40 minutes way to reach at college on bike even the road was also good but as per mummy's and Papa's instruction he has to go into the Bus. He has to travel for 1 hour and 30 minutes instead of 40 minutes. Because the bus will stop at three-four places. And the first stop is of Aakash so while returning the order to reach home is descending so he will reach last. He will spend more time in travelling and Aakash has felt for this. He thought that if it won't be suitable to him then he and Sunil will go by bike. Let's see for some days.

At Nisarg society's gate there were very less youngsters. Among them there were only two girls. Everybody settled down in the bus and bus on track. He come to know the benefit of first stop that he can get the seat which he likes. He reserved the next seat for Sunil. He wished 'hi' and smiled at young girls.

As he saw at girls he thought that "most of smart girls are in Arts, Commerce and almost in B.Sc. but in Engineering they are average. Engineering and beauty is fractious but what can be done? But one will have to spend the long four years in this desert."

Second stop was of Sunil's. there were many students from his stop. There were 7-8 girls. They were O.k. Even they can be liked as the time goes on ... but the last girl has attracted not only Aakash's but also everyone's attention. She has worn the stretchable black pent and sky blue t-shirt, heighted, brownish, open hair, and elongated circle face that girl was moving ahead with her own manner. Aakash was thinking that girl should sit with him but same time Sunil came and sat with him.

"Don't worry Aakash you are going to enjoy to see her everyday. If you are lucky then she may be in your class also. May be senior or may be my classmate also."

Aakash and Sunil was going first time in the bus so they don't know who are seniors and juniors. And it was difficult to find new and old students. Bus was full before it leaves the city.

College was big, elegant and beautiful. on the ground youngsters were looked into different colours dresses. All new students have to gather at community hall at 11:30 where principal will deliver a speech and other speakers will provide the information. They will explain the rules and regulation of college and orient them. The hall has the capacity of 600 students to sit together. Aakash and Sunil sat in this beautiful hall. They sat at the 7th and 8th row so that they cannot be into the eyes of teachers. Eyes of Aakash were searching to that girl who has the long hair, open hair, and elongated circle face. She came and sat with her friends before the two three row of them. She was not comfortable with her friends, he thought that they are new friends.

"Youngsters, now you are in new turn of your life. You will get more freedom rather than school. But all changes and freedom brings new responsibility. Now with the freedom you will be more responsible. There won't be any more teachers who can torture and who punish you but instead of that here explained, you will find professor who will guide you. You need to decide your own destination and your goal. College will support you. You have to follow the rules and regulation of college. You can wear the colorful dresses but it should be with the restriction. There can be the friendship between girls and boys with that you should not forget your limitations", spoken by principal. After that rules and regulations were explained by the speaker, even history of College and achievements of college. Aakash didn't find it much interesting so he started thinking that "if this girl will be his classmate then it will be nice! The uninterested engineering will be interesting."

Luckily that girl was the classmate of Aakash. Although the syllabus of all branches is same in first year but even though he has to sit in the mechanical branch in his class. Aakash sat on the bench. As the Principal has given the permission that girls and boys can sit together but girls sitting with girls and boys are sitting with boys. Exceptionally one or two among them. That beautiful girl was sitting with one girl. Aakash was sitting at the back side of 3rd bench. When he was looking at him he heard somebody speaking.

"Hello! I am Arjun Rathod . . . Can I sit here?"

"Sure," said Aakash and looked at him, heighted, physically powerful body, and long hair and well shaped eyes that boy. He was looking dangerous by his physical appearance but by his eyes he was looking lovable.

Today it was lucky day for Aakash. He comes to know the name of that girl. Her name was Priya Pathak. Even in addition the group for practical of 15 students she is in his group only. Aakash was very happy. He thought that now I will enjoy. But with that a possibility can also not be avoided that the education will be affected. Now there is just introduction part between them was remaining. But Aakash got that chance also.

One day in the Engineering graphics practical class there was the quarrel between the practical instructor and Priya.

"Ms Priya, you have to do a lot of work and you have not completed any one, and you have to complete 25 drawings. After observing your work I can say that you will not complete these 25 drawings even in 4 years." Instructor commented. In this response Priya replied that "Engineers need not complete drawings, they just have to understand and make them understand others. There are I.T.I draftsmen for drawing so there is no mean for this work." Instructor was not capable to give the reply to Priya's arguments. But he didn't allowed her logic in that. He said that "whatever it may be this is the subject and this is the syllabus for it and its compulsory. If you have any problem, contact to the principal and university."

Priya replied with style, beauty, confidence and daring. She was fearless. Aakash was impressed by this. As the practical was over he went to near her and said "Eexcuse me".

"yes," with gestures and by styling her hair she saw back.

"I like the engineering subject if you don't mind I can help you."

"Can I know your intention to help me out?"

"Friendship, Aakash mentioned clearly. Priya laughed and gave her hand and said, O.K. friends, I am Priya."

"I am Aakash" said Aakash and shook hand.

As wished by Aakash, the relationship with Priya was being developed. Aakash was the student of Gujarati medium and Priya was from English medium. Aakash was comfortable with subjects like Computer programming and Utilization, Engg, Graphic and Mechanics of Solids while Priya was not comfortable with them so he was helping her. And where Priya was comfortable there she helped to Aakash.

By helping each other in different subjects they come near to each other. Even they go for lunch and tea together in the break time. Sunil also met her in the break time. Aakash has introduced Priya to Sunil.

As the relationship grown up and the time passed Aaksh came to know that Priya is blissful daughter of an industrialist. She is the only daughter so she grown up in fondling atmosphere. And because of that she was very candid. She can say whatever she wants to share with someone she will say straight forward without any hesitation. It was easy for her.

Days were passing. The term is about to complete. It can be said that reading or Diwali vacation has been declared. And after that, the examination was scheduled after the vacation. It was for 25 days. The vacation was not for Diwali enjoyment but rather than that it was for reading. 2 days were remaining for the vacation, one of the Aakash's classmate Arjun Rathod has announced that "Friends, we have exam after this reading vacation, 25 days are remaining. So let's arrange one programme which will provide us relax for the exam.

"What will be the programme?" all asked together.

"The meditation camp for 3 days, which is already scheduled by my other friends. Those who are interested can join with us." Arjun said.

"Where is meditation camp?"

"In one of the Hermitage which is at Solen Shimla road. There is a facility of accommodation and food."

But whose camp it is? Who is going to conduct?"

"Osho's and it will be conducted by Swami Devendrabharti, you must have heard about Osho?" Many friends have listened to about him but only some of them have accepted. Many of them were not interested to join. But for Arjun's sake they were sitting. But Aakash was surprised. He was remembering Baba's talk about meditation.

He asked, 'What are the fees Arjun? And any other information? I would like to come and I am interested."

'The camp is for three days; on the same day when our vacation will start, same evening we have to reach. We will stay three nights and next day afternoon after the lunch we will disperse form there and fees will be Rs.800/- per person.

Which are the different types of meditation is going to be a part of this meditation? As per Baba's instruction Aakash was interested in Dynamic meditation. That's why he asked.

"Every day morning there will be Dynamic meditation, after that preaching and after afternoon there will be vipasyana or any other mediation. In the evening there will be kundli's mediation and in the night at 6.45 night Evening meeting."

Aakash was ready and he gave his name.

Second day when Aakash Sunil and Priya met for tea at that time they discussed about this.

'Both of you can also come for this camp we will enjoy."

'Have you read about Osho? Aakash asked priya.

'Yes, I read two three books."

"Have you heard about his mediation activity?"

"No I have not read but I have heard about it from one of his monk."

"Only that much! As that man looks like a logical, clever and scientist, he is not as practical in meditation. His Dynamic meditation is not logical but they are like drama. I don't want to come." Priya explained it very powerfully and logically that if Aakash has not remembered aura of Baba, he would have rejected for this camp. He has observed shine of meditation on Baba's face. He explained to Priya, "Even if you are right, there won't be any issue for three days. Do you have any problem for this?"

"Three days? One should be understood first and then someone can think about the meditation camp. And if I don't like the person I can't spend an hour for that person and this is about three days." Priya gave her ultimate view for this.

"Oh you are so angry. O.k. lets go and accompany me. Don't come for Osho but join for me."

"For you? Don't try to encash our relationship. Never try to force me. For me, my thoughts and my decisions are always important rather than our friendship!" she said and she stood up from the table and left from there and told him that "pay for the tea."

Aakash was shocked. He can't understand what to do? He was confused that how he can handle himself. He was fed up and putting his head on the table and sitting like that. As Aakash was shocked, it was observed by Sunil and he said that "I will come for meditation camp with you." Even though he didn't like. He gave his full support in sympathy for him.

On the day of camp at 5:00 o'clock in the evening, Aakash and Sunil packed necessary luggage and took white and burgundy colour cloths (Chauga) and reached. They got one combined room. The leaflet of rules regulation was provided to them. Arjun met them and he was very happy. He was very busy in the camp so he couldn't spend more time with them. So he felt bad.

At 6 o'clock every one wore the white colour cloths and gathered at the mediation camp place. Aakash and Sunil reached there. They were very eager to know about all these.

Swami Devendrabharti entered with smiley face and welcome to everyone. She started about talking.

'Human beings who follow the logical mind they believe that the meditation activities of Osho are illogical and complicated." Aakash was shocked. He faced the same conditions with Priya and the same topic was started by swamiji. So he was eager to know the answer.

'They are inspired by the knowledge, logic and speech of Osho, but they are not ready to accept Meditation of Osho. what's the reason? Because thoughts can be understood. They can be grasped by the mind. But thoughts can't grasp the Osho's meditation, therefore they are not accepted by the mind. But is it so that truth is only that which can be understood by the mind? Isn't there any truth which is beyond mind? Scientists have researched all the organs of human body parts, but they could not find any substance like love. So, is it so that there is no love? We all have experienced it, nobody can deny its existence. The whole universe has its existence well before it was investigated by scientists. Which shows that truth is beyond our reach and bigger than our mind and thought, it is very much mysterious. We can't fathom depth of it by our thought and mind. If truth is so little which can be understood by our mind then it will be smaller than mind and if the truth is smaller than mind then it has no value. Then it is not worth seeking. So, the truth is not only bigger than our minds but it is so vast which can't be ascertained by our mind and thought. However, we can only experience it. In which you can get a vast deep experience of its existence. You can never seek sea, for that you have to disappear as a drop, only then one can be ocean.

Such a mysterious, incomprehensible, vast and unknown truth can not be known by such a small mind. Its ways are without depts and not smooth. So, you have to forget your mind, you have to jump into reality, without thinking. Hence, with no worries, keeping your mind aside prepare to jump into reality. These meditation activities are for those who are ready to jump into reality. These mediation activities are not to be understood, but really to be experienced and enjoyed.

There was evening meeting at 6.40 and after that there was active meditation Aakash enjoyed in all active mediation camp. Especially he liked, evening meeting and Dynamic meditation, Osho's speech and Vipasynna meditation.

He remembered Priya throughout during the camp. He wished he would have convinced her as Devendra Bharti did him. Then Priya would have attended the meditation camp. It would have been a different pleasure if he would have enjoyed with her by dancing, eating, and passing three days, but it was not possible. She reflected on her for all three days. But she disappeared in the last session of meditation and suddenly there was only one flash of Kajal appeared. He was now thinking only about Kajal. He was feeling as if Kajal is there with him in the last session of meditation.

On the third day afternoon camp was completed. Now Aakash was restless and wanted to meet Kajal. He decided let him get two days less for reading, anyhow he madeup his mind to go next morning at Kabila to meet Kajal without fail."

In the evening he informed his mother Sushilaben "tomorrow I am going out for two days with my friend and will return thereafter."

Where, with whom, for what? What about exam? Avoiding all such questions and sarcastic remarks from his mother and replies thereof, he tactfully went upstairs and slept in readiness to visit next day morning!

9

akash got up early in the morning. The Sun was not risen fully, there was a storm and due to this there was glow lightness in the atmosphere. This time he wished to stay in the valleys of Himalayas for a night. So as per requirement, he reached there with necessary luggage. Still the rays of rising Sun were observing of different valleys and birds were singing sweet melodies and calling the sun.

Now, Aakash was well familiar of that place. But it doesn't mean that he will show to commute by Air, but he knows very well about the Valleys that from where he has to take turn and from where he has to go down. He also has idea about the time by which he can reach to the valleys of Himalayas. Today he went down and reached at the small part of Baba's residence. He saw that Baba was sitting for meditation on a stone. Slowly he kept his entire luggage at a side, closed his eyes and sat for meditation near to Baba. He started to observe his own breathing. By this it can be said that he was trying to concentrate on meditation without thinking. He was thinking that thoughts are so smart that they don't disturb that much in our daily life, but they do disturb us when we sit for the meditation. They all emerge at a time like anything, you can't remain unaffected by them. Aakash was not able to meditate. He was upset. Mentally he was not comfortable. He felt uneasy about what he was doing. He was feeling that he has spent for hours and hours in meditation. When he opened his eyes it was just for five minutes only. Baba was looking at the bright sun rays which were rising from the valleys.

Aakash Stood up. came near to Baba, he bent down for touching his feet. Before he could touch Baba's feet, he hugged him and said with a smile:

"Today wings brought to you or you brought the wings?"

"Wings have supported to my wishes."

"Can I know the reason behind coming over here?" Baba asked with a smiling tone. Rather than naming Kajal, he replied, "To see you." In fact, he wanted to see only Kajal after yesterday's meditation.

Baba asked "only to me?"

"No, to all of you" by saying he looked here and there.

"To all of us means? Do you know about others in detail rather than me and Kajal? Baba was trying to force him to speak the name of Kajal.

"to both of you and to meet Himalaya also."

Baba was continuously laughing, Aakash also joined with him.

"I have completed three days mediation camp of Osho. I enjoyed a lot there. There I was thinking of you so I came to meet you." said Aakash.

"Shall I ask again, only to me or to Kajal as well? Baba again started to laugh. Baba was right, There was only Kajal. Simultaneously, I thought of Baba also as I needed to ask him about something but it was not so important.

"If existence is beyond the mind and Osho's meditations are to go beyond the mind, why dos Osho speak like a logical and comprehensive scientist in order to affect the mind?" Aakash asked to Baba, the question had emerged into his mind after the Osho's Camp.

"If existence is beyond mind and Osho's meditations are to to beyond mind, even though when he speaks it seems to be logical and easy to understand, how it is that? Aakash asked the question he was thinking about when he was in the camp.

Because existence is not there in the mind but the mind is definitely the part of existence. So to jump into existence. The same mind can be used as a tool. Osho never preach to strengthen your belief, but he does so to propitiate your mind so as to enable you to go into unknown. He wants you to enjoy the experience of existence by taking aback, by pacifying, by shocking you and prepare you to set your mind free. This is Osho's compassion for humanity.

It was heavy preaching for Aakash. He nodded his head but hardly he could have understood anything. May be Baba perceived it and said "Don't try to understand it. Just keep it inside. At the right time the seed will germinate and you will realize it automatically. To get it germinated, just follow the meditation which will help you a lot."

By that time Kajal came with the breakfast. As she looked at Aakash her eyes were expressing happiness. She smiled at Aakash.

"When did you come Aakash?"

"Just now, today I am going to stay over here at night also."

"Good, let's have breakfast."

"You must have brought it for Baba only? If I will join, Baba will remain hungry." Actually he was also hungry but he told with some haziness.

"Generally we have breakfast together and if you join us, there will be no problem, nobody will remain hungry. Come fast without being smart."

Baba asked Aakash as if ordering. "I feel free with Himalaya. I would like to come here and like to stay with you. But I am always helped by you, I never become helpful to you. so obviously I feel some hesitations." Said Aakash.

"You need not feel hesitation, we don't give you anything from ours, it's from existence. We just facilitated to reach out everyone which is not that much important." Baba raised the hands towards the Himalayas valleys and explained. Then he went on:

"And really the existence wants you to come here and that's why you are coming, therefore, you have got the wings. And see how the wings bring you here only and that's why we have to admire the desire of existence."

Baba's statement was mystical. It was too difficult for Aakash to understand.

"Aakash, if you want to help, join with me towards the forest, we have to bring the fruits for all family members today. You just have to help. So that you may not feel bad." Kajal said, Aakash convinced and liked it. Baba also consented by just smiling and nodding his head.

Kajal and Aakash went to the forest for collecting fruits. They were going down by sharing and talking.

"Baba belongs to our world. When did he come here? How did he come ? Where did he stay in our world? What he was doing? Why has he come here?"

"You are asking so many questions. Your mind is working too much. Stop it or slow it down." Kajal Said.

"But there emerges lot of questions in my mind, so what should I do?"

"When Baba came here I was just 10 years, too young, so I don't know much about it. But he is the follower and the clergy of Guru Osho. His name was Swami Prem Prakruti, with love we all call him 'BABA.'"

"But where was he staying in our world? Why has he come here?"

"I don't know more about him but he is from Pune city. He loves nature and he loves Himalaya that's why he came here."

"But he was there..." before Aakash completes the sentence Kajal told,

"The rest you just ask to him. We never asked such questions to him."

"Should you not ask?"

"There is no need to ask, he is just with us that is enough. If he feels, he will explain by himself." By that time they reached near a fruit tree. Kajal went there and she stood near the tree by closing her eyes and after sometime she collected ripe fruits from different branches and started to go ahead.

"Oh ... there are more enough fruits on this tree then there is no need to go to another one?"

"Again question ... keep your mind aside for a moment. Haven't you observed that when I was asking the tree by my closed eyes, it granted me permission and I have just collected that much fruits accordingly?"

Aakash surprised and thought that Priya will surely be startled if she will listen these kind of illogical ideas.

"But if someday tree won't permit you for fruits then!" asked Aakash.

Kajal laughed again on his question, "remain hungry, learn how to trust on your own existence." He was surprised by what Kajal said so simply which was a great thing. Again they started to collect fruits from different trees. It was going to be an evening. Whole day they were moving from here to there. Going up and down, swooping. Aakash was tired by increasing weight of fruits.

"Kajal, you made me tired out by constant walking."

"You could have stayed with Baba but it was your wish to help us as you didn't like to get help at no cost, now you should have realized the meaning of hardwork. Otherwise even, we had no problem at all."

"That's right, I am tired but its also true that I have enjoyed."

"You are speaking ambiguously having dual meanings. You say that you are tired and enjoyed also!"

"It is true Kajal, I am tired and I have enjoyed too."

"Opposite but truth, isn't it! Same as Baba's talk for Osho," said Kajal and Akash understood the whole idea of Baba, the matter of opposites included in the existence! He is surprised by Kajal's perception! She is not well literate but the grasping power of Kajal is very high. Again this is the opposite truth.

As they reached up, Kajal stopped at the junction where three footways meet and she said to Aaksh, "you just go by this footway . . . you will reach Baba's place. I will go to that side its the way to Kabila place. You just stay with Baba over there. I am going to bring food for you." She said to Aakash and pointed the way.

Slowly, taking care, Aakash reached at the Baba's place which was flat. The way was rough but was not dangerous. He was tired. He sat on a stone and breathed and taken rest. Then he went into the cave. Baba had gone somewhere. As he was roaming from here and there, He was sweating after rambling. As the road was dusty the dust stuck to his body hence he wanted to take bath but where to bathe? As he was thinking, Baba came there.

"Son, take a bath. After some time there will be an evening meeting and every one will be there."

Aakash looked askance at him, "where to bath?"

Baba took him behind the stone where a stream was flowing. There was small stream flowing. Beneath water was collecting in a pit. The pit was overflowing and it became a stream and was cautiously flowing down. As if a natural bath tub! Aakash was enjoying the bath in under open sky and he was also enjoying the bath in the company of nature.

Baba also took bath. By that time people started to come there. They all were settled down at flat place. Aakash moved a bit and sat at the back. It was getting dark. Kajal came and went to the cave. She kept the food and came back and sat down. Two-three people broght odd musical instruments and kept them aside.

First of all Baba asked Aakash to get up. Baba introduced him to all the present. After that everyone was introduced to Aakash. Everybody welcomed him with a smile. But among them one person did not respond properly, who was well-built and was not at all interested in him—he was Bhimo. Aakash didn't understand his reluctant behaviour. May be, Aakash thought, that this was his lifestyle, by taking it that way he shook off the thought.

Baba also sat with every one in the group. The evening meeting started at the right time. As Aakash was experienced of evening meeting that it was started with music slowly. every one stood up and started dancing. Slowly music caught its rhythm. It became severe. People also started dancing excitedly. When the name of Osho was utterd in the evening meeting all of them raised theire hand and uttered ... The classical music is also played at three intervals. At last there were three drum beats on the drum. After that Baba sat on his place and looked at the stone which was infront of him as if some invisible person was sitting there, he bowed down and he started his preaching.

"I will express Osho's message as I have understood."

As there were no availibilty of cassettes and C.D, DVD, Baba himself started delivering the speech, Aakash thought. He had seen VCD was played in the Osho's camp.

Baba delivered a speech on LOVE. Love is unconditional. If there is any condition in love it is meaningless. There is happiness in loving. There are no expectations in love. If one expects something in love, it is not love, it is lust. Speaking further about love he said that love is not the union of two bodies, it is not quiet of two minds. love is union of two souls. Love, in itself, is so high that body and mind remain far below it. Love may include physical and mental pleasure. But love doesn't stop there, it is far above all these. It is so high that it is just near to the existence—Godliness. That is why if you want to attain God, love is the only way to get Him. People say that love is blind but love is never blind. lust is blind. The love is the light which helps you to reach God.

The speech got over. After sitting quiet for sometime slowly people stood up and started walking towards their houses. Kajal also went. When everybody left, Baba came near to Aaksh and sat and Said "My son let's eat something. Kajal has brought food."

They sat under the open sky to eat. It was beautiful sight. There was cool breeze flowing. The whole sky was full of stars. There was no moon. May be it was Amavas. (Blue moon) The stars were bright and visible very clearly. They were illuminated, dim, small, big, milky galaxy all were clearly visible. The light of town didn't obstruct it. Aakash was mesmerized. It was dark night, though the shape of trees and mountains were differently visible. The nearby mountains were looking very dark and the far ones were looking like covered up.

After having dinner, they went into the cave where the bedding was ready with the grass pillow. Both of them slept.

The next day when Aakash got up. There was sunlight everywhere. He came out and he saw that Kajal and Baba were having breakfast. He hid behind the stone and started watching. Baba's back and Kajal's face was at him. Its a wonderful scene to watch Kajal having breakfast. With complete awareness, slowly, pleasantly and involved in each and every activity she was having food. Aakash remembered his style. He was irritated.

He came out. He brushed at the place which he saw yesterday. He took bath and came out well dressed, but there was no Kajal.

"Baba, where is Kajal?

"Today she has to work in kitchen so she went. Let you finish up your breakfast, we will go to roam in the forest."

Aakash took his breakfast. Both went into forest. He tried to talk more for getting more information about Baba. Baba told and laughed, "I will share on appropriate time."

In the environment of valleys of Himalaya, Aakash was enjoying different and beautiful places. At each and every place Himalaya was revealing different types of beauty.

When we returned in the afternoon, Kajal had brought the lunch.

They all had lunch together. Took rest and after afternoon he took permission of both of them and saying goodbye Aakash returned.

10

Aakash got down on the terrace of his house before dark. He quietly opened the room, changed the clothes, sat down, made a show of doing something, read for the exam and then came downstairs.

"When did you come Aakash?" His mother asked.

"Why? I came before some time."

"Before how long?" As his mother had an investigating nature, Aakash had learnt to manage with her.

"Don't count too much of the time. There are exams after Diwali. I have to read a lot. So please give me food."

"That is alright. But I need to be informed about son." Sushilaben uttered with proud.

"Why do you inquire if you don't have trust on the values taught by you?" Aakash returned the same question in the court of his mom, so she got confused.

"I did because Sunil came twice in these two days to see you and even he was unaware about where you went which surprised me. So I asked."

Aakash got nervous. He repented upon not thinking that Sunil could come here and inquire about him. Now what should he reply?

"Mummy, I had gone to my branch mate's house and Sunil didn't know him so I didn't talk to him."

He finished the talk with a regret of telling lie. He also felt sorry for hiding matters from Sunil. Sunil was a childhood friend. They used to share all those close matters with which even their parents were unknown. He felt bad for hiding the matter. He thought of telling about this matter to Sunil at a proper time.

Days were less. And lot of time was passed in camp and Himalayan hills. It was certain that in Diwali too four or five days were to be wasted. Therefore, it was essential to make plan for study preparation. Aakash set the reading time table and began studying.

Aakash began reading again getting up early in the morning. It was only 9 o' clock in the morning and a sound was noticed of someone coming upstairs. He guessed about his mother bringing snacks so casually continued reading. The arriving person came nearer still snacks was not put on the table so he looked up and found that it was Sunil. Aakash got scared with his arrival. He had not even got time to prepare for lie. Now he got confused about what to say to Sunil.

"Hey, with whom had you been for two days with whom I am not familiar? Who has been your friend in the college in these days about which I am unaware?" Sunil was very angry, so he attacked suddenly.

"I had lied to mom" Aakash was now mentally ready to tell the truth to Sunil. "Although I tell the truth to you, you won't believe it. An incident which has happened and has been happening with me is unbelievable for me even."

"Stop beating about the bush, tell me straightway." Sunil was still in angry mood.

"I had gone to visit Himalayan hills."

"That is alright but with whom?" Still Sunil sensed that Himalaya began from their city only. So he might have gone in any temple, ashram or hotel of Himalaya. Aakash had understood his sense.

"I had gone alone and that too in the depth of Himalaya, beyond Manikarna. It was a place where nobody from this world could ever go there."

"How did you go then?" Sunil freaked. Excitement took place of anger. After hesitating for some time, Aakash said.

"I will tell you everything but promise me that you won't disclose this matter to anybody, as I have promised someone."

"Have I ever shared any of your secret with anybody?"

"That is right, but this is something which is different, strange and magical."

"Ok, it is my promise to you that I won't share this with anybody." Now Sunil had been extremely curious to listen to the matter.

It is mysterious for me too that I had gone flying in that hill where the native tribes of Himalaya live.

"I had gone there flying. In the Himalayan community of native people, I . . ."

Aakash told Sunil the whole matter from beginning to end. He only skipped Sandhya's chapter. He didn't intend to hide the matter of Sandhya but then he hesitated to inform him about his physical relationship with her.

Sunil was surprised for some time. He was not ready to believe him, he asked with doubt:

"If you could fly, then show me now."

"This is the only reason why I didn't tell you. I can fly only when there is intensity from my inner self. I cannot fly when and where I desire. This is the only mystery of this matter."

"But could anybody see you when you fly?"

"No, the moment my feet raise to fly, I get disappeared immediately. Again when they touch the land, I become visible."

"Give me chance some day to see you flying. And if possible, take me with you to travel Himalaya." Finishing the matter this way, Sunil talked about studying together. Sunil had been searching for him for the last two days to make schedule of reading only.

They decided to study together. They were to study at Aakash's home and it was more convenient for them as the syllabus of mechanical and electrical was almost similar in the first year. In between Aakash missed Priya. He missed her style, grace, beauty everything. He wanted to see her but last quarrel and the way she had cut his words so cruelly harassed him and he changed his mind. Now, it was Diwali time. At that time, He missed her a lot. His Diwali would have been memorable in her accompaniment. On the New Year day Aakash wished to meet her large-heartedly and promised to live together newly forgetting the past complaints. But Aakash could not dare, Priya also did not try to approach him.

It was examination day, the first day after vacation. A hope was there to see Priya without fail. But his assumption failed because the bus atmosphere was tense. Nobody was talking more than hi-hello. All started reading in the bus taking books of the concerned paper. Priya got on from the stand of Sunil. She greeted from a distance but didn't come near to them. She also lost in the book just like others.

Until the exams got over, no special conversation could take place with Priya. Aakash felt sorry for not being able to communicate with Priya openly, laughing and internally in person. Second semester began just after the exam was over. All returned to mischief and enjoyment getting relaxed from exam pressure. College campus was in full focus and bloom with the talks of exam, vacation, films, professors, politics and future planning.

It was possible to talk with Priya but in the presence of everybody on general subjects. Aakash was searching for a private chance so that he could talk to her personally. And he got that opportunity. Sunil had to go to one of the relative's marriage, so Aakash decided to reserve a seat for Priya in the bus so that peaceful communication may happen.

Next day morning, he reserved a seat for her in the bus. Bus arrived at Priya's stop. He saw Priya getting on the bus. He was watching her with a hope that Priya would notice and call him. Till then Arjun sat beside him saying 'hi' carrying a book from there.

He said laughing 'I know that Sunil has gone to attend a wedding.'

"Yes... but I had reserved the seat for one of our friends only." Aakash had to reply with a smile.

"How was your experience of meditation camp on that day?" Arjun asked.

"Wonderful! I really enjoyed it."

Then they had gossip on many topics, but Aakash's attention was not there. He hoped to somehow get the chance in the evening, but it couldn't happen even in the evening.

Next day Aakash thought of going by the motor-cycle so that after the college being over, he could get the company of Priya, if at all Arjun doesn't interefere. He intentionally created a scene of getting up late. "As today is an important class, so I will have to go to college and the bus is missed. Mummy, should I go on my bike?" Saying this he left on the bike seeking permission from his mother.

He took the bike on Kalka-Badi highway road leading to Chandigarh. As soon as he reached Saint Jo Church School, he heard continuous sound of horn from a car behind. He moved his bike on a side so that the car coming from behind could smoothly go. Although he did it, the car driver continued blowing horns. Aakash stopped his bike with uneasyness. Car came near to him. It was a Maruti Zen. As he had worn glasses, he couldn't see the car driver. Aakash was in a mood to fight like anything but as the window glass of the car was down, his mood changed to 180 degree. He got excited. It was Priya who was driving a car. She was alone in the car.

She asked, "Where are you going?"

"College."

"Why are you going on a bike?" Priya asked.

"As I got late today, but where are you going in a car?" Aakash asked in return.

"College, I also got late today so decided to go by car." Priya replied.

"Ok, see you in college then." Aakash said, although he was wishing eagerly that Priya should tell him to keep a car somewhere and go on the bike with him. On the contrary Priya said.

"Keep your bike somewhere and come with me in a car. Today I will drop you at your bike in the evening.—I will also have company."

This was called real love where there was a godly support. Aakash demanded a piece of sweet and he got the full dish.

He said: "But bike . . ." He looked around, "Where should I keep?"

"Keep it in the parking of a civil hospital ahead, no one will say anything."

"Yes, it's right. Ok, you wait for me at the gate of the hospital. I am coming over there after parking my bike." Saying this he accelerated his bike in full excitement.

Aakash sat in Priya's car from the gate of civil hospital. He looked at Priya, she had worn gogals. Her hair was open. She was in blue jeans and white T-shirt with a lining open shirt upon it. Priya was looking like a heroine of a movie. Stylish! Aakash spoke out. "Vow!"

"What?" Priya asked with surprise.

"You are looking dashing driving a car."

"You need not surprise in that as I have been driving it since 12th standard."

"Great! Why do you go to college by bus then?"

"You also have the bike, why do you come by bus?" Priya boomeranged.

"As per my parents' opinion, there is safety in the bus."

"Yes, I have the same story. In addition I am a girl and that is the second reason. But I am a 21st century girl which they are not ready to understand."

"Your parents worry for no reason about you. Actually others should get afraid of you." Aakash told in a slightly joking mood.

"As I denied accompanying you in the Osho camp, that is why you are taunting, aren't you?"

"No ... no, it is completely your choice to join or not to, but your attitude of denial had made me afraid of you." Aakash told clearly.

"See; let me be clear about myself. I consider emotional blackmail or such a response completely childish. If you wish to convince me, do so by logic and science. But never make use words like 'for my sake'. Even my parents can't impose upon me their moral values."

It was really difficult to answer Priya as she was very clear and logical. Still my mind was not ready to believe her to be true. Her logic, honesty, beauty and style were such as would be ready to face any challenge for her. Aakash had also accepted this challenge to win her. Changing the topic, Aakash told:

"Ok, let us forget the matter now. Tell me how did you fare in exams?" Saying this they started talking about exams, vacations, films and hobbies.

The relationship between Aakash and Priya was developing with a particular care on some specific matters pertaining to Priya by Aakash. Even in their friend circle, all believed Priya to be more comfortable in the company of Aakash. Aakash was happy and proud on his relation with Priya.

After three days, the result of first semester was displayed. Sunil had also come back from out of the town. But surprise! Sunil, who always used to get 2-3 percentages less than Aakash, he scored 3 percent more from Aakash this time. Priya was even lesser than Aakash by 2 percent. But it didn't make any difference to Priya. She was neither upset. She considered boring and unnecessary subjects responsible for her low result. But Aakash envied Sunil. He repented for his fewer efforts. His regret was visible in his behaviour, body and face.

"Congratulations Sunil," As Aakash told, so Priya also greeted.

"Hey buddy! Saying this he put hand on Aakash's shoulder and said: beautiful accident may happen sometime."

"No . . . no, it is not an accident. It is the result of your efforts. You are growing clever now." Aakash uttered with suppressed and dry tone of voice.

"You are also clever, man. But you have been behind this time because of paying attention into three directions." Sunil said.

"What do you mean by efforts of three directions? I didn't understand." Priya asked.

"One is college, second Himalaya and the third is study of Logic, right Aakash" Sunil said it in the tone of taunting. Aakash could get the point of college and Himalaya but couldn't comprehend the study of logic. Confused about it, he looked before Sunil, he pointed towards Priya. Aakash laughed and said:

"So you are spying on me, ha?"

"I didn't understand anything." Priya excited with suppressed anger.

"Hey, he is just joking due to my childhood habit. I am fond of nature and logic. So I read on these subjects many times during exam. So he is mocking mentioning my too much interest."

They got relaxed with communication and canteen tea, but Aakash was yet not out of his painful envy. He was hurt by feeling jealous of Sunil's more percentage. Sunil is a childhood friend. He has always been in his support in good and bad times. It is only he who has taken utmost care of Aakash's happiness and suffering. When he got to know that Aakash was hurt by Priya, he accompanied him in the camp though he didn't desire to go. Still he was jealous of his close and best friend Sunil. Aakash felt bad. He got angry and ashamed of his own self. How inferior he was! He repented over thinking that he doesn't deserve love from anybody. He started hating himself. It was painful for him to fight with his own heart. He looked for consolation, help and understanding. He recalled Baba. He felt there is only one person who would bring him out of this pain and that is Baba.

He went home. He told his mom that he is going to Sunil's house and will return tomorrow evening. Saying this he left for Sunil's house on the bike.

He told Sunil "You wanted to see me flying, didn't you? Let's go then, I am going to Himalayan hills. Take me at a lonely and quiet place, on the riverbank near the stones."

"But what is the reason of sudden going?" Sunil asked.

"It's because of a voice raised from inside."

Both began. They searched loneliness in the middle of the stones on the riverbank.

Aakash stood on a stone. He bowed down giving a sight toward the sky. Wings grew out. He was lifted and got disappeared.

Sunil was mesmerized. His eyes broadened out of surprise. It was unbelievable but what he saw was true.

11

'Jealousy' Baba said. 'Why does man envy of the near relatives?' When Aakash arrived at Baba's area, he heard these words. He could not decide that how can he derive the same solution or answer of the problem from Baba through which he is passing through. Is it a co-incidence or sign of nature or miracle? Baba was addressing to the crowd sitting on the stone. Everybody was at the backside to Aakash. He silently went there and sat at one side of the crowd and started listening to Baba who was saying about his pain.

'The one whom you don't know, the one with whom you are not deeply associated; you never envy them. The more the relationship strong, the more envious you become. The intensity of jealousy is more and therefore suffering is also large. Man gets envious of his closed ones more than the strangers. You become happy knowing about the adventurous bravery of the community with whom you are not familiar with. But you become jealous knowing about the same braveness achieved by a man from your community. A small child who loves his mother and loved by her, who has not learnt the lessons of jealousy; still when his mother gives birth to another child and loves and takes care of him, he is filled with resentment from the other child. Why? What's the reason?'

'Yes, I have also come to know, understand and search the same from you.' Aakash thought. Baba's preaching a sermon was going on. 'When you are associated with somebody, suddenly you begin to build an image and define that relation. And when that imagination or definition breaks, you are hurt. And this suffering may come out in the form of jealousy too. This assumption may not be created intentionally by thinking or understanding. This assumption is stored in your unconscious mind taking benefit of your oblivious situation. When it gets the situation against your assumption, it is awakened. For instance, we just saw that a child is envying to his real younger brother. Because he has assumed that he is the only proprietor of mother's rights. In the same way, you draw an inference that the friend who always scores less is created to remain behind from you. But when he precedes you, your confirmed supposition is broken and jealousy is felt.'

'You are right, Baba. My friend Sunil who always used to score less than me in studies has preceded me. And I have been suffering from his jealousy. I am also hurt for breaching the trust. But what to do? I am relieved knowing from you that this is the common psychology of most of human beings.' Aakash addressed mentally to Baba

'You will get relieved listening to me, but that is not the solution, it is only the knowledge about a disease. For instance, while carrying a bier to the cremation house, people change their shoulders due to tiredness. They are relieved by changing the shoulders. But the burden upon them is not lessened. This relaxation is for a few moments. Once again, a new reason will grow up and jealousy will be active. How long will you continue changing your shoulders? The true solution is to get free from this disease.'

Aakash felt Baba is scholar in reading mind. He has read my mind. What I am experiencing is expressed by him through words. Now Baba, please tell me the curing of this disease.

'To become aware of the deed is solution. Whenever you feel jealousy, don't try to justify it. Just observe it without interpreting it as right or wrong, fair or unfair. The way we observe the things we are not connected with, although we make decision of right or wrong in that matter too. But watch it without taking any decision. The helpless mind would make maximum efforts to interpret right or wrong, just be the witness of it and observe without getting trapped into it. The day you will learn to be a witness, you will get completely free from this or such diseases.'

'But how to be an observer? Although aspiring to become a viewer, what when this conscious mind catches us? Mind does not give time. Aakash developed this question into his mind from the experience of meditation. But he need not express it.

'It would be possible to be a spectator, only and only through meditation. Continue doing meditation. You have got habituated to look and live externally. You have forgotten the inside way. The internal road is full of junk and darkness; you will have to go inside. The more you will go inside, the clearer the inside way will become. The lamp of your awareness will illuminate. There will be brightness and everything would be lucid.'

Baba's oration finished. For some time, everybody sat in that amusing atmosphere. Then slowly they dispersed according to their wish and returned towards their camp. Kajal told Aakash coming from the opposite direction, 'I am going. Stay today, we will meet tomorrow.' Aakash held her hand and asked, 'Can't you stay here today? ... Please stay.'

Aakash had agony in his eyes. Kajal was in a mood to stay but at the same time, someone caught her hand and said,

'come on now, there is no need to stay.' It was a stout Bheemo who said this.

'I want to stay' Kajal said.

'I said don't stay, don't I? Bheemo said with a suppressed anger. 'If Kajal wants to stay, let her stay here, Bheemo. She has not stayed with me for long time. I would also be happy if she stays here.' Baba's voice came from behind. The camp people respected Baba a lot. Nobody argued with him. His word was like obedience to all. Bheemo was also not exceptional. He left Kajal's hand and went away.

'Now there was only Kajal, Baba and Aakash there.'

Aakash bowed down Baba and said.

'Baba, I do meditate but I don't feel any effect yet. Teach me to meditate in depth.'

'Dear son, just continue to meditate . . . everything would be alright at its time. Nothing is in our hands except meditation. Continue your efforts having faith and without getting disappointed.' Saying this, he pointed towards the sky full of moon and stars. And said, 'Let us meditate here! When shall we get such a pleasant atmosphere?'

'Should I arrange for your food?' Saying this Kajal was about to go.

'Kajal, why don't you also practice meditation?' Aakash said.

'Son, you perform, you need it. Kajal will do when she desires.'

Aakash felt surprised that the man who insists everybody to perform meditation, how can he give freedom to Kajal? Why doesn't he insist her?

Both performed Vipashyana meditation in the cold flowing breeze of moon night in the accompaniment of mountains.

Kajal arranged the food and all had it together. They talked happily then and slept.

Waking up in the morning, Aakash took bath under the stream and performed meditation in the accompaniment of Baba. Kajal brought snacks there and the three of them had it together. After having snacks, Kajal said.

'Do you want to come in forest? Today we have to go long.'

'No . . . today I want to leave in some time. I will leave after sitting with Baba sometimes.'

'When will you come back?' Kajal asked.

'When wings carry me here, I will . . .' Aakash laughed saying this.

'OK I am leaving then.' Kajal bid farewell saying this.

Aakash went to have a small walk with Baba in the jungle. He discussed with Baba about his internal problems. Baba explained away him the weaknesses of mind. Aakash felt good listening to Baba. He derived new enthusiasm to do meditation.

After coming back, Aakash left seeking Baba's permission to go. Wings grew and he flew in the sky.

But today a strange thing happened. He lifted in the air. But today he flew in the opposite direction instead of the common direction in which he flew often. He went deeper in the hill instead of going in the direction of mountain crossing. He got frightened but nothing was in his hands. After sometime, he got down slowly and gradually.

He got down slowly in the shrub behind a tree. As he looked before, Bheemo and Kajal were standing before each other at a distance. Aakash was able to hear their dialogues as the wind was coming from the direction in which Bheemo and Kajal were standing.

'I know why you stayed yesterday at Baba's place?' Bheemo said.

'OK.' Kajal replied in a single word.

'You did not stay for Baba but for that Aakash.'

'What problem do you have even if it is so?'

'You can't give more importance to anybody than me.'

'Why? Is there any such rule?'

'Yes . . . I have made it from the childhood! And you are compulsorily obliged to this rule because I also follow it.'

'It is your wish to follow the rule but you can't impose it upon me, I am the owner of myself.' Kajal said proudly. Bheemo tried to convince her thinking that threatening won't work.

'Kajal, you are mine only from the childhood. We have grown up together, only I have a right on you. He is a foreigner, how can you pin your hope in him? He will use you but not love you ever.'

'There is no need to talk about Aakash; let us talk about our matter. I don't agree on what you are.' Kajal said firmly. Now there was no ability in Bheemo to argue or convince, therefore he came on forcing.

'What do you mean by you don't agree? I am simply talking and you are showing your smartness? Kajal I can do all forcing, I can make you mine forcefully.'

'That is your illusion.'

"It is not illusion; I can make you mine just now." Saying this he went near her. He caught both her shoulders strongly. "You can get my body forcefully but you have no solution to get my heart and mind." Kajal replied.

'Oh come on! Once I gain body, then mind and heart will automatically be achieved. Everything would be under my control within four or five attempts.'

"OK then have my body and see whether you can attain mind and heart?"

Saying this Kajal stayed there straight. Bheemo got confused for some time.

If there was any girl of city and is forcefully compelled by someone, she would have shouted for help in that case. She would have tried to run away from there in order to save herself or would have tried to quarrel or face to the opposite person. But here, Kajal was behaving as if was inviting Bheemo. Aakash got annoyed at her. He got angry at her foolishness.

Bheemo threw Kajal in the sand catching her hard and placed on her body. He started kissing on her lips. He made her naked and Kajal stayed there as a dead body without giving any expression closing her eyes.

Aakash could not tolerate this. Aakash, who was afraid like anything from the threatening of a bully at the time of Sandhya's relationship, did not get afraid from a bull like Bheemo. He did not think what Bheemo could do him. He ran and kicked hard in the abdomen of Bheemo who was laying on Kajal. Bheemo was tumbled down from Kajal's body. Aakash leapt upon him and started beating him from his hands and legs haphazardly. Bheemo was more strong compared to Aakash. He stood up and leapt back on Aakash with his wild power. Aakash had extremism while Bheemo had wild power. In that fight Bheemo was injured less but condition of Aakash was critical. If Kajal had not come in between and stayed with determination between Aakash and Bheemo, then Aakash would have been half-dead. When Kajal crossed around Aakash to save him, Bheemo stopped beating Aakash fearing that Kajal is not hurt.

As the situation got worst, Bheemo left keeping both there in the straight ascending of rocks and disappeared in the mountains. Aakash was still in his fanaticism. Although beated a lot by Bheemo, Aakash ran behind him but due to stumbling down and getting exhausted he laid there and fainted.

Kajal went him running. She sprinkled water on him. She brought the roots of some tree and crushing it with stone applied where he was injured. Carrying Aakash's head in her lap, she sprinkled water on his face once again and made him drink water. When Aakash opened his eyes, he saw that Kajal was sitting over there leaning with concern. Aakash remained quiet and watched Kajal and started looking around taking a long breath. There was nothing around except sand. He surprised.

'Kajal, from where this aroma is coming?'

'Don't worry about smell. What was the need to leap upon him?'

'He oppresses you, behaves like a tyrant and should I do nothing?'

'You are not aware of Bheemo's power, Aakash.'

'So I should only watch however he behaves with you.'

'He is not able to do anything. Is there any way to go further than body?'

'Is there no worry if he uses the body?' Aakash was shocked with surprise. He tried to stand up in shock but fell down due to pain.

'Yes it is. But body is not that much important. Mind and heart are more valuable.'

'You are speaking rubbish. It seems that you don't understand anything.' Aakash could not clarify. He even could not accept Kajal's belief.

Aakash was relieved enough due to Kajal's herbal root. But some rest was inevitable, so laid there keeping his head in Kajal's lap. He was also enjoying the fragrance. Aakash said.

'Kajal, but for whom had you stayed last night? Tell me.'

'On my own wish.'

'Why don't you tell me truly that you had stayed for me?'

'Why? Can't I stay for Baba?'

'You can. But you stayed for me last night, didn't you?'

'What Bheemo was asking with quarrel, you are asking lovingly? What is the difference?'

'But . . . I want to know?'

"What will you do knowing that? Even if I tell, you would believe only what you wish to. Then it is of no use to know."

"It is tough to comprehend your complex thoughts. Leave it aside." Aakash stood up saying this. Kajal brought plants and applied at those places where she had put medicines on his wounds. She asked him to drink some root liquid forcefully and then allowed him to go.

Bidding farewell to Kajal Aakash left for home.

Jealousy which Aakash had brought was passed over to Bheemo and had gone home carrying Kajal's doubt.

12

Today Aakash's attention was not to the sky, not to the Himalaya nor to the splendor of trees, rivers and lakes. He was not able to comprehend or accept Kajal's behaviour or her relation towards Bheemo.

He could not understand why Kajal did not oppose demands from Bheemo? Why did she give in to Bheemo's demands without any resistance? Why did she not express hatred or rage towards Bheemo? Was she in favour of Bheemo's demands? Did she really not consider anything wrong in having physical relation with Bheemo? Did she have love for me as Bheemo expressed? If she had, then why didn't she agree to it after Bheemo went? If I would not have been there, had Kajal allowed Bheemo to do what he wished?—With all these thoughts, his mind got irritated. But to whom should he share with all these? Whose help should he take up? Kajal is dear to Baba, so there is no meaning to ask him. Will Osho provide its answer as always he does?

Would a woman of the city allow touching her body to the man whom she does not love? If such situation increases, that woman would surely oppose that man vigorously, but not surrender. No matter that man has to attempt raping her. But Kajal was offering her body willingly without any opposition.

Putting on his thinking cap, Aakash reached on the same mountains from where he had flown yesterday. Aakash caught an auto rickshaw from a distance and went Sunil's home.

Sunil was frightened seeing Aakash. 'When did it happen? How did it occur? With whom did you have fight?' All these questions were thrown at by Sunil. Aakash discussed everything to him.

Sunil took Aakash to their family doctor. Doctor also wondered observing such strange bandage made of plants. Removing all, he cleaned the wound, applied lotion and tied white cotton bandage. He wrote tablets for pain killing and asked,

'When did this accident event happen and how?'

Aakash replied the made-up answer. He said 'I had gone into jungle for strolling on bike. Due to bike getting slipped, I fell down. As it was slop, I went down in the jungle tumbling.

'When did it happen?'

'Just today, only before four hours' Aakash told the correct time thinking that doctor may assume the time from the wound.'

'Who bound this bandage of herbal roots and leaves?'

'Why? Anything wrong had happened?'

'First tell me who had done all this?' doctor asked insistently.

'There were some rural people who did this observing my situation.'

'What makes me surprise is that observing your wound I suppose that your situation should have been worse than this. You should even not have been able to stand up. But these herbal roots have recovered you quickly which is wondering me. I want to meet the man who has done the treatment and will have to learn from him.'

'Oh my God!' Aakash was amazed with Kajal's treatment.

'Mr. Aakash, would you make me find out those people?'

'Certainly ... on some day. I will take you there after getting well. Aakash and Sunil escaped from there saying this.

Sunil dropped Aakash at his home. Sushilaben got infuriated watching his bandage and knowing about his accident of tumbling down from bike and getting slipped. She scolded and instructed a lot on how to drive a bike to Aakash. Aakash heard everything very quietly and nodding in affirmation came in the room and slept. But the doubt about the matter regarding Kajal did not allow him to sleep.

Next day in the evening, Sunil had come to meet Aakash while returning from college. Aakash told:

"Sunil, do you know why I had gone to meet Baba immediately?"

"No."

"I was suffering from jealousy toward you. For the first time, you had got 3 % more than I did and I should have been happy for that but I envied you." Aakash began crying saying this. He cried taking Sunil's hand into his hand.

"I also envy many times to you but then it does not make any difference in our friendship. It happens for some time, it is forgotten then. We are still the same as we were." Sunil consoled him sympathetically.

"This is your greatness buddy. But I am weaker than you. I do not deserve your friendship. I am selfish." Aakash was still upset about feeling jealosy.

"Now you will not have to envy me." Sunil said smiling. "Now I am also in love like you with at least one, I can also see her while reading."

"Who is she?"

"She is Nisha Kothari."

"Isn't she that who is fair, tall and always wear Punjabi dress in your class?"

"Yes . . . she is the same. But you don't have to pay attention on her this much so that you can illustrate her fully. She is going to be your Bhabhi."

"C'mon buddy . . . do you doubt me?" Aakash thrashed Sunil saying this.

"Tomorrow I am going to introduce her in our group."

"Not tomorrow, but day after tomorrow, I will come back from the day after tomorrow." Aakash said. On the third day, Priya met him in the bus and lectured him about the matter. She instructed him to drive carefully while scolded him to drive rough. What did doctor say? What did he do? Which treatment he gave? . . . She took these details. Other familiar friends also expressed sympathy. Aakash became happy to see the feelings of all to him.

Afternoon in the canteen, Sunil introduced Nisha to the group.

Slowly the group increased. Arjun also joined. It was a competent group of 8 members. We passed the academic happily and mischivously. Every day in the canteen, all of them met and had a discussion on novel topics.

One day in Delhi, an event occurred which found a tremendous discussion in newspapers, on TV news channels, in every area and street. Taking that event into consideration, sociologists, psychiatrists, journalists, chairmen of great trusts, orators of women association organizations had a huge discussion on TV news channels. How can youngsters, colleges, canteen, Aakash and his friends group get excluded from the discussion? Today the same topic was discussed in the canteen.

The event was of a Delhi gang rape. In Delhi, a girl was raped in a closed bus. She was found on the road in disarray and ragged condition. Fortunately, she was alive. The men who helped that girl and carried her in the police station; they were aggressive to lodge police complaint, catch the criminals and give them strict punishment. And the police was ready too. But that girl was not ready to lodge complaint. She only requested police to carry her home. Police also wondered. Police went her home with a purpose to convince her family members to report a police complaint. Family members were shocked witnessing girl's situation. They became sad but worried on the news of girl's rape getting spread. They asked police not to write complaint and hiding her identity. At that time a boy came there. Police tried to talk to that boy considering him a family member but he broke the engagement with that girl and left infuriating on a girl and her family members. That boy was a fiancé of that girl. Rape was not a new event for Delhi but to a victim girl getting raped resulting into break up of her engagement was a shock although she was not at fault. The actual criminals were those rapists and still the girl was being blamed. This event had come into focus accidently therefore had been the reason of discussion.

'The victim girl is also accused in this case.' Trupti said who was much precautious and caretaker in life.

'How?' Sunil asked surprisingly.

'The first reason is that she should not wander alone at night, and second is she should not sit in anybody's car without thinking.' Trupti clarified.

'And in case it had happened forcefully, she should not surrender willingly. She should roar out the whole road. She should break the glasses of car through her hands and leg.' Priya spoke.

'Priya, as you perceive the situation, it may not be that much easy. The condition in which she has been found, it seems that she would have made maximum efforts to oppose them. But the criminals were in more numbers and more powerful, therefore she could not protest.' Sunil said.

'If she had made efforts, then it is wrong to consider her accused.' Priya said.

'Would Kajal be considered accused, if she did not protest to save herself?' Aakash thought internally.

'Although the girl was not at fault yet her fiancé left breaking engagement with her.' Nisha said 'Why women have to suffer for all injustice?'

'What is the fault of that boy who accepts a girl as wife whose virginity has broken up? And life is for living not for gaining social medal. A new involved member in the group Prakash said aggressively. All nodded in affirmation with him but Arjun said.

'So did that boy loved the girl just for the sake of body? Is there no meaning of heart? Is body wholesome? If body is everything, then a wife is no more than a prostitute forever. Actually it is an insult to a woman.' Arjun said.

'But what is wrong if pure body is expected apart from heart?' Prakash uttered.

'The question is not of body purity. The question is of giving importance body only. Where there is love, true love, body and mind serves no purpose at all. Love precedes body and mind. This was a bodily affection only, it is wrong.' Arjun retaliated.

'But that boy would always recall the virginity destruction while loving his wife which would eventually destroy his love.' Aakash uttered.

'You have continued giving importance to only few parts of physic which is stuck to your mentality. Therefore it is pity otherwise hands, leg and head are also not detached from Kamashastra. We don't consider anything wrong, when someone touches our other body parts. There is nothing wrong when someone perceives badly through mind and thoughts. Why we have stopped in these two parts only? Love is the process of going beyond the physic. Love is to be focused; the problems of body would automatically fade away.' Arjun responded.

"What a thought, man! There is a power in your argument. But the answer is idealistic which is preferable in listening but impossible to implement." Prakash responded back.

"I hate that lover who cannot accept her beloved forgetting an accident happened against her will." Priya gave her opinion.

"Still our society, especially men has not developed maturity in this belief. But they need to think and evolve in this direction. They should search love beyond body and mind." Arjun said.

"Buddy . . . these thoughts are given by Osho." Aakash said.

"Yes, this understanding is given by my mentor." Arjun politely said.

Aakash got more confused. But there was no solution, he had to confine the thought, the event and its memory within.

Again came exam days. It was 20 days reading vacation given. Everybody returned from the outside world into their world. They got busy in their exam preparation. This time Aakash felt more burdens of exams. It was perhaps due to more preparation, being unclear with Priya's relationship, Bheemo and Kajal's event, because of food, hot blazing, or any other reason; but it had a contrary effect on Aakash's body.

He had no desire to eat anything. He felt senses of vomiting. It appeared as if he had a minute fever. He was feeling weak in the lack of food. He gave the last two papers with difficulty.

Aakash felt it was happening due to physical and mental overload. After the exam being over, once he will go in Himalaya hills for 4-5 days and stay in fresh air, pure food, in Baba's accompaniment and wander with Kajal in mounts, he will get healthy soon. But it happened contrary. As Aakash came back after giving exam, he had lot of vomits and fell down due to weakness.

13

Aakash's parents got frightened seeing him stumbling down. They did not doubt about any serious illness. They felt it was due to exam burden and lot of efforts. So they called their family doctor at home. Doctor gave medicines assuming weakness and normal fever.

Apart from taking medicines for two days, Aakash did not recover. In fact, his condition got even worse. He was taken to Dr. Gupta, an M.D. He asked for some tests. From the test reports, he judged that it was an effect of typhoid, therefore he was asked to be admitted in the hospital. Aakash was admitted and once again his treatment began.

Aakash's friends were coming to see him. Arjun, Nisha, Sunil and Priya. Friends tried to talk to him but he had got upset from inside. He even did not like to talk with anybody. He used to take very less food. Whatever energy was left, it was due to medicines and bottles. Priya often used to come. She inquired him, asked him to take care, take the medicines in time and get well soon which Aakash liked. Sunil was continuously in his service in the morning-evening. Many times, Nisha also came with Sunil in the evening. There was no recovery even after four-five days being passed. On the contrary, one day his condition got worse and he had vomiting. All frightened and decided to carry him in a multi specialty hospital situated in Chandigarh.

He was taken into huge global hospital of Chandigarh into ambulance. He was admitted in ICU. On the basis of blood, urine and other tests done, it came to notice that Aakash had hepatitis named disease, which was a serious type of jaundice.

Doctor informed that he was brought very late. The disease was serious. Life was in danger. We will try our level best; all is in the hands of God. Aakash's mother had taken a vow to go to Vaishnodevi on his getting well. Dhara's domicile was in Chandigarh so it was relaxation. She along with her husband had come there. Treatment began in emergency. After keeping Aakash for 48 hours, he was shifted into special room. He was continuously put on bottles and was given doses of medicines. After five long days, his condition ceased to get worse but was not recovered well. Dhara used to come every day in the morning and evening. Sunil was there for the whole day and night, Arjun also came once in the morning. Aakash's father used to come in the evenings due to job. His mother could come once in two days because of domestic and socially decided responsibilities. Actually, she was at ease due to Sunil, Dhara and Arjun's presence.

There was no recovery seen even after spending seven days in the hospital. One day in the noon, Aakash was sleeping in his bed closing his eyes. Sunil had just left to get refreshment. There was nobody in the room. Aakash was alone and at that time somebody thrashed the door and entered. Aakash did not open his eyes presuming any nurse. Aakash was in no mood to open his eyes. He preferred to close his eyes due to weakness and disinterest.

"Aakash."

Aakash was taken aback hearing the voice. He slowly opened his eyes and saw that it was Kajal standing before his eyes in the same one cloth crossing from the whole body to knees and Baba was in maroon robe gown.

Aakash felt delighted. He became immensely pleasant from inside seeing Kajal. His disease had made him disinterested toward all food items and people. Still he became happy to see Kajal and Baba. He was about to stand in an excitement. He tried to sit holding Kajal's hand but did not succeed. He stretched his hand to touch Baba's feet but he even could not bend down. His body did not give support.

Baba said, "Son, take rest. Touch my feet after getting well soon." Saying this he and Kajal made him sit on the support of a pillow slightly raising him up. Kajal sat beside his bed and Baba on the table beside his bed. He was amazed watching them in the city and in the hospital.

He asked, "Kajal and Baba, how did you come here?"

"We just came. But tell us what has happened to you?" Kajal began investigating Aakash intensely saying this. She observed his palm and nails holding his hand. She tested his leg and its nails. Raising the eye lashes saw his eyes. She checked his mouth. When Kajal bowed down to check his moth, Aakash felt the same fragrance which was felt by him during the time Kajal had taken him in her lap after fighting with Bheemo. Basically, Aakash had an allergy of smell but this scent was so divine and charming as if did not belong to this world. He lost into fragrance for some time. His mind was not that much active to ask Kajal about the perfume.

Kajal saw a heap of tablets on the table and bottle attached through injection.

"But I want to know, how did you come here from such a long distance?" Aakash asked but ignoring his question, Kajal took information from him that when had happened what? What was felt? Etc . . .

Aakash slowly informed everything in detail what had happened before exam and the 12 days after his exam. Aakash was feeling sense of freshness after such a long time for the first time. As if Baba and Kajal had brought Himalayan bloom for him with them.

Observing these strange clothed men in the hospital, when a scared nurse came to inquire; Aakash informed him that they were his relatives. After nurse left, Kajal stood up and said, "Baba, I am coming" she left the room saying this.

"Kajal, where are you going?" Aakash tried to call her shouting but he could not shout loudly. He tried to speak once again, but before that Kajal left.

Baba said, "Don't worry. She will just come back."

"But how did you reach upto hospital? How did you come to know about my being here?" Aakash once again asked the same questions. Now it was time to inform him in detail. And until Kajal comes, they had to talk on any matter. Thinking so Baba said:

"We reached here due to Kajal's strong determination," Baba continued taking a pause, "She brought me here making an old-aged man run."

"But why did Kajal compel to come here?" Aakash was wondering knowing that people who are not interested in the external world, why would they persist to come here?

"She might have doubted. Generally she does not have an attitude of inquiry. But before few days ago, she told me, "Baba, Aakash's exams might have been over, yet he has not visited us. Why has he not turned up here for a long time? Etc . . .""

"I was about to come but this disease . . ." Aakash spoke indicating his body.

"I told her that there might be any reason. When he aspires and gets free, he will come to us. But you were not seen for two days even after then, so her concern increased and she asked me again and again and I used to ignore her.

She told me, "Baba, something has surely gone wrong. We must go. You have to come with me." I avoided that too for two days. At last I had to give in before her force and we left.'

"But how did you reach from there to here? If there had been a way, then the men of this world have also reached there." Aakash was highly eager to know that how they came without any way.

'Again your mind is getting active to ask questions.' Baba laughed saying this and said further, 'there may be some ways which you are not able to find out but we know about them. Therefore our community is still saved.'

Aakash thought that it is not appropriate to ask about the way so he asked:

'After how many days did you reach here?'

'We reached Kasol at the third day. Usually it takes five days to reach, but Kajal has not allowed me to rest. She neither sat quiet for a minute nor allowed me to have rest. At the passing of few minutes she would tell me, let us go fast or it will get late.

'Then?'

'Fetching taxi from Kasol, we reached Kalka via from Bhuntar to Mandi.'

'But how did you get the address of my home?'

'While having a fight between Bheemo and you, your school identity card had fallen down from your pocket which Kajal had given me. Your residential address was there in it. On the basis of that we reached directly your home.'

'Aakash understood that Baba had come to know about his and Bheemo's fight. But how did Baba respond to it then? It was not possible to ask about that under the circumstances, so he kept quiet. He recalled that his pages had fallen down here and there during fight which he had collected but there was no need of school identity card after going into the college, so he did not consider it.

'Then?'

'We went your home. We asked your mother about you, she began crying. She talked about your health and this hospital.'

'Had you introduced yourselves?'

'Yes . . . I told that I am a follower of Osho and Aakash is familiar to us. Therefore she gave the address and offered tea and snacks. I had a desire to have tea and snacks but she (Kajal) did not allow me to have it and brought me just hungry here.' Baba laughed saying this.

'Although Kajal brought you here hurriedly, but she left us here talking. What is the reason? Aakash was surprised about where could she go?

At that time the door opened and Kajal entered into the room bringing roots of any tree and leaves. Sunil and Arjun both entered just after Kajal, but hesitated to see two unknown people. there. They could make a guess from Baba's attire that he was surely a disciple of Osho. But Kajal seemed totally unusual belonging to different world.

Aakash called out Sunil and Arjun and introduced to Kajal and Baba.

'Sunil is my childhood friend and Arjun is the follower of Osho and my college-mate too.'

'This Baba is Osho's follower and Kajal stays in the Himalayan community, she is my friend.'

Both felt amazing watching Kajal's eyes which were naturally filled with splendor, deep and beautiful. Kajal's splendor had a kind of simplicity, love, soul and charm.

'Sunil and Arjun please help me crushing these roots and leaves, I want their extract.' The way Kajal talked to them with a kind of authority, both were shocked. They forgot that they were learned and were following the instructions of an uneducated girl.

With the help of Kajal, both brought the extract from the leaves and roots and filled it in a bowl. Kajal asked Aakash carrying that liquid.

'Aakash, drink up this liquid.'

'But what is this?'

'It is Herbal root.'

'From where did you bring it?'

'There is a rivulet under the hospital which has a jungle like place' ahead at rivulet, from bushes grown up on the hills.

'But what would happen with this?'

'You will get well.'

'Did you go to take this?'

'Yes, but no recovery is felt from doctor's medicines, will it recover me? What if something goes wrong . . . ?

'Now have it without asking many questions. Sunil and Arjun, please convince your friend.'

Educated men will never take any risk to ask his friend to have that herbal root liquid made by a rural and uneducated girl during the time of serious illness and hospital treatment. But they were convinced by Kajal. Sunil recalled the statement made by doctor during the time of Kajal's domestic treatment done after Aakash's fight with Bheemo. But Arjun who had no idea about this was also convinced.

He said, 'Aakash, have it. You will surely recover, I am sure.'

Sunil also nodded in affirmation. Aakash had to drink that herbal liquid.

'See, Aakash, after three four hours a kind of yellow liquid may come out from your mouth and nose which will continue for the whole day, it may come out till next day morning but don't get afraid of it. Don't consult any doctor or have any kind of concern. You will surely be recovered.' It seemed that Kajal's eyes and voice had got emotional while saying this.

At that time, door opened and Aakash's sister Dhara came. Dhara also wondered watching the strange kind of people there but before she inquired, Sunil introduced her to them.

'Didi ... I have given Aakash to drink herbal root extract. He will get well soon. Don't worry about anything. And don't even call any doctor.' Kajal said. Dhara also got impressed with Kajal's innocence and ease. She liked Kajal a lot.

'From where did you come?' Dhara asked as she was not familiar with any of Aakash's such relatives.

'From Kasol and now leaving for Kasol.' Baba and Kajal stood up saying this.

'But how will you go?' Aakash asked. He was still surprised how did they come by taxi and will go back? Hence they might not have currency of this world.

'In the taxi' Baba said. Aakash wanted to ask about money but did not find it appropriate.

But he said, 'you have come from a long journey. You seem exhausted, have snacks and tea and then go. Didi has brought domestic snacks for us. Have it.'

Kajal gave affirmation through eyes, so Baba sat. Both had refreshment and left.

Kajal told while going.

'You will get well soon and will come to meet us within 8-10 days too.'

Dhara and Arjun were lost in thoughts, especially by Kajal's attire. Kajal did not seem to belong to this world. If she belonged to other world, how did Aakash come into her contact? It was a surprise but they kept silence.

14

'akash, how do you know this Kajal and Baba? They stay around Kasol. When did you go there? The way they were having concern for you, it appeared that they are familiar very closely to you. When did you go close to them?' Dhara asked.

'Didi, it's a long tale.'

'From her attire, Kajal did not seem to belong to Kasol. I have been to Kasol while going Manikarna. But I have never seen any such dressing. They might belong to any internal area but how did you get acquainted with them so closely?' Dhara was Aakash's sister. Her mind has also been active due to half-a-through information. Arjun was also wondering. Aakash looked at Sunil. Sunil nodded his head in agreement. Aakash said:

'I will tell you everything, but promise me you will not share this with anybody. Otherwise their lives may get harmed.'

Dhara could not comprehend. How can one get harmed knowing about where he resides and how he/she came into introduction? Still she offered promise due to eagerness of knowing the story. Arjun was also firm in his promise.

Aakash told everything about his flying, his reaching there, these people's introduction, their world being totally contrast to this world. He concluded saying that 'I don't understand how and why do I fly? I am a great devotee to nature and Himalayan splendor—which I can fulfill due to my wings sprouted miraculously with the biting of an unknown bird. But why do these wings carry me only in those hills? Himalaya is enormous. But why do wings take me there only? What does existence wish from me? To whom does it aspire to gain? To that Baba? To that Kajal or to that community? Or some other mystery is there. I can't fly on my own wish. Only when something strikes from inside, I can fly then. Actually, it is not any miracle but a carrier only to reach from one place to other. My wings do not give me any special power which might be useful to human beings, society or to the world. I cannot understand why do I go there directing by existence dependently?'

Aakash spoke a lot. It was surprising that he had spoken so long and loud very healthily for the first time after getting ill.

'You go there due to Kajal.' Arjun said. He was saying this looking into the void.

'Don't forget that Baba has taught me to perform Osho meditation. It may happen that existence carry me there to climb on the stairs of self-enlightenment.' Aakash uttered.

'If we explore, we will get many other reasons as well, but I also liked Kajal's reason.' Sunil said, 'Kajal is startling yet simple that touches the heart.'

'I also liked Kajal in the first glance. She appears very charming, excellent and dear." Dhara said.

'Aakash is fortunate that Kajal has strong affection toward him. I see my sister into her.' Arjun said.

'Do you have a sister?' Sunil asked.

'I don't have, but had. She died in a car accident at the age of sixteen.' For the first time Arjun shared his personal life, otherwise he did not share anything about his private life.

All kept quiet. Atmosphere got serious. Two hours passed and Aakash began feeling burning pain in his nose and scuffing in his throat. Slowly white liquid began to come out of his nose. Aakash had to get straight in his bed. He sat hanging his legs on the edge of the bed. Sunil kept spittoon on the floor. Aakash lowered down his head on spittoon. Slowly more liquid began coming out. From white, it turned into red. Yellow cough came out at a particular interval of time. If Kajal had not alerted, he would have surely get worried. But the way she told, it happened at the exact time. Dhara fondled Aakash's back, eyes were also burning during the discharge of yellow liquid. Aakash's back was paining in this time of physical weakness due to continuously sitting. He was fighting back tears due to the pain and burning sensation. It was a frightful scene, but all had trust in what Kajal had said, especially Arjun had firm belief. All kept taking care of Aakash turn by turn during the whole night. That liquid continued flowing out during the whole night, only it stopped in the early morning. Exhausted Aakash slept fast then after.

After Aakash slept, Dhara, Sunil and Arjun were also drowsing. It was 11 in the morning and doctor came on the round. There was a nurse with him too. Aakash was sleeping. All seemed to drowse. Nurse knocked her pen on the bed so that they note the arrival of doctor. Doctor awoke Aakash. Aakash's sleep had not been complete yet not incomplete, he awoke. Doctor checked his eyes, mouth, hands and leg and said loudly, 'excellent, Mr. Aakash, you have got enough recovered. It seems new medicines are more effective than expectations and good enough!' He spoke with proud and looked around. Others had also awakened but still were in sleep a bit. All remained silent.

Aakash's parents came before evening. They also wondered seeing Aakash getting recovered. Aakash demanded food willingly who used to avoid and spoil his face in the name of food. Grams and sugarcane were considered good to be eaten in this disease, so he was given. After having them, he demanded once again, which was a pleasant experience.

Aakash was recovered a lot till next day. Doctor was astonished when he came on the round at 11:00 o' clock in the morning. He was not ready to believe that his changed medicines have resulted so effectively, still he did not want to let the credit go. He said 'Aakash, I am confident that you will soon get discharged from the hospital. My new medicines have shown their effect.'

'Sorry sir . . . but I have not taken your tablets yet. The tablets which you prescribed was brought by my friend Sunil at 3:00 o' clock, but before that I made an experience of herbal root which delayed your tablet.'

It was a time of surprise and defeat for doctor, yet doctor means doctor!

'Aakash, Ayurveda is not science, but experiment only. It may soothe you but not get you well. It may happen that your recovery is the result of our long treatment.'

Aakash was silent knowing that it was in vain arguing with doctor. He was discharged on the very next day. Hospital in charge Dr. Khanna remarked, 'it is a miracle for me—it is unbelievable yet result is there before us.' He thrashed softly on Aakash's back saying this.

His mother said on the way to home, 'My son, this a miracle of taking vow of goddess Vaishnodevi.' Dhara informed her about Kajal and her herbal root treatment.

Aakash was quickly recovering. He was getting energized. He was wishing that Priya comes to meet him, inquires his health, and express feeling for him, and feel happy knowing how he recovered. He was lost in thoughts of Priya and his door room opened, it was Sunil. Aakash said.

'Friend . . . you have come. But I was waiting for somebody else.'

'Whom? For Priya?'

'Yes buddy . . . but it is she who doesn't turn up.'

'And this heart is not ready to accept the fact.' Sunil finished the line.

'Sunil, why does she not turn up?'

'Perhaps, she may have no idea about the seriousness of your disease.'

'But when I was in Kalka, she had visited me. I have got badly ill and therefore will be admitted to Chandigarh was known by her.'

'Yes. Perhaps she might not be able to tolerate your pain—as she can't bear it, she doesn't come.' Sunil mocked.

'Oh, come on buddy . . . I am waiting for her tonic to get completely well and you are joking?

'No. Now it's her turn to arrive. One cured you and the other will come to energize your health.' Sunil also indicated to Kajal.

And Sunil turned right. On the very next day, Priya reached by her car at 11:00 o' clock. She came hastily in open hair, black jeans pant, and pink top and wearing gogals. She got information about Aakash and reached his room. When she came, Aakash was reading something sitting on chair-table. She spoke immediately after coming.

'Come on . . . buddy, patient should be in the bed and instead he is on chair—table.'

'Yes . . . pain also got tired waiting for someone, so went away and I got well.'

'It is alright whatever happened. But you are benefited in my late arrival, right?'

Priya was smart in communication. Her arguments were although unacceptable yet difficult to challenge.'

'May God bless to that country girl who gave herbal root to me and I recovered, otherwise . . .' Aakash left the sentence half-a-through. He intentionally spoke country girl instead of Kajal so that Priya doesn't doubt.

'Great! It is good that miracles happen. I thought this is the result of my prayer done in Taj mahal.' As she talked about the love temple Taj mahal, so he generated some hope and thinking that he should not extend the joke, Aakash said:

'You take everything in joke, but I was serious.'

'You are right. But what would have happened with my presence here? It was doctor who had to do everything.'

'But . . . I would have felt good.'

'There is no comparison between your sense of feeling good and my situation. I had been to Delhi to my maternal uncle's home. His friend had come from America. I had to go to Agra and Mathura with them, therefore could not come. What can I do in that matter?'

There was no meaning to convince Priya. There is a big difference in journey and illness. What if her closed one had been ill? But how to convince her?

Priya left after gossiping for some time. But one thing was sure that Aakash was feeling fresher after Priya's visit.

Aakash became completely alright within two-three days. Aakash wished to visit Himalayan hills and meet Kajal and Baba. Now family members had also known about it, so there was nothing to hide like. He took permission of his mother and got ready to go next day.

As there was no point to hide anything so there was no need to fly hurriedly. Therefore, Aakash left at 8 comfortably having snacks and tea.

He was about to fly. At that time, he recalled that it was nine days past when Kajal came in the hospital and gave herbal root.

15

Aakash reached in the charming Himalayan hill while flying, but instead of getting down on his usual place, he started going down from that place; where it always appeared to him a river like flowing something. Slowly he proceeded to get down on one side of the river. The more he went down, the clearer the river appeared. Water was of blue colour, as clear as the sand beneath was visible. There were uneven-rough, small-big, black or grey coloured stones between the flow of the river. The river appeared ephemeral due to mountainous slopes as compared to the river flow of level area. It appeared flowing with a speed. And in that also, where water was getting obstructed, sweet music was generated due to obstacles and white bubble was seen. Somewhere breadth of river was narrow, while somewhere large. Somewhere it was rock slope or somewhere breadth of sand.

There were beautiful trees of pine, apple, guava and plums on the mountainous slope at the two sides of the river. On the stone of that river bank, Kajal was sleeping covering her face with one hand in order to avoid the direct sunlight, pressing other hand under her head, stretching one leg and the other curving through knee. Kajal's sleeping on the stone in this style was making the whole of splendor charismatic. Aakash went to her getting down.

"Sit down, Aakash, I have just taken bath; let me dry out myself and clothes."

"No problem." Aakash began observing the magnificence of nature saying this. He began strolling. Aakash felt cool response from Kajal. For a moment, he felt that she ignored him. Kajal then settled to sit. She turned and twisted her body to shake off idleness; stretched two hands raising them higher in the air bending from waist. Aakash felt if camera had with him.

Kajal asked Aakash, "come here Aakash, let us sit here."

"No, it's hot now. Let us go under that tree." Aakash was right. Sun was blazing due to pure atmosphere and height. The sun had also been higher.

Kajal stood up. Both went near the tree and sat there on the stone.

"It is really amazing of these Himalayas, this river, mountains, this invigorating air and trees." Aakash uttered glancing all around.

"Yes . . . it is really incredible to live in Himalayas."

"But I wonder why do birds are not found in much amount here? I have not noticed any other bird except crows."

"The one who can bear this cold and atmosphere, survives here"

"So, are there no other birds here except crows?"

"Apart from them, there is a Devvani (robin) bird here which is mysterious and wonderful.

"How does it look?"

"Golden fur, violet body, and red beak, it is a sparrow kind small bird."

"But I have been coming for a long time here and yet not seen it."

"Do you want to see it?"

"Yes", Aakash said. And Kajal made a different sound from her mouth, and the bird as described appeared on her shoulder within moments. It cannot be said that it came flying because it had suddenly appeared on the shoulder.

"How did it come suddenly?" Aakash was yet not able to understand from where did the bird come? So he asked confusingly.

"It disappears while flying and becomes visible while sits—just like you."

Aakash lost in thoughts. He felt that he had seen that bird somewhere. He said, "I think I have seen it somewhere."

"You have seen it in your childhood. As it bit you, you are able to fly today."

Aakash recalled. He recalled the dream and childhood as well into which he observes the wounded bird lying on his terrace and does its treatment compassionately. And during that time, he had bitten him through beak. Aakash spoke.

"Yes . . . it is absolutely right. I retained everything, but why couldn't I fly from the time it bit me?

"This bird also cannot fly so many years from its birth until it gets young. And this is their difficulty. Until it can fly, it is visible because of which it becomes prey to other animals. Therefore, these birds are in very less amount. You were also bitten by this bird in childhood because of which you could fly in your youth."

"That is right, but why can't you fly? The bird knows you and becomes visible at your call even."

"But it doesn't gnaw me."

"Try out so that it bites you."

"This bird has never nibbled anybody. It bites to any one person only among lakhs with the aspiration of existence." She put her finger in bird's mouth saying this but it didn't bite.

"Then why did it bite me?"

"With the desire of existence. Do you know why is it known as Devvani? Because it delivers us the messages of existence. For instance, natural calamities, heavy rainfall, earthquake etc. it provides symbolic indications to us through its behavior and yells."

"It is really amazing. But what can be the suggestion of existence in biting me?"

"If it wasn't desired by existence, why had it bitten you coming from a long distance of Himalaya to your town?"

"But Kajal it can be co-incident. It might have forgotten the way and reached from Himalaya to my town where he had a collision with other bird and have fallen down on my terrace and bitten me out of fear." Aakash recalled that it had bitten him after some time of the treatment while staring. "I will call it co-incidence only."

"What educated people like you call it co-incidence; we call it desire of existence."

"But what difference does it make?"

"It makes a huge difference, Aakash. Co-incidences exist only outside while existence is connected with entirety."

As Aakash found Kajal's talk incomprehensive, he stopped there and asked.

"Then why do I come only at your place by flying? When I came for the first time, why were your people ready to kill me instead of considering it existential wish?"

"It is only known by existence why do you come here? It is also inexplicable to me. And one more thing, those people had doubt about your arrival here, but when you said you have reached here flying and started looking for wings, I suddenly recalled Devvani bird and explained Baba about it. Therefore, Baba rescued you."

The whole scene appeared before Aakash's eyes, he mesmerized.

"Did you come in the hospital on some message from existence?"

"Don't you get tired thinking a lot?" Believe that I came co-incidentally and saw you ill. And whatever sense I had, I treated accordingly and you got well."

"No . . . but what made you worry to come here? Baba was telling . . ."

"That Baba knows, how he observed my restlessness. Leave all this. I am hungry like anything. If you are also hungry, then come and let us relish fruits and enjoy the pleasure of Himalaya."

Both ambled in the jungle till evening. They had fruits and enjoyed and then came to Baba climbing up. Kajal was laughing but Aakash was panting for breath.

Baba was delighted to see Aakash well. He smiled looking at Kajal.

"You have really got well within nine days and have been as healthy as being able to climb the mount."

"Yes . . . it is the miracle played by Kajal's herbal roots, Baba." Aakash said.

"And what about my contribution?" Baba said smiling.

"Baba, you came there but why didn't you stay with me? You belong to that world, don't you?"

"Therefore I didn't want to stay. I have stayed a lot, now I like here only."

"Baba, where did you live earlier?" Aakash again began investigating.

"That is not more important. Tell me, do you practice meditation?"

"Yes . . . but not daily. I do it when have a mood. Many times, I don't perform meditation for long, while some time, I do it continuously for long without any reason."

"Why? Don't you enjoy it?"

"It is not the matter of enjoyment, but I witness no change inside in spite of doing meditation. Anger, antagonism, aspiration, greed, jealousy, I see everything stable there. Do I mistake while meditating?" He found it improper to doubt about meditation looking Baba's personality.

"Don't practice meditation considering desire, anger, greed and jealousy. Enjoy it. Result will follow. It is the internal (self) journey. It helps to be more insightful."

"I will try to perform it every day." Aakash also decided to enjoy it internally. Baba's persona was such that everything was acceptable in his presence, whatever he asked.

It was evening now. The community people began to gather and the evening meet began with music. Baba was speaking.

There always occurs misunderstanding in love due to attachment and habit.

Many times we perceive liking as love. We consider someone's fluency, style, graciousness, speech, behavior, logic, thoughts, study or information enough to love that somebody. But the liking comprises of one part only, no matter it is less, medium or more. If the resemblance of liking is more, it is possible to be with each other for long. if it is less, it may not be for very long. If it is least, you may enjoy it for a little time. Where there is liking, disliking is also there. The moment we decide someone's accompaniment based on choice, the part of disliking becomes active and strong immediately. And it becomes so extreme at a long time that it destroys completely to your sense of happiness. In the same way, considering habit as love is the second big misunderstanding. When one lives or has to live with someone daily, an attitude of adjustment is developed by living with each other. To avoid conflict, one doesn't consider dislikes. But it is also not love. Relationship developed out of habit doesn't involve warmth or depth in it. We fight at the point of disliking, but again get together due to habit. Love developed out of habit is like addiction, which we follow it compulsorily although not liking it.

What is love then if it is not habit or liking? Love is entirely into which the value of acceptance is bigger than liking or disliking. Those who love each other may disagree to their choices but they do not oppose each other's disliking. They accept each other with their limitations where love is beyond habit and liking-disliking. There resides amazing and unsophisticated pleasure in it. Majority of people live due to liking and habit. Only the extraordinary ones can experience true love.

With this Baba finished his perception. The community people dispersed one by one. Aakash had sat on his place lowering his head down. At that time someone touched his shoulder. It was rough and strong hand. It was Bheemo standing in moon night as he saw raising his head and eyes. There was a sense of apology in his eyes and face. Bheemo didn't utter words, but his silence was communicating a lot. It appeared that he was about to cry. Aakash also put his hand on Bheemo's in response and patted as if he had also forgotten the past. For some time, communication was done in absence of words and then Bheemo left. Aakash had such a deep sense of experience in the silent communication for the first time in his life.

16

I n all creations of the God in this universe, woman is the most mysterious creation. Scientists have been able to invent from big animals to small insects, from visible mountains, forests and rivers to non-visible microorganisms too. They have travelled from the earth to galaxy. They have also made observation from the Peak of Himalaya Mountain to the depth of sea. But they have failed to meet the challenge of knowing women. Nobody dares to challenge knowing women. Oh! It is okay if one is not able to know her in a day or in some time but even after so many years married life, the man repents for not being able to know a woman.

Aakash's father also used to share the same thing about her mother but Aakash considered it as a joke on his part. But today, he has been passing through the same experience. He could not understand what Priya wanted. Some time he felt that she loved him while some time, he felt that she consideres him not more than a common friend. Priya was endowed with the mysterious trap around her. It was always mystifying to guess how she would perceive and respond to your thought. In case of Priya it was possible as she was an educated metro girl brought up in the hypo critic society. But Kajal was a common girl nourished in the nature of a small community, still was inexplicable to

Aakash. Generally she talked about everything but when it came to discuss about her or about feelings, she became completely quiet. Either she would change the topic or laugh at it. It is really puzzling to decide what she desires. Generally, it seems that she has relentless affection toward Aakash. But it is difficult to acclaim her affection with love as her affection is for the whole universe; she considers every happening as a game of existence. And she looks with persistent affection to it without any complaint. So, in the game, the existence of Aakash becomes clear. She has affection toward Bheemo too who attempted to rape her. She has not broken her relation with him even after such a cruel act on part of him. Anybody else in place of Kajal would have banished him from the community but Kajal has treated this matter in general just like other matters. She might have told Baba about Aakash and Bheemo's quarrel and fight but have hidden about the attempt to rape. Otherwise someone would surely have punished him.

Aakash felt, it is OK if I don't understand Priya and Kajal. But even I cannot understand myself. Do I love Kajal or Priya? If I love Priya then why do I get curious to meet Kajal? Although I tell everybody that I am infatuated due to Baba, Himalaya and desire of existence but is the desire to see Kajal not prime in all these? If it is not so, then why did I wish to hide about Kajal from Priya?

Once again Aakash felt . . ." No no, I like Kajal but not as a beloved but as a friend only. I like her company but my love is only for Priya; because I like to think about her. I like her style and wish to do anything for her." In this way, he came to a conclusion to save himself from the harassment and complexities of thoughts.

Still his days were passed with Kajal and Priya. Aakash, who did not miss the company of Priya in college, went to meet Kajal in the hills of Himalaya during vacation without fail. He went there as if he was pushed by someone. It was also known by the group of Aakash that he was infatuated toward Priya as he did not oppose Priya even though she argued wrong, behaves stubborn or arrogant. Either he would favour Priya or kept quiet but never opposed her. In the case of Priya too, Aakash's importance was much. She liked and accepted Aakash more than others. Still she was smart in maintaining a kind of distance. If Aakash tried to over express his feelings, either she stopped or broke him in between without any hesitation. She never shared her personal matters or programs with anybody, just like Arjun. She joined friends in the party and sometimes she threw a party to friends. Although she used to enjoy and make others have fun, it appeared that she had encircled a limit around her, which no body can cross.

Sunil was not able to understand Aakash's two-way journey, yet he kept quiet. Once he expressed his desire to come with Aakash in the Himalayan hills and meet Kajal, Baba and enjoy the splendor of that world which was unaffected by the modern world.

Aakash said, "Buddy . . . I would also like to take you there but those people don't prefer and wish any outsider in their world."

"But you can try for me. Talk to Baba, if he permits; I would be able to see it."

"This time I would surely ask him." Aakash said. Aakash expressed Baba about Sunil's desire. Baba thought for some time and then said. "OK, you can bring him here. As the existence wishes!"

Aakash shared the good news of getting permission with Sunil. Next time when Aakash was to go, he had called Sunil at his home the previous night.

Both woke up early in the morning and got ready. Sunil was so excited to view the new world and to meet Kajal, Baba and unknown place of Himalaya.

Coming in the spacious area, Aakash prayed folding his hands and wings grew out. He lifted Sunil widening his hands and as he wished or tried to fly, wings disappeared. As two-three efforts to do so, failed, Aakash had to cancel Sunil's wish to take him there. Sunil was disappointed but they were helpless. So Aakash left alone for the Himalayan hills and Sunil watched him with an upset face.

Days passed. Aakash's days were passing in college, Priya, Kajal, friends and practice of meditation. In this way, the last year of engineering turned up. Everything happened very normally. The relations were getting deep but did not seem clear. Everything was normal, there were no big crises. Life was passing through in the contradiction, in confusion and happiness. In all these, one day . . .

As Aakash was getting ready to go to college, he got a call from Priya. She was frightened during the call.

"Aakash, my father has met with an attack and we are going to Chandigarh hospital" she cried saying this. Aakash was thinking what to say to console her and Priya kept the phone off.

Aakash perplexed what to do? Did she inform to other friends or not? What should I do now—to go college or to Priya. He called Sunil. Sunil said.

"Stupid, you should not think much, just come at my home on bike. Till then I inform everybody. We should stand by Priya. We will go to Chandigarh hospital."

Sunil was clever in social matters. He was more smart than Aakash in all these. He was impressed with Sunil's smartness.

Within no time, all gathered at Sunil's home. Aakash had not asked in which hospital Priya's father was taken to. So it was difficult to decide where to go. This also resolved by Sunil. First he called at Priya's home but no one received the call as being nobody at home. Then he rang up at her factory, it was received by her father's secretary who informed about the hospital.

Aakash, Sunil, Arjun, Nisha, Trupti, Prakash all got arranged on bikes and reached in Chandigarh Heart Institute and Hospital in Chandigarh.

When they arrived at the hospital, they saw red light outside the operation theatre room. And Priya, her mother, her younger brother, relatives and friend-circle all were waiting in the lounge here and there. All were looking worried. They were in chaotic attire and hair. It appeared that they might have not got the enough time to get ready. They were looking at the red light of operation theatre again and again after few minutes being passed. Some visitors were whispering something in a group standing in the corner. Priya was lying on a waiting bench raising her legs and placing head upon knees. She was in night suit. Her mother and brother were sat beside her worriedly. All went to Priya.

"Priya" Aakash called her softly and put his hand on her shoulder. Priya raised his face; her eyes were swollen, sleepless and weepy, hair dispersed. It was surprising that Aakash found her charming even in that serious situation; today it was affectionate beauty unlike usual stylistic and intelligent beauty. Priya suddenly stood up. She hugged Aakash hard with her two hands and keeping her head on his shoulder began crying. All friends encircled her. Nisha began moving her hand on her back. Someone brought water and asked her to have it. Priya calmed down. Aakash had been full of emotions not seeing the situation of Priya but sensing her special feeling toward him. He was not able to utter words. Whatever was to be asked by him was inquired by Arjun.

"How did it happen suddenly?"

"Last night at 3:00, papa had pain on the left side of his chest. He perspired although sitting in an A.C. room. We got scared observing this." Priya began slowly and then told clearly looking straight before Aakash. "Mummy woke me up. I immediately rang up our family doctor Dr. Desai and asked him to come." Taking a breath, she informed further, "He came and suggested to admit papa immediately in the hospital. We called out ambulance and came directly in Chandigarh hospital. It was due to Dr. Desai's contact, everything proceeded quickly, and we got urgent treatment otherwise . . ." Priya sobbed again saying this.

Their discussion could have continued like which treatment was given, when was he taken into operation theatre, how many blockages are there etc . . . But the door of operation theatre opened and doctor came out. All went running to doctor.

"Congratulations Mrs. Pathak" Doctor informed addressing to Priya's mother, "Everything has been over without much trouble. But we will keep him in ICU for two days to have precaution care. And then we will discharge him, is it alright Mrs. Pathak?"

All were relieved and comforted now. Faces became stress free. Discussions were held. Priya also seemed fresh now. New guests were arriving to inquire the condition and the old ones leaving. All began scattering except the family members. Sunil and Aakash stayed for long.

Next day in the morning, Aakash called Sunil informing that he would go to hospital in the morning before coming in the college and would visit Priya in the evening after college hours. So he would prefer bike to bus as it will be more convenient.

Sunil had a desire to accompany Aakash. He didn't wish Aakash to go early on bike in the morning and go back lonely to home in the late evening. But he did not want to be an obstacle in Aakash's developing love, so he showed unwillingness to join him. And perhaps Aakash understood it too.

Every morning Aakash reached hospital at 7:00. He sat with Priya and her family. After finishing other minor works over there, he went to the hospital. After departing from the college in the evening, again he went to the hospital. He discussed with Priya about the what was taught, shared the events of the college and left for home late in the evening. It was good on part of doctor that he didn't test Aakash as a lover much and discharged Priya's father within two days as said. Priya's father was relieved from the hospital with the instruction of food preserve and prescription of necessary medicines. Doctor gave advice to rest for some days at home for the sake of safety measures.

Once again all the friends went at Priya's home to meet her father during his rest period. Aakash also visited twice-thrice.

Everything was normal now. Priya was about to begin coming in the college. Aakash and other friends were excited to welcome Priya. Aakash got up early in the morning and got ready. He was about to catch the bus and Priya rang him up.

"Aakash, I will go to college by car. Will you give me company? Come at my home on bike, we will go together." Priya didn't wait for Aakash to reply yes or no and asked to come straightforwardly. Aakash liked Priya's obstinate attitude for him a lot, no matter Aakash's inflexibility was not liked by Priya at all.

Aakash also recalled that when he had asked Priya during his serious illness "why didn't you come to inquire about my health"; he was given with logical yet unacceptable answer. He was disturbed for this, but he didn't want to lose the opportunity of Priya's affection. So he reached happily at Priya's home. Both left for college by car from there. Priya said on the way.

"Thank You Aakash for your generous support in my affliction days."

"There is no need to show gratitude. Who else will help a friend if not a friend?"

"Your warmth really soothed me."

Aakash's heart began lifting. He felt assured that Priya was in his love. He wished to thank the heart-attack. He also recalled the words told by Priya at the time of his illness "what was my need, whatever was necessary was to be done by doctor; on the contrary I had been an obstacle to all." Aakash had a desire to ask "I hope I had not been a barrier to anybody there." But he didn't utter anything. He didn't want to lose the opportunity. He spoke even modestly.

"Priya, whatever I did was not only for you but have done it for me too."

"Means?" Priya dazed.

"I also enjoy supporting you."

"Really? But is there any special reason of this?"

"I did it for a relationship which exists in the absence of reason."

"Don't converse philosophically, speak straight."

". . . because I like you."

"But I also like you." Priya said. They talked on many matters, but Aakash had been emotionally full only with this sentence. He was in the seventh sky. He got excited to share this news with Sunil, Kajal and Baba but at that time the words of Baba's sermon "Liking, habit and love" cracked. The liking word uttered by Priya disturbed him but she might not be aware of the in-depth knowledge of words therefore might use 'liking' word. Or she may have used this word purposively as being a woman to express her feelings of love. He pushed Baba's sermon in depth of his mind thinking this.

The members of their group had begun to observe their relationship in a special way after the event of Priya's father's attack, the way Priya had cried in the hospital hugging Aakash and described that incident looking straight to his face. Priya and Aakash had come close too.

Aakash also shared the conversation with Sunil held in car. Aakash also shared his desire to marry Priya with Sunil. He also shared his determination to talk on this matter to his family members. Sunil found him over excited. Sunil advised Aakash to wait for some time and make some more clarifications. But this event was enough for Aakash to make his future plans.

He was curious to share with Kajal about Priya's love. He was in the search of opportunity.

17

Dhara had come to stay in Kalka-parental home-with
her son for the last few days. Dhara's husband had
to go on deputation in the head office Delhi with
regard to his company's work. As Dhara did not want to
lose the opportunity of staying with Mummy-Papa and
brother and so had come to Kalka. On one Friday, she came
in Aakash's room and said.

"Brother, I want to meet Kajal, will you take me there?"
Aakash was also thinking to go but was avoiding it. As
he believed that her sister would feel bad if he goes in the
Himalayan hills keeping her here. His heart got excited
with Dhara's proposal but calmed again.

"Sister, but how can I take you there?"

"Why, you can lift me while flying. We will leave in the
morning and return by evening."

"But wings do not allow me to fly carrying others."

"How can you say that?"

"Sunil had also expressed desire to fly just like you. I
had tried to fly carrying him with me, but we could not fly."
Aakash clarified.

"He is your friend, but I am your sister. As we are
similar by blood, that bite of bird may allow me to come.
Dhara was also skillful to exhaust the mind like Aakash.

"OK, we will try out tomorrow. Come up early tomorrow in the morning. We will make an effort."

"If the effort succeeds, I will be able to meet Kajal and will see the newly wonderland of Himalaya, otherwise you alone may go. At least I will see my brother flying." Dhara went downstairs to sleep saying this.

Next day, Dhara could not reach at the predicative time on the terrace due to her baby but came at 8:00 in the morning. Aakash was punctual about timing but didn't want to displease his sister fouling his face. He was also skeptical whether he would be able to fly carrying Dhara. But he didn't utter before Dhara's stubborn. And even if he would not be able to fly carrying her, he was permitted by Dhara to go alone. So he was happy.

Dhara came, Aakash stood up on the terrace. He prayed folding hands and wings grew out. Dhara watched the incident delightfully. Aakash tried to lift Dhara twice-thrice, but at every new effort the wings disappeared the way they had moved out during the time of Sunil. At last Dhara asked him to go alone. And he tried, lifted up from the floor and vanished. He began flying toward Himalayan hills saying 'bye' to Dhara. Dhara watched it with astonishing expression.

This time also he flew toward a river. He was going on the upper part than last time where stream was gushing abruptly due to sloppiness and stones and water was flowing fast. There were the same pine and other trees around. He saw that Kajal was sitting on a narrow stone placed near the shore in between the flow. She had curved her knees and putting face upon it, was facing the water flow. She was looking utterly charming. She had sat keeping the uniformity of splendor with river, mountain, and Himalaya just like a statue. As if there was no human being, but an invention of Himalaya's newly majestic existence. Aakash continued staring her for some time from a distance and enjoyed the scene without fluttering eye-lash. After some time, he proceeded near shore taking utmost care of not sounding even his foot. He didn't want to create any barrier in Kajal's cogitative condition. But he didn't understand how Kajal knew about his arrival and said:

"Come ... Aakash." Kajal directed her face toward Aakash.

I was coming utterly quiet taking care not to make sound. How do you come to know?" Aakash uttered this sentence only to express sense of wonder as he was already given answer of this by Kajal earlier.

"Come here. You will enjoy watching the water flow sitting on the stone." Kajal said.

"But won't the stone be narrow for two people?"

"No, it won't be any problem sitting near to each other."

"OK. But how should I come?" Aakash indicated on the stone situated in the middle of water.

"Get down in water carefully supporting the branch of tree from the side of shore. Come ahead supporting the branch, as soon as you come this side, I will stretch my hand fetching which you will reach here."

"Is water too deep?"

"No"

"Then I will come without taking help of any support." Aakash spoke with manly attitude.

"It is not so easy as you perceive it to be. Do as I say."

"Oh come on now. Now I have also been usual to this place." Aakash got down in water wearing off his boot and socks. But he had to take support of branch immediately due to the speed of water flow, slippery and rough land. Kajal laughed loudly watching this. Stretching one hand to

Aakash and keeping other on the stone, Kajal supported Aakash in climbing up the stone.

"Do you realize now, Aakash?"

"Yes, there is nothing wrong in accepting fault rather than hiding it." He placed closely beside Kajal saying this. He sensed the usual intoxicating, lovely and charming smell from her. He saw here and there, but there were no plants or flowers around. He moved his face to know from where the aroma was coming? Kajal asked observing him. "What are you searching for?"

"It is really lovely fragrance. I am finding out from where it is coming. I think it is coming from you. Do you make use of flower sap?" Aakash wanted to use the word 'perfume', but said 'flower sap' thinking that Kajal won't understand it.

"No"

Aakash sensed that it was Kajal's own fragrance.

Aakash said, "Kajal, why do you sit near the river shore most of the time?"

"I am akin to river, river-flow, and the music formed from the collision of water with stones." Kajal said.

"You like river-flow much, what if this flow will stretch you away with it?" Aakash said jokingly. And today Aakash was in a very good mood too.

"If river-flow and Himalaya wishes, it will happen." Kajal responded.

"But this flow comes in our world." Aakash said.

"Then I will go there with it."

"But would you be comfortable in our world?"

"Comfort zone doesn't matter much, what matters is the desire of existence. And you will be there in that world, then why should I worry?"

"Yes. What if this flow stretches you somewhere else?

"Then come to take me there."

Aakash kept quiet. For some time, they enjoyed the jingle of flow quietly. Aakash spoke after some time.

"Kajal, I have come to share good news with you."

"What is it?"

"I am in love of a girl named Priya Pathak and going to marry her." Aakash was saying this staring the river-flow. If he had looked before Kajal for a moment, he could have noticed a cloud of soreness crossing through Kajal's face and eyes for a moment. Kajal didn't utter anything. Aakash said further.

"She has been studying with me in my college and classroom for the last three years. I aspired her heartily which I could express verbally before few days only. And she has also given agreement."

"Great, when are you going to marry then?"

"After the college being over. I was curious to share this news with you." Saying this Aakash talked about college, Priya, her father's illness, and friends for long. It continued till evening and then they came on the shore where Kajal had already put a basket ready full of fruits. She took the basket in hand and said.

"Are you coming to give this good news to Baba?"

'Yes, but I am in no mood to go on foot.' Aakash saw toward higher mountains saying this.

'Then what shall we do? You reach by flying and I will come on foot.'

'That also does not seem appropriate.'

'Then fly carrying me.'

'But how?'

'Why, lift me with basket and then fly.'

'But it is not possible. I had tried many times to fly carrying Dhara and Sunil, but as I lifted them, the wings disappeared.'

'Then try once more or get ready to walk.'

Aakash got ready to try it once again unwillingly. He raised his hands in the air, prayed and wings came out. Widening hands, he carried Kajal with basket. But to his surprise, wings did not vanish away this time and he could fly. Not only he could fly, but went toward the decided ground of community.

They got down on the small ground situated outside the community. Aakash's wonder was not resolved yet. Questions raised in his mind.

'Kajal, how did it become possible? I did not succeed in flying while carrying Dhara and Sunil and how could I fly carrying you?'

'You should know this; I have no idea about flying.' Aakash became quiet but he got confused due to this miraculous happening. So Kajal said,

'Come on now ... without thinking much. Let us go to Baba putting this basket aside.'

Both went to keep the basket. They met father. And they left to meet Baba greeting after familiar people of community.

Once again it was the same narrow, rough, and manually invented path on the edge of mountain. On one side, it was higher and straight climb; somewhere it was a mountain full of rocks and covered with trees. And on the other hand, it was a straight sloppy valley which was covered by pine trees and rocks. In the middle, there was a stream upon which path was constructed arranging stones upon it. It was really dangerous like stunt. If walking people would have been aired on TV, the viewers' would have watched it breathtakingly. They would have appreciated it with a great round of applause and TRP of the show would have induced for free.

"Kajal, it is advisable to make a wooden railing on this track in order to lessen the risk."

"But there has been no accident among us, what is the need of this then?"

Aakash wondered yet spoke, "But there may be accident on some day. Any old or child may fall down from here."

"Small child or old people walk catching hand while adults walk playfully. We see no danger in this."

"What is the reason of not seeing danger?"

"It is due to bare foot. The touch of our soles alerts us about possible danger. Our legs have got used to these rocks; therefore, they save us sticking through floor during the time of danger."

"So you mean to say that you people are really not afraid."

"Yes . . . as we don't fear, we don't lose confidence. And as we don't lose confidence, we can naturally walk here. And as we are natural, danger no more remains danger. We are able to walk through this path even when it is dark."

Aakash recalled that after the evening session being over, all might go through this way. Aakash found Kajal's thoughts higher and weird. He thought these people are not aware of the use of science and technology. But if I convince Baba, he will consider and get wooden railing set. He was in these thoughts and his leg slipped. He was about to stumble upon, but Kajal came to his rescue before that and saved him as usual.

"Second reason of not falling down is we don't think while walking." Kajal laughed saying this.

"But how long will you save me in the same way?" Aakash said this recalling the river-flow event.

"Till you continue falling down." Kajal again laughed saying this.

Both reached to Baba. Aakash informed everything about the track and said:

"Baba, what I opine is that there is nothing wrong to make use of science and technology for facilities and comforts. But Kajal and community people don't understand this."

"I believe that it is wrong to make use of science and technology for amenities and comforts. Have people been happier with the use of science and technology? Has he been stress free? Actually, human being has been ignorant, lazy and luxury oriented due to it. He has been losing his abilities. The use of science and technology should be used for development, not for disgrace.

"What is wrong if human being wears boot. On the contrary, his convenience increases to walk swiftly and safely due to this." Aakash thought he had thrown a right arrow.

"Human being has lost the sensitivity of his foot soles due to boot. He has lost the enjoyment of earth touch and its message."

"So do you want to say that these people should live ignorant in the deprivation of science and technology?"

"Do you think that they are unaware of science and technology? But they have mutually and smartly decided not to use science and technology. They are so sensitive that they have already visualized the coming calamities and dangers which are not seen to outside people. Therefore, they don't want to have any contact with the external world or don't want to allow any person from the outside world. Only I and you are exceptions." Aakash listened to it mesmerizingly. He realized that many times education and life skills have no connection with each other. He had also understood it from Kajal's just now. Baba was really a nature lover.

"Baba, I have come here to give good news to you."

"What is it?"

"I am in love with Priya Pathak..." Aakash told everything and said further, "I have come to get your blessings."

Baba looked at Kajal. Kajal lowered her eyes. Baba said:

"May you derive deserving happiness."

Aakash left for home getting blessings from Baba, after talking to them and taking kind consent from Kajal.

18

They were studying to be an engineer. This was the last year for being an engineer. This time, semester exams were to be scheduled before Diwali, especially for the final year students. Everybody had to work on a project during Diwali vacation. Students had to find out their favourite companies and if they do not become able to do this, it was to be arranged by the college. This was an important project work for field training. Credits were to be given of this project in the final semester results. And report of this project work was to be submitted when the college reopened.

There was a double responsibilities, students have to prepare for ensuing exams before Diwali and finding out companies for the field work project. Priya was to do the project work in her own company. She has already submitted the permission letter to conduct the project work signed by her father on the letter pad of her company. After searching out many places, Sunil had got into Siemens India Ltd. situated in Badi and Aakash and Arjun had got the permission letters from a company named Plasto Tech. Plasto Tech was also a big company situated in Badi.

All got engrossed in the preparation of the semester exam to be held before Diwali vacation and in the project work for field training in the vacation then after. Nobody could enjoy Diwali vacation peacefully nor could they remain in contact of one another.

Colleges began again after Diwali. Now this was the last semester. Aakash thought that he will have to talk to Priya regarding their new life after college in this semester only. He was looking for opportunity which he got after a month.

Today workshop class had been over a bit early. Therefore workshop students had been free early. There was almost an hour left in the arrival of college bus. Priya and Aakash went in canteen to wait for it. Both began chatting.

Only four months, and then our college journey will get over, right? Aakash asked Priya.

"Yes"

"What are your plans after college being over?"

"About what? Confused Priya asked for further clarification.

"Are you going to study further or doing job or taking care of house getting married?" Aakash had been able to talk on this matter after a long time rehearsal and efforts.

"It is fixed that I am not going to study further for master degree. It is also final that I am not going to do any job. And in case of marriage, I am not in hurry yet."

"What will you do then after being an engineer?"

"I will decide it after discussing with my parents. I may join my father's business. What have you thought?"

"We have no other option except pursuing job. And we have neither experience nor capital for business. And I have no desire or suitability to study further. And in case of marriage, if I find a good girl like you, I will marry."

"Then start searching for a job and a girl."

"I have bright chances of getting a job as many factories have been established and are yet to be established many more in Badi. And I have already searched a girl; I am just waiting for her 'yes'.

"Who is that fortunate girl?" Priya asked eagerly.

"You" Aakash said daringly.

"I ?" Priya asked with wonder.

"Yes . . . why, is there any problem?"

"Aakash, I think you are getting our friendship in wrong sense."

"Why?"

"We are only good friends."

"If there is only friendship, then why we always remain close than others? Why others connect our names with each other?" Aakash was dying with the fear of losing.

"As you are my close friend than others. But you need not misinterpret our close friendship." Priya said arrogantly.

"I have done it, tell me about you."

"I am not prepared for marriage yet. When I will, I will inform you." Priya bluntly replied Aakash.

"I will wait for your positive answer." Aakash said as if consoling his own self and then kept quiet.

Aakash had been disappointed but didn't consider him a failure. He thought that Priya is moody and she would have replied this only because she might not be in a mood. She has also not denied yet. She has only said that there is no hurry for marriage. I am ready even if she asks me to wait for a year. No matter she said that I consider you a good friend only and don't misinterpret our friendship. But always friendship is turned into love. If she considers me only a good friend, and not more than that; why did she hug me and cried at the time of her father's heart attack among so many friends where her other she-friends present too. It is certainly love. And she will realize it; only some time is required.

The last semester exams came and finished away. A farewell party was held with the co-ordination of the whole college for final year engineering students. Everybody was happy and sad as well. They were excited for future too. They were happy to get new identity and sad as well for spending four years in the college and departing from friends. Aakash thought I will ask once again to Priya in loneliness on this emotional occasion. But Priya didn't come in the party on that day. Everybody was missing her presence, especially Aakash. Everybody was inquiring Aakash about Priya's absence, but he himself was ignorant like all.

Inquiring, it came to be known that Priya had gone to her maternal uncle's house in Delhi just after the exam being over. Priya even didn't turn up to get the exam results. His father had come to receive her result. All got busy in future planning. Aakash, Sunil, Arjun, Nisha had certainly been busy in finding out jobs.

Sunil and Nisha declared to get marry each other but after getting jobs. All asked Aakash about his marriage. Everybody clearly indicated for Priya. But he always avoided by replying that he wanted to give preference to job and getting settled first.

Suddenly everybody got Priya's wedding invitation one day into which it was informed that she is going to marry USA settled Dr. Kishor Bhalla. Wedding was arranged in the prestigious hotel of Chandigarh and reception in the hotel of Delhi after three days of her marriage.

For Aakash it was intolerant shock but he had to keep the face smiling. Nobody was sure about his love for Priya except Sunil. Everybody remarked too: "Buddy . . . we used to imagine you in couple and how did it happen suddenly?" Responding friends, Aakash gave the same answer given by Priya but this time in his own favour that "we were only good friends. If you consider us something more than friends, it is your misunderstanding. What can we do ?"

While replying, he lacked confidence too but there was no option for others except accepting it. As the answer was logical. Sunil knew that Aakash had broken from inside.

There was no more gap than 3-4 days in getting invitation and marriage. Aakash avoided meeting everybody in those days. He used to remain in his room only. He pretended being busy in his work. But he couldn't cheat his childhood friend Sunil.

On the very next day, Sunil had reached Aakash's home in the room situated on the first floor.

There was no need to utter even a single word. Finding Sunil there, Aakash had cried a lot hugging him open heartedly. His suppressed pain was transforming into the form of tears. Sunil also allowed him to cry for some time. He moved his hand on Aakash's back. As Aakash relaxed, Sunil asked him "how did it happen?" Aakash had given assurance about his love to Sunil earlier.

"I don't know. Last time when we had a discussion, she told that there is no hurry for marriage. And when I asked her about me, she told she will reply after thinking for some time."

"We will inquire about the reason of this happening." Sunil thought Priya might have been pressurized for marriage. But Aakash was assured that she was not such a girl who can be suppressed by anybody. He said: "There is no meaning. This decision of marriage might be Priya's own decision. I really feel bad that she used me. She mocked my feelings and made me ridiculous."

Aakash was still evaluating Priya's answer as per his comfort zone.

"OK, forget what has happened. There is no way out without accepting it. Behave healthily tomorrow in the marriage, otherwise everybody will come to know about it."

"I don't want to attend the marriage." Aakash said.

"If you don't come, everybody's doubt will get converted into confirmation."

Sunil was right. Next day in the evening, all the friends reached in the hotel of Chandigarh getting ready where marriage of Priya and Dr. Kishor Bhalla was arranged. On one side, wedding was going on, while on the other, guests arrived in the marriage were relishing multiple dishes of dinner. Aakash and friends had dinner, till then wedding had been over. Dr. Kishor Bhalla was in turban, traditional choodidar (a type of Indian wedding attire) and mojdi (a type of light shoe) and Priya in the attire of a bride was looking beautiful. First, they took blessings from elders, and met their relatives and family members. Then, Priya approached toward friends with Kishor Bhalla.

Aakash's body shivered completely. He was confused thinking whether he would be able to bear Priya as someone else's bride. What if he loses control over his suppressed feelings, artificial smile and his physical healthiness? He got scared. As Sunil noticed Priya's arrival, he consoled Aakash as if encouraging him to remain calm.

Everybody congratulated turn by turn and offered gift. Then Priya began speaking addressing to everybody. "Meet Dr. Kishor Bhalla, my husband. He is from USA." And saying this, she introduced him with Aakash first "This is my close friend Aakash Patel." And then she introduced everybody with Dr. Kishor Bhalla turn by turn.

"It is really nice meeting you all. Priya talks a lot about all of you, your group and your mischief." After some time Dr. Kishor Bhalla said "Especially about Aakash". He looked before Aakash saying this and added "Priya says that Aakash has really been helpful throughout my college years."

'Priya and doctor, you have given us a big surprise. Priya got disappeared after the college being over and immediately this surprise . . . . We are still surprised.' Arjun said.

'Yes, the situation was such that we had to plan everything very quickly.'

'But how did Dr. Bhalla came in your life? You did not give us any hint.' Nisha asked to Priya.

'If you remember, I had gone to Delhi when Aakash was badly ill.' Priya looked to the faces of everybody saying this but as she noticed a slight confusion on their faces, she looked before Aakash.

'Yes . . . in third year vacation.' All remembered when Aakash told.

'At that time Kishor . . .' Priya had been that loving to Kishor Bhalla that she addressed him as Kishor only. 'And his parents had also come to visit Delhi who are close friends to my maternal uncle. They had stayed at uncle's home. During this, I met Kishor and we went to the journey of Agra, Mathura, and Vrundavan together then where we became close to each other. Kishor and his parents were impressed with my mischievous attitude and I got impressed with Kishor's amiable nature which got converted into preference for each other while watching Taj Mahal in Agra.'

'She was telling me that she prayed for my health in the love temple of Taj Mahal while the fact was that she was building her own palace of love there.' Aakash thought internally.

'Then they went back to U.S.A. But they chose me for Kishor which they conveyed to uncle. Uncle talked with

Mummy-Papa. All decided together and Kishor and his parents came to Delhi in this vacation and Mummy-Papa pushed me there. They selected me. They proposed me for marriage and I had no reason to deny so I also said yes. Immediately marriage got registered. We visited American Embassy after travelling where Kishor informed that he has married me being an American born citizen and expressed his desire to take me in America. He presented all the documents. And Embassy permitted.'

'But you could have informed us.' Nisha said.

'That is right. But as I was allowed permanent residence by USA Embassy, mummy-papa decided to arrange my ritual marriage and Kishor's parents planed to give reception. So I could not realize where time passed in preparation and shopping of all these. Actually I felt shortage of time.' Priya completed her explanation.

'So you are going to settle permanently in U.S.A. right!' Sunil asked.

'Of course, there is no other way out. It is the duty of a Hindu woman to follow the footsteps of her husband, right!'

Saying this, she laughed in coquetry and watched toward Dr. Bhalla crossing her eyes.

'When will you leave for USA now?' Arjun asked.

'We will leave within four-five days.' Dr. Kishor Bhalla said.

'You should take Dr. Kishor Bhalla for visiting the wonderful Himalaya of India staying here for some time.' Aakash said unwillingly as if doing formality.

'Thanks, but it is not possible this time. We will come some other time. And as Priya's parents are here, it will continue coming here.' Dr. Kishor Bhalla replied modestly.

All returned late night. While returning, Sunil asked Nisha to sit on the rear seat of Arjun and made Aakash sit behind his seat. Sunil did not drop Aakash only upto his house, but upto his room too. Again finding loneliness, Aakash cried before Sunil and said.

'How immodest she was in her laughter! And recognized herself a Hindu woman!

'What is wrong in that? She has not hidden anything from you. It is possible that misunderstanding was on your part regarding her relationship.

And within seven days after Priya's departure for U.S.A., Aakash received a letter by courier on the very next day from Priya clarifying his misunderstanding. Priya had written that;

'Dear friend Aakash'

Reading 'friend Aakash', he gave an ironic smile. He read the letter further. In my opinion, mistake lied on your part to misunderstand our friendship. I had always tried to remove this misunderstanding on my behalf. But you had always developed an illusion to love me.

What is love? In my opinion, love is liking, convenience and nothing special than the habit developed out of convenience. It is a beautiful title given to mental and physical necessity. You were fulfilling my liking and necessities as a friend therefore I was comfortable with you. And I was there in your choice and necessity, so you liked to accompany me to which you gave the name of love. Perhaps I might be your greatest choice and necessity, but my preferences and needs were more than your limitations.

I am born and brought up in luxuries. I am used to utilize and consume luxurious pleasures from my very childhood. And this has been my needs now which were not possible in your house, your family or with you. How is it possible for me to develop love in the absence of all these necessities?

Even I wish to share this with you as a friend too. You need to understand the impossibility of love anywhere in this world. The more convenient the liking and need, the more sweet the relationship is. Tell me truly, if I were ugly full of spots on my face with chicken pox, having large number of glasses and wearing incongruous clothes, would you make the mistake of loving me ever? Have you ever come to know about love between a beautiful and an ugly person in this world in past or present? You have surely not listened about that. As something which is titled as love begins from body and ends at predilection, preference and convenience.

Dr. Bhalla was the best match for me who was able to give me all pleasure I wished and was desirous to give it. He has all resources and convenience which could fulfill all my needs. He is a gentle and handsome man having smartness as per my preference. And he has high status in society. What more do I wish than this?

Therefore, I have taken this decision. What can I do if you create misunderstanding about me on your own and get hurt? I can only pray to God that he gives maturity to my friend so that he can understand and accept this world.

Fare you well. I would like to enjoy visiting my old friend while coming in India. I wish you would also like.

Now

Priya belongs to Dr. Kishor Bhalla only.

Aakash recalled Baba's words of love, liking and habit while reading letter. What he could not understand through words became possible for him to get it through experience.

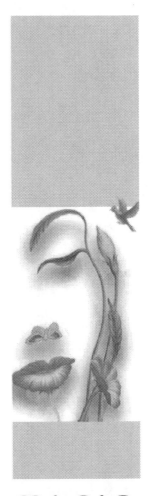

KAJAL

19

Aakash was infuriated with Priya's letter. Of course, Priya's letter was hundred percent right in terms of presentation, her rights and logic. But in terms of relationship and emotions, Aakash found it completely inappropriate. Aakash felt that Priya made use of him cherishing his feelings. He was a toy for Priya. She played with it till needed and then left throwing him aside. Priya had played with his self-respect. She has proven her intellect foolish. It was intolerant for Aakash to get through this wound. Many days passed to this event and yet he was not able to come out of this.

Priya herself was central in her life. To her, there was no value for others' feelings and existence. Everybody were objects to her no matter it was a car or a person. There was no difference for her. She had value for her needs and comforts but had no value for those who let their comforts and needs go for her. Even if she is honest, so what? Can honesty be so cruel? She used to define each situation as per her convenience. Aakash thought when 'I was ill' she said 'what could I have done, if I would have been there. It was doctor who had to do everything.' But when her father was ill and I used to go, she said 'you gave warmth to me'. The pain of proving out fool was stronger in Aakash than the pain of losing love.

Aakash was lost in thoughts and more thoughts the whole day. Priya's sting was running through his body as a poison. He should meet Sunil and Arjun. He should go to meet Baba and Kajal so that the effect of sting lessens but it was not possible for Aakash to do so. He lay in his room, in the room of his mind and himself enclosing completely.

In this way, when he lied in his room the same way, Sunil and Arjun came there. Arjun spoke:

'Buddy . . . you are not seen for long.'

'It's nothing buddy, I just don't go anywhere.' Aakash uttered.

'Now we have vacations only until we get jobs.' Sunil spoke.

'Is it really nothing or have you not come out of Priya's shock yet?' Arjun asked.

Aakash looked at Sunil, as if was asking 'who gave all this information to him? Have you given him?' Sunil nodded his head saying no with fear.

'Don't doubt on Sunil. The way you changed witnessing Priya, considered Priya, did all her work immediately, from these not even I but everybody knew about your soft corner. So there is no meaning to hide anything. I had seen breaking you completely in Priya's marriage. Therefore I have come to know about it.' Arjun clarified.

Sunil said, 'Arjun came at my home, asked about you that why Aakash is not seen? What does he do, etc . . . ? So I said, he does nothing, is just at home. So he told: I know and you might too that he is in shock due to Priya. So let us go to him and we came here.' Sunil clarified.

Now there is no meaning to hide anything. And the way Arjun had come closer in those four years; Aakash found to open his heart before him and showed them Priya's letter. Both read the letter.

'In my opinion, both were in confusion. You made a mistake to consider her dearly loved and she considered you as a close friend. Yes . . . if she had wished, she would have clarified your misunderstanding but she continued with this and you got in and in deeply as a result of which this mistake is constructed.' Arjun put his point.

'That is alright, but how to get him out of this pain and thoughts? He seems to go in depth day by day instead of coming out of it.' Sunil said.

'You are right. Aakash is a man of mind and thoughts. The more he will think, the more he will get confused and the more he will get confused, again it will lead him to think more. And further he will think, he will involve himself deeply in it.' Arjun clarified his psychology.

'What is the solution of this?' Sunil asked. Aakash was hearing the discussion about his situation with a wavering mind.

'He needs a support who can get him out of this with feelings and love.'

'We are there to help him out.' Sunil said.

'This problem cannot be worked out externally, our feeling would affect him upto some extent only. His pain of love won't get wounded. He needs a woman who can cure his wounds with love.' Arjun shared his knowledge.

'But from where to bring such woman?' Sunil expressed the confusion.

'Yes . . . that is right.' And suddenly he jumped out of excitement as if recalled something and uttered, 'what if we bring Kajal here?'

'Kajal!' What has Kajal to do with this problem?" Aakash jumped.

'As the situation is opposite overthere; You consider Kajal a friend and Kajal considers you so much.' Arjun spoke.

'How can you say that?' Aakash inquired.

'As I have seen the ocean of love in her eyes for you, therefore . . .'

'Even I also think so.' Sunil said.

'Oh come on buddy, she has love and affection for everybody. She has love for everyone whether it is a young one of leopard, birds, trees or any person or even to a wrong doer. So it can't be said that her love is special for me.' There passed leopard, Devvani bird, fruits being taken with the permission of trees and Bheemo before Aakash's eyes. He felt that as they have seen Kajal once only therefore they don't know about her nature.

'You are right. But why I am telling you that she has special feelings for you because she came upto here in your disease only for you. And she had come to know about your disease on her own, you had not informed her through courier or mobile. She had got the message on her own.'

Aakash also kept quiet. Sunil was in complete agreement of this matter. Now, how to bring Kajal? The trio got involved in the discussion on the issue of difficulties to be faced in bringing Kajal here.

'First of all, I am dependent on mummy-papa and if Kajal also gets dependent upon them after coming here, mummy won't agree to accept her in that case. If I had a job, situation would be different but in the absence of any job, there can be no discussion. And you know that beggars have no other choice.' Aakash spoke.

'Yes . . . buddy, you are right, that is why I and Nisha have decided to get marry after getting jobs.' Sunil spoke.

At that time, Aakash's mummy called him out.

'Aakash, come downstairs. There is a courier in your name.'

Aakash went down. He brought the cover up in the room. He was very happy with the cover opened in his hand.

'Hey buddy . . . one question is solved. I have got a job into Plasto Tech Company as a junior engineer.'

'See, God is also with you in this good intention. You have got the employment for Kajal,' Arjun said.

'OK, if Dhara gets ready and you people support me, we will be able to convince mummy but how to tell Kajal about it?' Aakash shared his confusion.

'What to worry for? Just go and tell her that I want to marry you.' Sunil replied.

'It is not that easy friend! I had gone to them and talked about my marriage with Priya with a great proud. Now how can I go to Kajal and propose her?' Aakash disclosed the main point.

'The way you had expressed your love to Priya, in the same way you have to do it again.' Arjun uttered.

'And are you not aware with the consequences of it?' Aakash told.

'But here lies the difference. The other person also loves you.' Sunil said.

'It is believed by you. It may not be the case actually.' Aakash replied.

'So what, you won't get hurt as you have no expectations from her.' Arjun told.

'But there is a chance of being insulted, and it is also tough to bear now.' Aakash informed about his condition.

'There is a difference between Priya and Kajal. You should first talk to Baba; he will guide you properly after listening the fact. He won't humiliate you.' Sunil told.

'Yes . . . this could be done.' At last Aakash got ready to try.

Next day Aakash left to meet Baba. He deliberately went late so that Kajal may have left giving breakfast to Baba till he reached there. He did not want to face Kajal.

When Aakash reached, Baba was sitting on the stone closing his eyes just after finishing his walk of the jungle.

'Baba' Aakash said softly.

'Oh son, when did you come? Kajal has just left giving breakfast to me.'

'I want to meet you.' Aakash said in a bit disappointing tone.

'Why do you seem so freak, is there anything odd? Is there a problem in love?' Aakash knew that Baba was asking about Priya.

'Yes . . . it is about it, Baba . . . Priya has married somewhere else.' Aakash choked with emotion.

Aakash told the whole incident. He talked about his being into delusion. He was feeling easy sharing this with Baba.

'Priya is honest; misunderstanding was on your part. You have misunderstood and perceived her friendship as love. It is clear from your sharing that Priya was transparent in her thought.

'Still it is impossible to come out of the wound to which I considered love for so many years. As only she was everything to me and for me.'

'Time is the only solution to all the questions.' Baba said that in order to avoid this question.

'This wound will destroy my heart and make my life a poison.' Aakash uttered.

'That is right. So what is the solution of this in your opinion?'

'I need a person who can fill me with love.' Aakash told clearly.

'Then search for that person' Baba replied.

'I have come to you to demand for such person.'

'Who is that person?' Baba could guess it but wanted to confirm.

'Kajal, I wish to marry her.'

'If you had demanded love for the sake of love, it would have been appropriate but you demand love to get cured from your suffering-pain as a medicine which is wrong.'

'You are completely right. But I have a faith that one day I will also cultivate an ability to love being loved by Kajal.'

'But it is only possible if Kajal loves you.' Baba was saying it just for the sake of saying although he was ascertained about the happening.

'You can call Kajal and ask her.' Aakash said.

'Let us wait till she comes bringing lunch in the noon.' Baba said.

Kajal came in the noon. Her eyes became painful observing Aakash's sadden face and freak body. She asked:

'Aakash, why have you been like that?'

Aakash shared the whole event about Priya and asked at the end:

'Kajal, will you marry me? Will you come with me?'

'Yes' Kajal answered in one-word.

'Are you aware that you will have to stay in the city? You will not find this Himalaya, these rivers, trees, streams and these people.' Baba wanted to make her aware with the situation.

'I have no problem.'

'Do you remember the decision to leave that world was taken by you only once upon a time? Baba was asking as if wanted to confirm.'

'Yes, I remember and still I would go.'

'My crazy daughter, there reside people of mind, you won't get people of heart. If they don't understand you, they will do injustice to you. They may harm you more than you assume.' Baba uttered this to measure the vigor of Kajal's decision.

'But I will be there only. I will take care of her.' The people of that world are not fully worthless. If there will be any problem, I along with my parents, friends and family will stand by her.' Aakash interfered. Aakash recalled Kajal sitting on the river bank who was ready to be flown with the fall and was ready to enter into that world with that fall, only relying upon him.

'But have you asked permission from your parents?' Baba asked.

'Only if everybody present here agree, I will ask permission from them. I am hopeful that they will accept Kajal.' Baba looked at Kajal. Kajal nodded in affirmation. Baba smiled.

He looked before Aakash as if conveying 'as you wish'.

'Who will convince father and community? Baba said.

'This task of convincing should be done by you, Baba.' Kajal and Aakash said.

Four-five persons from community were called which included father, Bheemo and others. Observing Bheemo, Aakash felt it will really be tough to convince these people.

Baba informed them about Aakash's proposal and Kajal's desire. This kind of incident occurred for the first time in the community. So opposition was obvious. Someone commented too 'we had denied accepting this boy on the very first time. See, hasn't he created this question today?'

'The issue is not about that question. He will not abduct Kajal secretly from here. He wants to take her proposing modestly and with your permission.' Baba said.

One man asked, 'but what if Kajal doesn't know about the worldly rituals, attire, and food of that world?

'We will teach her that. Even though she does not learn, we will manage.' Aakash replied.

After a long altercation and Bheemo's little opposition, all got convinced with the efforts of Baba and Kajal's firm decision.

Aakash now left to get permission from his parents.

20

The situation overturned to Aakash's assumption. Aakash had imagined that it will be tough to convince community people, Baba and Kajal but it got easily resolved. Kajal got convinced without any logic-argument and doubts. And he guessed it easy to convince his family which proved tough.

Coming back from the Himalayan hills, Aakash visited Sunil's home to plan the strategy for here. Arjun was asked to join and the three of them began discussing on what to do.

'As far as I assume it is tough to convince your mother. If your mother says yes then it will be easy to get consent from your father. He won't get involved in much dispute. So the main question is how to convince your mother?' Sunil said.

'His mother is social activist. She is a member, worker and leader of organizations like Women Strategy, Women Development Cell. She would certainly support or she must provide her support.' Arjun reminded them.

'I wish she responds in the same way but I have a doubt, we should not take risk.' Aakash told.

'We can apply one idea here; let us get agreement from Dhara didi. If she agrees, it will be easy to convince to your mother.' Sunil excitedly shared his thought.

'Yes . . . buddy, mummy-papa usually doesn't avoid Didi's opinion.'

'So let us leave for Chandigarh to Didi,' Sunil said. Arjun, Aakash and Sunil were at Dhara's home after an hour. Dhara was at home.

'How are you here, brother?' Dhara asked.

'I just wanted to meet you.' Aakash uttered.

'Is there any urgency?' Aakash's sudden arrival with Sunil in the noon gave surprise to Dhara. So she worried little.

'Yes, it is like that.' Aakash spoke.

'Didi, you know Kajal, don't you?' Sunil directly come on the point.

'Yes, is she that girl who saved brother from serious illness in the hospital?' Dhara told.

'Yes, what is your opinion ab out her?' Sunil asked.

'She was good but in which sense do you ask me?'

'For Aakash' Sunil told her directly.

'What do you mean?' Dhara asked getting confused.

'As Aakash wants to marry her . . .' Sunil uttered.

'She was a good girl but when it comes to marriage we have to think about so many other things.'

'Could you give any example?'

'Culture, rituals-customs, caste and other'

'Is there no value of her love toward your brother?'

'No, that is the most important thing but other things are important too.' Dhara spoke with clarity.

Arjun said, 'If we talk about love, we all have witnessed it. It was proven when she came from thousand kilometers away to cure your brother giving medicine to him. Her eyes had expressed it. Second point is about culture. Culture is for those who value, maintain and love domestic life, and it will be my guarantee. And the remaining discussion is about rituals-customs; they can be taught and developed.

And if talking about caste, consider her as my sister, I promise to consider and accept her as my sister throughout my life.' Even Sunil could not understand why Arjun got so emotional. Whether it was due to his friendship with Aakash or there was something in Kajal?

'But brother, will mummy-papa get convinced, especially mummy?' It was clear that Dhara agreed now as she was talking about mummy-papa.

'It is your duty to convince papa-mummy and especially to mummy.' Sunil imposed upon Dhara and Dhara got ready too.

She said, 'I can't assure but I will try to convince.'

They all left then preparing strategy for the next day.

As per the plan, Dhara came to her parents' home on Friday pretending to come co-incidentally. Her mother got surprised but thought that she was a daughter and had all the rights to come any time. After having dinner, all were sitting in the living room to watch television. Suddenly Arjun and Sunil arrived there.

'Oh Didi, when did you come?' Sunil asked.

'Just today in the evening'

'How did you come just all of a sudden?' Sunil asked the question which her mummy could not ask.

'Daughter has no need to take permission from parents to come at their home. Your friend has not married yet that focuses Bhabhi's rule.' Dhara said looking before Aakash.

'No no, even if there was a rule of my friend, he won't do any such thing that you would have to take permission.'

'I have trust on brother but nothing could be predicted about Bhabhi. She may have power over him.'

"But he should not bring such Bhabhi. Bhabhi should be brought of your choice, it will have no problem." Sunil spoke in the mocking tone.

'When will such Bhabhi be found?' Brother studies now, show us some girl so that we can select.' Dhara said.

'We are looking for her too but she should be suitable.' Dhara's mummy told.

'Why do you worry? Today boys find them out on their own.' Dhara said.

'We have no problem if he finds her out on her own.' Dhara's mummy told.

'Your son has already decided. You just have to give permission.' Sunil placed the point.

'Who is she?' Sushilaben asked surprisingly.

'She is Kajal.' Sunil replied.

'Who is Kajal?' Sushilaben puzzled.

'She is that girl who had come and cured brother with the herbal roots in the hospital.' Dhara said. Sushilaben slightly recalled. At that time a sage like follower and a tribal kind girl had come to inquire about Aakash in taxi.

'Do you know her?' Sushilaben asked Dhara.

'Brother meets her on regular period of time, but I saw her on that day in the hospital. But she appeared good to me. And at least she loves brother.'

'But that is not enough. We will have to know about his family. We will have to see her caste and social status. One should not fix a merriage considering only a girl.'

'In my opinion, feeling of love for each other is more important, all the rest is secondary.' Arjun interfered for the first time in familial matter.

Sushilaben didn't like his interference and said 'everything is to be seen. What would happen if something goes otherwise tomorrow? What if she doesn't obey family? If all the relatives are practical and reputed, any problem can be solved easily.'

'Mummy, the girl is really good but about other things . . .' Dhara got hesitated saying this.

'I take all the other responsibilities for rituals to any problems. I consider her my sister from today onwards. I assure you for the solution of all questions possibly get raised in future.' Arjun spoke with all his zeal. Aakash and Sunil startled. If Sunil talked about considering Kajal a sister due to Aakash, it was understood. But on what basis and with what feel was Arjun taking the responsibility?

'Aunty, even I could assure you about Kajal and she is really very good. Aakash will be happy and she will behave lovingly with everybody.' Sunil spoke.

'Still it is not good to hurry without knowing her family members.'

'I know her. And that is enough. I want to marry her only, and this is my final decision.' Aakash said in wrath.

Aakash's father got scared with his anger. He interfered in the matter thinking that the boys of today's generation can do anything if their desire is not taken into consideration.

'Be practical Sushila. 'If Aakash likes her, we should have no problem with it. We don't have to live long now. If she takes care of us till we live, it is enough for us.

'No, it is necessary to know about the social customs.' Sushilaben wanted to have dignity, status which could be exhibited in the society and rich in-laws for his son so that she can impress others by all the usual pomp that surrounds occasions such as the royal wedding.

'Nothing but a girl. And clothes will also be given to her by us. There would be no celebration and rituals in marriage. Her parents would also not come here, now tell me do you accept or not?' Aakash told getting irritated. Her mother was shocked as all her dreams were getting into vain. She had dreamt that the only son who is educated well and had a good job, we will marry him in such a dignified family which will also make us proud in society. But Aakash broke all those dreams very easily. Still she uttered:

'It is not easy to come from the rural community and directly handle the married and domestic life.'

'But you are very much here, Sushila. You are there to help her. You were also not learned and still you have learnt everything today. She will also learn.' Sureshbhai tried to calm Sushilaben.

'My issue was different. I had guts.'

'See, although there was nobody to teach you anything and still you have learnt and reached in many organizations and trusts today, haven't you? In the same way, you could also train your daughter-in-law. If she gets your support and training, she will be succeed as you did.' Sureshbhai told fondling Sushilaben.

'It always makes a difference from person to person, mind it.' Sushilaben spoke with little proud.

'It is completely alright. But there is no worry getting mother-in-law like you, you have an ability to convert a metal into gold.' Sureshbhai finished the discussion appreciating Sushilaben at its extreme.

At last all got convinced and it was decided to bring Kajal next day.

Next day, Aakash and Dhara went to the market and purchased clothes for Kajal only on the guess of measurement.

Arjun came in the evening. He had come to share good news that he had also got the job in Plasto Tech as a junior engineer into which Aakash had got it. He forcefully made payment of clothes which were purchased for Kajal to perform the duty of a brother.

Next day, Aakash left to move toward Himalayan hills in the community of Kajal. He lent down at Baba's place directly.

It seemed that Baba was waiting for him. Soon Kajal came bringing snacks for Baba as usual. All had it quietly but there was a heaviness in today's silence.

'Dear, kindly send Bapu, Bheemo and two-three persons. I want to talk to them.' Baba told Kajal who was collecting the dishes.

'And take these clothes with you. Get ready; we will go in the evening.' Aakash told Kajal handing over a bag of clothes.

After Kajal left, Aakash realized that how would Kajal get to know how to wear Sari, blouse and petti-coat. He shared his problem with Baba. Baba said.

'Don't worry, everything will get managed.'

At that time Bheemo, Bapu, other two women and one man came there and bowed down to Baba. They stood beside him.

'Son,' Baba said, he put his hand on Aakash's shoulder. He got emotional and kept quiet. After some time, Baba spoke clearing his throat.

'Aakash, Kajal is the dearest daughter to all of us. My morning begins with her and my evening sets with her, take care of her. She has got ready to enter in your world only because of you. Take care of her that she doesn't get hurt and wounded through her heart.' His eyes got wet. He spoke wiping eyes with his hands. 'She has no understanding of your world. She has only heart and no mind. Kindly take care of her, you have to be her support.'

'Aakash' a heavy hand was put on Aakash's shoulder. When Aakash looked, it was Bheemo. 'On that day you were saved because it was Kajal to save you and you had fought with me to defend Kajal. On that day, it was my mistake. But if anything happens to Kajal, there will be nobody to save you from me.' Saying this Bheemo kept quiet going one side with wet eyes.

'Bheemo, now Aakash belongs to all of us. He has taken Kajal's responsibility now. You should not behave in this way with him.' Bapu said.

'Aakash wondered whether all of them were aware about the happening of that day. How would have they responded? Which procedure they would have done on Bheemo? He spoke keeping all these thoughts aside.

'I will take care of Kajal and would not do anything which may break her trust.'

At that time, Kajal and other community people came late in the afternoon.

Kajal was ready in Sari, blouse and other ornaments. It was bun on one side of her head instead of hair tied. Kajal was looking beautiful in Sari.

When and where would have Kajal learnt wearing Sari? Aakash felt to inquire about it. The way Kajal had got ready removed Aakash's illusion that she would look odd in the external world.

It was time to leave now. Kajal began meeting everybody one by one. She was hugging them. There were only tears without communication. Kajal was meeting with children too bending down and hugging them. Kajal hugged Bheemo too. Bheemo cried hard. She met Bapu. He moved his hand on the wet-eyed face. Kajal hugged Baba. 'Dear' Baba could only utter this. He was moving his hand on her back with tears in eyes. At the farewell occasion of Kajal not only did the people of community but trees were crying too. Wind also stopped in a corner as if wiping tears. The river flow stopped making noise on that day getting completely quiet although flustering with stones. Sounds of birds and beasts stopped coming too. Suddenly Devvani bird appeared on Kajal's shoulder without making noise. Tears were visible in its eyes. Kajal patted it. Himalaya seemed completely unvoiced showing that Kajal was not only the daughter of community but was a daughter of the whole Himalaya. Kajal ran and hugged pine tree. A tree was giving farewell bowing its branches down to Kajal. Kajal's farewell occasion had created such an impact upon the whole of atmosphere that it had been completely gloomy. It appeared that the whole of Himalaya, trees, river, birds, beasts, mountains and stones were crying.

Aakash looked up in the sky and prayed gathering his two hands and wings blew out. Aakash carried Kajal in his two hands and began flying in the sky, with Kajal.

21

During the whole flight, Kajal was completely quiet lying in the hands of Aakash hiding her face on her chest and closing her eyes. There was innocence on her face. The way she was in the arms of Aakash, indicated that she had extreme trust upon Aakash. There were no signs of future concern on her face. There was a grief of separation from the close ones but there was a happiness of unification too.

Whenever Aakash looked at her face, he felt love on her, on her innocence and on the trust put by her upon him. Perhaps Kajal was unaware of the cruelty, deception and calculations prevailed in the external world, therefore was certainly free from all worries. She was entering into the world of mind from the world of heart.

Slowly they got down on the terrace of Aakash's house. Aakash came downstairs taking Kajal with him. Everybody was sitting in the living room with eagerly waiting eyes assuming that Aakash may come with Kajal anytime which not only included Dhara and her mummy-papa but Arjun and Sunil too.

Kajal touched the feet of mummy-papa first and then went to touch the feet of Dhara but she took her in her arms and hugged. Kajal looked at Sunil and greeted him. She identified Arjun too. She gave smile and greeted him too but Arjun came and hugged her. Everybody continued looking at Arjun with surprise. Mummy welcomed Kajal with rituals. All had dinner together and after having it, Sunil and Arjun left gossiping some time.

Aakash and Kajal came upstairs in their room. Both were mentally and physically tired. Aakash was concerned about future and about Kajal's acceptance by the world. Kajal had burden of beautiful nostalgic memories. Both quietly went to the bed. Aakash played with Kajal's body. He got excited while playing and Kajal surrendered him without any opposition or arguments. Aakash took pleasure of jungle's wonderful splendor. Within some time, Kajal slept fast. Aakash was looking at her for some time. Kajal had taken care of Aakash instead of getting tired a lot and a pain of separation from the relatives and family. Aakash felt extreme affection toward her. Aakash slept late after watching Kajal and playing with her hair for some time.

When Aakash got up next day, it was late morning. When he looked beside him in the bed to awake Kajal, she had already gone down getting ready. After some time, Kajal entered with tea and snacks in her hands. Her wet and open hair was playing upon her face. Kajal was looking fresh. Aakash tried to catch her but she ran away informing him to come down after getting ready.

In the afternoon, when Aakash, Dhara, mummy-papa and Kajal were having lunch, Sunil came at that time.

'Aakash, Kajal's arrival is really lucky. See, I and Nisha have got job into Siemens India Ltd.'

'Congratulations, friend! Now tell me when are you going to marry?'

'Within short period of time. Everybody is ready from both the sides. We were only waiting for jobs. We may marry before joining the job so that we don't have to avail leaves during the job.'

'When will you probably marry?'

'Perhaps within 15-20 days as we will have to join job after 30 days.'

'Yes ... make it fast as I will also join Plasto Tech within 15 days.'

'Congratulations, now both of the brothers have got jobs. But brother what will you gift me from your first salary?' Dhara asked looking at Aakash.

'What do you want, tell me?' Aakash told.

'I want a beautiful dress.'

'OK, done.'

'I don't need anything from one salary, but I want a gold necklace from so many salaries.' Sushilaben said.

'Sushila, a gold necklace? What will do with it at this age? Don't be selfish. Don't think about you only. Think about everyone like me.' Saying this Sureshkumar looked at Aakash and uttered, 'Son, I wish to purchase a four-wheeler for a long time. If you become economically sound, we could purchase it so that we all can travel together.'

'OK, I agree to you too, papa.'

'Kajal you should also demand something. Brother has got this job only with your destiny, so you have a strong right.' Dhara spoke.

'Don't reward destiny. This is the result of your brother's efforts.' Sushilaben said angrily.

'Still ... if you wish something, please do ask for.' Aakash told Kajal stopping his sight at her.

'I don't want anything.' Kajal got busy in work saying this.

From the next day onwards, life became routine. Kajal got up in the morning, got ready and said Aakash awaking him, 'get ready and have exercise and meditation, and I bring breakfast for you.'

'Please sit with me for some time and then you can go.' Saying this Aakash started playing with her body.

'Today papa has to go to bank early and mummy has to go in some meeting. From today, kitchen is my responsibility so I have to work. Now get ready after meditation.' Kajal went down saying this.

Aakash began thinking.

She has just come yesterday and how easily has got mixed up. She doesn't find anything unknown. When she was in Himalaya, she stayed belonging to Himalaya. And after coming here, she has been used to this world. How simple! How innocent! How affectionate! How responsible! She was wonderful as wife too. She also took care of his meditation and exercise. She was eager to give all kind of happiness to him. Her figure is also well formed. Her skin is shiny, strong yet delicate. Aakash was in the seventh sky of his life.

Both were having lunch in the noon and Sunil came there. Sunil and Nisha's marriage were decided after 15 days.

Sunil said, 'Friend, you will have to be with me in all my shopping for marriage and its arrangements.'

'Yes . . . nowadays I am completely free, so don't worry but Kajal . . .'

'Kajal has also to accompany us as Nisha will also be with us. In that case, we will get chance to stroll together and play mischief along with shopping.'

'Yes friend, I have to purchase so many things for Kajal too.'

'So we will start form tomorrow. We will go to Chandigarh tomorrow in the morning.' Saying this Sunil left.

On that day, Aakash took Kajal at the temple situated near the river bank. Both sat on the stone near river bank.

'Kajal, this is a beautiful place. I like it a lot.'

'Yes it is. It is really lovely.'

'Kajal, don't you get surprised watching everything? Does it not make any feeling to you watching these vehicles, houses, roads and facilities? You behave in a way as if you have been staying here for long.'

'Now as I have to stay here, so it will be good if I accept everything as soon as possible.'

"Acceptance is different form learning. How can you manage with gas stove? How did you learn to use tooth-brush in place of neem-stick? How did you learn to make variable food of this world within two days? How did you learn to wear Sari?" Aakash expressed his surprise which held for the last two days.

"You should also get surprised on how did I become able to identify your boot? Baba had said that I don't like external world, so will I be comfortable now with it? You should have felt surprise too knowing about our knowledge of the railing construction. You should have even thought how did we come to meet you in taxi?"

"Yes . . . you are absolutely right." Aakash wondered.

'The reason is that I had stayed in your world for three months." Kajal answered.

"Really . . . When . . . ?"

"Before six months from your first meeting with me."

"But . . . how had you come here? For what? Where did you come? With whom did you stay?

"Quiet Aakash, don't you know that Baba belongs to your world? After coming in our world, he convinced everybody that the way I have come here on my own wish experiencing the outer world, you should also decide about your stay here after experiencing the outer world. There is a value of decision taken willingly not compulsively. So everyone got ready. Everybody was sent turn by turn. Some stayed in your world for 3 months, a few for six months while returned staying after 12 months. I returned within 3 months."

"But when did you stay and with whom?"

"Baba has a factory in Poona. Our arrangements were made there. We were given a small room to stay there. Everybody was taught some work of factory and they were asked to work there."

"What did you do?"

"I am a darling daughter of Baba so I was kept in Baba's guest house and I was taught to make food. I learnt cooking there. I also learnt using gas, wearing Sari and dress."

"But why did you go back after three months?"

"As I could not learn the sense of calculation in everything, so I went back."

"Why have you returned with me now?"

"I have come back to experience once again." Kajal spoke looking before Aakash.

"What was the name of Baba's factory?" Aakash asked.

"I don't know." Kajal replied.

"What else did you do in Poona?"

"I saw Osho's ashram and Poona."

"What is the real name of Baba? What is his biography? Why has he come in your world leaving a big factory?"

"I don't know all this. You should ask Baba about all this. I only know his one name which is given by Osho. It is Swami Prem Prakuti."

"I tried to ask him but he didn't tell me."

"You should ask him. He will tell you. Now you are a son-in-law."

Aakash wondered listening to this new story of community people. Aakash also understood from where the taxi charges would have come.

From the next day, Aakash-Kajal and Sunil-Nisha began to go on shopping and made arrangements for the marriage. Along with the shopping of Nisha-Sunil, Aakash could get the chance to purchase things for Kajal too. He bought saris and Punjabi dresses for her. Kajal had to purchase pant and T-shirt too due to the over insistence of Aakash. Aakash also wondered thinking that why he was so excited to see Kajal in pant and T-shirt. Perhaps he wanted to fit Kajal in the image of Priya in the depth of his heart.

15 days passed by in merriment. All four enjoyed too much and Kajal could get enough knowledge—good information of this world too.

Aakash's job was to begin from the very next day of Sunil-Nisha's marriage. It was the last day of holidays which was the day of Sunil's marriage too. The whole group of college gathered at reception in the evening. Priya was in America so she was not to arrive. Therefore, there was no point for Aakash to be in any difficulty. Still he was anxious of his friends' queries on his marriage with Kajal. And it happened accordingly. After reception being over when all arranged on the chairs in a group to gossip, at that time Sunil introduced Kajal to all.

"This is Kajal, Aakash's wife."

"What, when did you get married and you didn't even inform us?" Most of them cried out loudly with one voice.

"It has taken place before some time only." Aakash replied in flat tone.

"Is it love-marriage or arranged one?" One of the friends asked.

"It is actually a love marriage happened with the permission of parents." Aakash told.

All continued staring in astonishment as everybody sensed Priya to be his love and Kajal's arrival in his life was a great surprise to all of them.

"Hey, when did you fall in love? Is she a school friend?" Everybody knew about his college-life.

"No, Kajal belongs to the internal hills of Himalaya."

"People are fond of loving Himalaya and you fell in love with a Himalayan girl?" Someone teased.

"By the way, what is Kajal's education?" Someone asked.

"Nothing" Kajal uttered and there was a complete silence. Aakash hesitated. Sunil and Nisha became quiet. Kajal was looking at everybody with curiosity. She was not able to get why there was stillness among them. Arjun stood up and came near Kajal. He spoke putting his hand on her shoulder:

"Kajal is my sister. Is there a value of intelligence or love in the relationship between husband-wife?"

"Of course of love" Someone spoke.

"The same thing is important for Kajal too."

Everybody had a sense of respect for Arjun. All kept quiet with his statement. The whole matter of discussion got over with a sense of inquiring nothing if she was Arjun's sister.

While returning, Aakash told Kajal.

"What was the need to inform about your illiteracy?"

"As they asked the same, therefore . . ." Kajal replied innocently.

"It would have been OK if you had kept quiet. I would have managed." Aakash spoke. Kajal got the idea that Aakash didn't want to reveal about her illiteracy to anybody.

From the next day, Aakash's job began. Everyday Kajal woke Aakash up early in the morning and asked him to perform meditation and exercise after getting ready. She prepared breakfast for him and lunch to carry in the office.

She watched him till he becomes invisible on his bike turning from the corner of his street. As soon as he came back home, she took his bag and offered a glass of water and cold-drink.

Days passed in joy and merriment and one day Aakash was pleased reading Sushilaben's speech about her daughter-in-law in the local newspaper. He began feeling proud for his mother. She had written "I have tried to set an example in the society. When people run for dowry and false societal status today and trade their sons indirectly, I have made my only engineer son to marry with a girl of his choice who belongs to the Himalayan community and is illiterate. I have no importance of external luxury or status. Love and cultural values play an important role to me. My son's happiness matters a lot to me."

Social activists and journalists had admired Sushilaben open heartedly.

While for Kajal this news was of no importance at all. Only her duty was at all important for her. She was completely dutiful. She was devoted to that extreme that nobody in the house including Aakash too was aware of her own desires. She was loyal day and night.

It had been a month to Kajal's arrival. She expressed her desire before Aakash to meet Baba, Bapu, community and Himalaya.

Aakash said, "We will go there on Saturday. We will stay there for a night and return on Sunday. Even I want to know about Baba's early life from him. Please insist Baba to tell me about his early life if he denies."

"OK." Kajal tapped on Aakash's head as if saying "Don't scratch your mind much."

22

Kajal expressed the desire to go early on Saturday so that evening sermons could be attended. No matter Aakash too liked evening sermons. So they left little early. When Aakash reached near Baba's residence on the flat surface with Kajal, everybody was coming to one's places as the evening sermons were to begin. The music players were placed on the instruments. Aakash and Kajal quietly set themselves among all.

All danced in merriment. They listened to Baba and began dispersing lovingly. All noticed Aakash and Kajal's arrival. All came quietly and hugged and kissed Kajal and went away. Bheemo stood quiet coming before Kajal.

Kajal said, "Bheemo, just wait here. I am coming in the camp. Aakash is going to stay here. Let me meet Baba."

Kajal went to Baba catching Aakash's hand. Baba was waiting for Kajal. Kajal hugged Baba. She cried for some time and Baba was moving his hand on her shoulder.

Kajal spoke, "Baba, Aakash is eager to know about your arrival in our world and how you became the follower of Osho."

"What will he do knowing all this? If my life becomes helpful to him, it is meaningful to share in that case only, dear."

"If not now, it may be helpful someday." Aakash said.

"Do you have any problem to share Baba? I have already told him that you belong to Poona and your name is Swami Premprakruti. I have also told him that you arranged a place in Poona to give opportunity to make a choice of the world here and the external world. And I have also stayed in the external world before this."

"Oh, so only information about me remains now. OK I will tell today as Aakash is going to stay here today." Baba had heard Kajal and Bheemo's conversation.

Kajal and Bheemo went to the camp. Aakash and Baba sat on the stone in the open yard after having dinner. Aakash had got the opportunity to sit in the company of Baba in the splendor of nature, in the accompaniment of cold breeze and under the twinkling stars after a long time.

"Baba, how did you become the follower of Osho?' Aakash asked Baba after a long silence.

"As Kajal has told you that I was a successful businessman of Poona. But before coming in the contact of Osho, I was searching happiness in bungalows, modern cars, clubs, big parties in hotels, in the wine bars and in the foreign journeys. But every time the more I consumed all these things with excitement, the more I became disappointed after it. Actually I was not unhappy at all. I was healthy too. Industry was running without any kind of concern. Staff was really efficient. Wife and children were also good. Although having all these, there was a feel of emptiness continuously residing within me. A kind of sadness prevailed inside. As soon as I was in club, hotels, on a foreign tour or had a new car, I was happy. Happiness reached at the pinnacle too, but as the time passed by, I fell down more strongly. The tide of happiness turned into ebb tide.

To remove this inner sadness and lack, I wandered in many religions, cults and met many saints and priests but all talked about renunciation. They talked about donation, about removing sins and cursed pre-birth deeds. This was something I could not believe, I could not accept such things at all. Still I tried to discard the luxuries of my life and made efforts to live in simplicity, but the body which was accustomed to use luxuries and materials for so many years deceived and made me more disappointed. At that stage of my life I was told to go to Osho by someone who considered him a fit guru for me. He is also a guru for rich. He stays in an ashram like five star hotel. His ashram is full of comforts and facilities. Foreign people arrive here in troops. He claims not to teach a religion but religious conviction. He is considered a revolutionary saint. In addition, he stays at Koregaun Park in Poona."

I had read little about Osho in newspapers. I had read his one book also. I thought to visit him with a hope of returning within three days if at all don't find myself comfortable and will start searching for something else. And nothing was to be lost within three days.

And once I went, I stayed there only. I was coming in and going out from his ashram but ever remained with Osho.

"What happened in those three days that you could trust him and had a faith in him?" Aakash's curiosity roused.

"I remember clearly when I went in his ashram on the very first day, morning sermons were about to begin. All followers were placed there in their saffron dresses. It was a Buddha hall covered from net all around. There was a small stage on which single sofa was placed. Beside it, there was a microphone. There was eagerness in everyone's eyes. At that time, a man in white attire and a hat on the head entered the stage. He was Osho who had a smile on his face and appearance of greeting toward all. He was walking in such a way as if a feather was flying on the earth—very delicately as if walking on the earth without troubling or putting weight upon it. He sat on his seat and spoke with reference to someone's question:

"There is a need to comprehend the difference among happiness, entertainment and delight. Generally, we mean the same by all three, but in reality there is a huge difference. Let us first understand happiness. Happiness is associated with body and senses. For instance there is happiness in food, sleep, corporal union and happiness of water if it is received in thirst. But that happiness is not eternal. The moment it is fulfilled, it gets over. Once again it is there when one is hungry, want to sleep or have desire to have physical pleasure, he feels dissatisfied. The desire of achievement creates excitement. It creates dissatisfaction and envy if not fulfilled. But it is a fact that such kind of pleasure is momentary. Second is Entertainment which is associated with mind where we are observers only and not any subject or participant. This is the prevailing trend in India. To watch TV, serials of mother-in-law and daughter-in-law and getting hurt, happy and sad etc ... Entertainment is meaner than pleasure wherein you are not a subject. To gain pleasure, you have to be subject at least; it has that much value too. But entertainment is illusive. It creates an illusion of experience which is dangerous. It keeps you away from a real experience. And till you don't die on your own, it is not possible for you to get the heaven. Third is delight (bliss). Happiness and entertainment are belongs to outside and associated with external things. While delight is associated with you, it is with the self. And true bliss is never attained without knowing the self and getting stable into it. Unless you get the understanding of self, it is not possible to get delight from external materials and comforts."

Baba said, "I was amazed listening to Osho. It was as if he knew my question and was replying to that only. His voice, pronunciation and pause taken between words were so wonderful that I could not realize the time. It seemed he just began and finished. Still it raised one more question in my mind was that why then God arranged in such a way that people get inspired to find happiness-pleasure in the external sources? I was attracted toward Osho. Next day again in the morning, I reached to listen to him. To my surprise, the sermon of second day was: Why do people get inspired to search happiness outside?"

"The reason is people are habituated to find the reason outside for so many past births. As a result our senses have been completely external and we have forgotten the way to lead the senses inside now. And the happiness lies inside. The thirst of happiness inspires us to search but our habit inspires us to search outside. Thus, we try to find it out in materials, facilities, corporal union, and in food but at last it turns out to be momentary and therefore more emptiness is experienced. In order to avoid this emptiness, people try to involve themselves in activities. This activity begins in the name of happiness finally resulting into ego fulfillment. If you believe that the one visiting a river bank, or wandering into forest or performing social righteousness do it with a desire of gaining happiness, then it is wrong. They might do all these to keep themselves busy." Baba said internally. "Osho really uttered correct expressions. I now realize that to keep myself busy I was also doing all these things like going on tours, celebrating parties, but all this was to find happiness. But how to find happiness within? The answer of which was given in his sermon the next day by Osho."

"Now the point is how to get happiness? How to move towards inside? How to lead the senses to inside which are accustomed to go outside? Whatever work you do, the activity you perform, it should done by heart, from your inner-self, it means you must have aptitude for the work you do. But in most of the cases, your deeds are generated from your ego and attachment. They are performed to defeat others, to execute, to get succeeded, to earn more money and to get more and more facilities. Only this is the fundamental matter. You should find out your aptitude. To find that aptitude out, if you need to find it out 5-6 disappointing attempts or if you have to sacrifice your time or property, it is worth. This loss is nothing in comparison to the amount of loss of many births and rebirths."

Now how to find aptitude? And it appears more difficult in the contemporary world where people are behind social, political, power and property. But you should perform meditation. Do it continuously. As soon as you engross yourself with meditation, you will be able to experience more clearly the inner-self. Meditation would serve like a lamp to show the internal path and with the achievement and help of aptitude and with the help of meditation; you will be able to get your ecstasy and delight.

"I was completely dumbstruck." Baba uttered. "Osho's sermons had entered somewhere across my inner self. I became curious to meet Osho and to be his follower. I requested the coordinator there. He asked me to come in the evening taking bath. He instructed me very strictly not to touch Osho while meeting. I reached in the evening and bowed down to him. An unworldly aroma from his body began spreading on my body and mind. I became intoxicated. Osho put his finger on the forehead-the command wheel or the domination spot, a space between the two eyes and I don't know what happened to me. My eyes became full of tears. I lost somewhere. I reached in the divine, unworldly universe far away from the external world. I don't remember how long it continued but when I awoke, I was informed that my name was Swami Premprakruti given then onwards."

"That is alright . . . but how did you come here in Himalaya? Where Osho talks about "Jorba the Buddha", but you have come away from the world to live here." Aakash too had begun reading Osho along with meditation.

"Due to Osho . . . I began visiting Osho ashram regularly. I handed over the charge of my profession to my son and employees. I used to stay in ashram from morning to evening. I worked for ashram, listened to Osho's sermons and performed meditation. I had begun to get an unprecedented peace. In that peace, I could be able to see my path. But as long as Osho was alive, I could not imagine going away from him. On 19 January 1991, Osho left the world. Till then I was in Poona. With his departure, I became free from my self-created bondage. And about which I got to know later on while Osho could foresee it in advance. Therefore, he had named me as Swami Premprakruti. To me, nature was my love. I left to go to Himalaya. Wandering into Himalaya, I could meet the people of this community. They accepted me and till then I am with them."

"But Baba as you were accustomed to the external language, materials and facilities; how then did it become possible for you to adjust here?" Aakash asked.

"Actually I could get the real pleasure here only. I do not recall that world now ever and although these people respect me as a saint but the fact is that I get to learn a lot from them compared to what they learn from me."

"What, how come?" Aakash asked surprisingly.

"We live through and in mind but heart is the only inner way. And these people live heartily. Heart has no language but deep understanding. You will wonder that these people could communicate with trees and birds and are able to comprehend each other while we fail to comprehend the fellow human being. Love is the slogan of these people."

"Love resides in our world too, Baba! We do love our dear ones! We love our sister, brother and parents too."

"Ours is not love. It is a culture. It is an assumption, arrangement. Our love does not flow from heart but from mind. And therefore it is made up of words and selfishness. It is made of necessity and body. True love has no words but only responsibilities. It has true devotion and if needed it is ready to make sacrifice too."

It was good to listen to all what Baba had to say but Aakash's experience was not vast enough to comprehend everything smoothly. Aakash kept quiet. Both slept late night.

Next day Kajal brought snacks for both of them. Everybody had it together. Baba asked Kajal about her life, what is going on? Do you have any difficulty? Are you comfortable? In reply of all the questions, Kajal said.

"Aakash is with me! What difficulty can I have then?"

After meeting with Baba, Kajal asked Aakash to walk in the jungle and to enjoy the river bank. Aakash felt that Kajal is missing this place and I should allow her to enjoy everything completely.

He said, "Let us go."

Both went to forest. Kajal called Devvani bird making a sound. She loved it and made it familiar with Aakash. It went on Aakash's shoulder. It seemed that all the trees were in full mood getting the company of Kajal. Wind was flowing in merriment. Himalaya, its rocks, stones which were silent, but they seemed to be in full gaiety. The whole atmosphere was had been alive.

Kajal was dancing, moving, singing and talking with the trees on the way. Kajal was very happy. She saw the leopard on the way; it came near her and began to rub its body with Kajal's. Kajal also introduced it with Aakash. Aakash was afraid of it but as Kajal was with him, leopard rubbed his body with Aakash's and he was moving his hand on its back.

They went to sit on the river bank. They sat together on the same stones. Kajal sat silent watching the flowing water.

She said, "You see Aakash, I came in your world flowing with this water."

"Yes" Aakash said.

Again they kept quiet. After sitting for an hour, they returned back to Baba. Bheemo, Bapu and others had started coming. Meeting all, they left for the city.

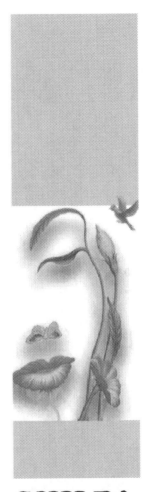

SHILPA

23

Plasto Tech was neither small nor too huge. It was all right. It was a Poona based company which had 200 workers, engineers, 2-3 managers and a staff of 15-20 other members. This group had one company in Poona and the other was located in Badi. The important functions performed by it were injection molding, making tool dies on the basis of it and to do product assembly as per the requirements of customers.

When Aakash and Arjun joined the company, construction work was going on at the first floor. Entering into the gate, there was a beautiful garden on one end. There was a car parking behind the garden. On the other end of the gate, there was a canteen which was separately divided for workers and staff. There was a two-wheeler parking then after. The factory building was in the middle. There was a path from where two vehicles could pass through together and plants around it. In front of canteen road, staff used to sit in the factory building. There was a store beside staff room wherein tools and material were kept. There was a 50-60 injection molding shop floor after it. And there was an assembly shop after it. And there lied finished goods godown behind it so that truck could carry goods into it and could go out through factory road.

It was only after joining the company, Aakash and Arjun could get to know about what kind of construction work was going on at the first floor. Die in the company was made from the main office of Poona. But many times, there raised a problem of maintenance in the running production or there occurred a need to make changes into it as per the demands of the customers because of which die used to be sent in Poona. As a result, the work which was able to be done in two days took 20-25 days in sending and receiving. In addition, it took extra repairing time. Expenses of sending and bringing it back, inconveniency suffered by customers and the loss in production led the company to make a decision of constructing small tool room in Badi. It would to be easy for the company to handle common work of maintenance and making changes as per the customers' demands into it in Badi now. With this objective, work had begun on the first floor by company where there were also arrangements to be made for staff and tool room was to be built in place of present staff space.

Aakash enjoyed his work. He got to know and learn new things. In rest of the time, he used to enjoy Kajal's company. In the Saturday-Sunday holidays, they along with Sunil-Nisha went for travelling and have fun. Once they visited Shimla, second time they went to Pinjor garden or sometime they would go to watch movie in Chandigarh multiplex. And once in a month, he would take Kajal to visit community in the Himalayan hills without fail.

Three months passed in the same routine. Toll room was constructed in Plasto Tech, machines came and staff office was made on the first floor. New recruitment began to be done for tool room.

One day, there came a circular from management to meet in the canteen at 4 o'clock in the afternoon. Generally this kind of meeting was held when there was a new recruitment of any staff. Tea party was arranged to introduce a new employee at 4 o' clock in the canteen.

A staff of 50 members including director, G.M., engineers and manager gathered in the canteen and director would make a new employee familiar with everybody turn by turn. "This is Shilpa Shah" director addressed everybody saying this. Shilpa Shah was dressed in black pant and black lining T-shirt having a white background. She had slight grey hair which was tied. Shilpa was looking like a Spanish girl who had fair skin and long face-cut. She had a narrow chin and sharp grey eyes. "She is joining as a tool room engineer in our company from today." Director finished the introduction saying this. Everybody started meeting Shilpa turn by turn while sipping tea and gave their introduction.

"Hi... I am Aakash Patel—Production Engineer" Aakash stretched his hand saying this. Shilpa stretched her hand too with a smile. Shilpa's teeth were like foreigners, slightly yellow and coming outside still she was looking really charming. On that day, he could not get chance to have more talk in the function as others too were in the queue to introduce themselves to her but he could get to know more about her next day during lunch time.

Shilpa was taking her lunch sitting alone on a table and Aakash reached there.

"May I sit here?"

"Yes" Aakash sat there stretching a chair before she could say it moving her neck.

"I have pursued my B.E. in mechanical from Chandigarh Leet College of Engineering. And You?" Aakash started introducing in detail just after sitting.

"I have done my B.E. in Mechanical from Punjab College of Engineering." Shilpa uttered smilingly.

"Very Good—it will be enjoyable" Aakash said this out of excitement.

"Of what"

"Of working together"

"Why so?" Shilpa asked widening her eyes.

"It's because when two people of the same age meet, it is enjoyable to work together" Aakash could immediately think of the reply. He pointed Shilpa toward old aged people glancing around the canteen.

Shilpa laughed.

Arjun also came there finding Aakash on the table. From the very first day, they had an informal friendly introduction. And till the lunch getting over, they got familiar with one another so deep as if knowing one another for long.

It is not only magnet which attracts the iron, youth also attracts youth. And there were very few officers in the staff falling into the age category of 22 to 30.

Aakash had to meet Shilpa often with regard to the problems of die-tooling. Initially Aakash felt that Shilpa was very slow in making any decision or bringing any solution. As when he went to her taking the problem of die-tool, Shilpa asked him to submit the details first and told that I will think on what to do, how to do and I will inform you when it will get over but she could never exhibit her work in time. She managed to accomplish easy functions with the help of her subordinates. But where it was complication, she became slow out of nervousness and it delayed the work. Aakash had to follow up Shilpa frequently as there was a pressure of production schedule upon him. Some time he thought of complaining to his boss but he found it insignificant to lodge a complaint against Shilpa. Therefore he himself took interest in the die solution. He discussed with Shilpa and both worked on its solution and the work began to be done quickly. In the beginning, Aakash felt that Shilpa lacked self-confidence but slowly he could realize that she was poor in technical knowledge too. But the only weakness of Shilpa turned out to be the reason for Aakash to go near Shilpa. They began meeting often. Perhaps Shilpa also realized now that Aakash had known about her poor technical knowledge. Therefore she always appreciated Aakash and fondled him. She tried to catch him emotionally. She often used to say "Aakash it seems that you have pursued engineering in real sense of the term." "You are genius." "You are an in born engineer." And so on. One day investigating about Aakash's childhood, she asked, "Did you determine to be an engineer from your childhood, Aakash?"

"Yes . . . As a child whenever my father brought anything, I would open it before use even if he brought pen for me. When he brought bicycle for the first time and then bike, I had opened it up. I have always been interested to know about how a particular thing works rather than how to make use of it."

"And I have never had any interest in engineering. I have done it unwillingly."

"Why you had to do it unwillingly?" Aakash asked.

"I have always liked to work with money and people and how to bring out work from them. And we are jains, so money and its calculation is there in our blood. And we have a jewellery show room in Chandigarh. Thus, I have been playing with money from my childhood. And as our family has much importance of religious and social functions, I am nourished with people and their psychology. This is also one more reason why I was interested in it. Actually I wanted to pursue B.Com. and then do MBA but papa wanted me to be an engineer and therefore made me opt for science in 11-12 standard. When I got less percentage, I felt I would be saved now. But he made me take admission through management quota and finally made me an engineer."

"And as you became engineer, I could get the chance to come in your acquaintance" Aakash finished the talk laughing.

"No, you met me after being an engineer and now I am learning real engineering, so I am at more advantage than you." Shilpa told.

"No . . . no . . . It's not completely like that. You also know something. It's only that you might face some difficulty."

"Tell me straight away that I am dull. I won't mind at all. The fact is that I have been able to learn only that much which could be learnt through labour and cramming." She playfully moved her eyes saying this and laughed secretly.

Aakash was also at profit in Shilpa's being weak. If she knew more, he would not have got the chance to go nearer to her.

They had now been closer as the time passed, yet Aakash never talked to her about Kajal. Perhaps he would never talk about her but one day Aakash, Arjun and Shilpa were sitting in the canteen during lunch time. At that time, Arjun saw a sabji of potato and bitter gourd in Aakash's lunch box which he liked a lot. As Arjun used to stay alone, he took his lunch in the canteen. But Aakash and Shilpa brought home made food. Relishing sabji from Aakash's lunch box, he uttered, "Vow, what a sabji! Who made it, mummy or Kajal? I have never had such a tasty sabji in my life." As Arjun appreciated the sabji, Shilpa also tasted taking it from Aakash's lunch box and she also complimented:

"Really, it's delicious, simple yet tasty, who made it?"

"Kajal" Aakash replied shortly.

"Who is Kajal?" Shilpa knew that Aakash's sister Dhara stayed in Chandigarh.

"Kajal is my wife." Aakash informed unexcitedly. He didn't like the matter raised by Arjun.

"You have never told me Aakash that you are married?" Shilpa said.

"It's because you have never asked about it." Aakash told.

"I considered you and Arjun bachelors just like me."

"I am bachelor and perhaps will remain forever." Arjun said.

Arjun's thinking of remaining bachelor was too great, it was surprising too. Still Shilpa focused on Aakash only and asked:

"Apart from this, if you wish to inform about children, you can Aakash." Aakash felt Shilpa asked ironically.

He replied shortly. "No, at present, we are two only. Ok, now I will have to leave." Saying this he quickly left for his shop floor.

Aakash thought that now there will be no interest in maintaining relation with Shilpa. Now Shilpa won't precede the relation ahead. But nothing such happened. She remained the same as earlier. On the contrary, she preceded one step ahead.

One day after getting free from company, Aakash left for home and saw that his bike was punctured. He thought of taking the bike at a garage located at a little distance and go home after getting it repaired. As he reached near the main gate pulling his bike, he heard the horn of a car from behind. Car stood beside him. Putting the glass down and neck out of it, Shilpa said:

"What happen, Aakash?"

"Puncture" saying this and expressing boredom, Aakash stood there near the bike.

"Do one thing" Shilpa said. "Keep the bike near watchman's cabin and put the tier out of it. Take it and come with me in the car. We will leave the tier at garage for repair and I will drop you at your home in Kalka.

"But you have to go to Chandigarh. It will be wrong to go by Kalka."

"No, not wrong but long. Instead of Panchkula, I will drop you at Kalka and go to Chandigarh through Pinjor. It will be only 15 kilometers long, won't it?

"But why you need to go so long? I will keep my bike here and go in any other vehicle. And if possible, I will go getting it repaired so that I don't have to take trouble tomorrow." Aakash said.

"Tomorrow I will come to pick you. I will come via Kalka. Ok, please sit now." Shilpa insisted.

"Again you will have to come taking a long route." Aakash said to express courtesy.

"And don't worry about a long route. I am a daughter of Vaniya. I will have tea and snacks in return of it. And I will also get a chance to meet everybody in your house, especially Kajal." Shilpa laughed saying this. Aakash could not deny. He left the bike there and sat in the car putting tyre out of it. After giving the tyre for repair, they left for Kalka.

"Do you regularly come in car?" Aakash asked.

"Of course, I had a condition with papa that if he wants me to do job, he will have to purchase a car for me and that too without driver so that I can enjoy it my own way."

"What is the meaning of this job if your salary is less than your car expenses?"

"I will get experience. An educated—engineer girl could get a perfect match. I have got this job through papa's reference. Otherwise it was not possible to get such job on the basis of my percentage and knowledge." Shilpa clearly mentioned.

Both reached Kalka while talking. As per the directions indicated by Aakash, they reached his home. Kajal quickly came out running but hesitated a bit observing a girl on the driver seat of a car along with Aakash. Kajal was looking dashing in bun and sari. Aakash introduced indicating before Kajal.

"Shilpa, this is Kajal, my wife and Kajal this is Shilpa, we do job together. Shilpa gave her shake hand but Kajal greeted her joining her hands and welcomed her."

"No, I am in hurry. I will be late. I will come some other day." Shilpa uttered.

"You have come upto here. You may not have eaten anything from noon. Please have some snacks and cold drink and then go." Kajal knew Aakash's habit of having snacks and cold drink in the evening so she insisted. Shilpa could not deny and came inside. Aakash's mummy Sushilaben was watching TV. Aakash introduced her with Shilpa. Kajal went to prepare snacks. Aakash went to get fresh so Sushilaben asked her out of formality.

"Where do you stay?"

Aakash came back getting fresh. Till then Sushilaben had got completely excited in her communication with Shilpa.

"Oh, so the jewelry shop named 'Woman Paradise' in Chandigarh belongs to you?

"Yes . . . auntie, my papa Subhashbhai handles it. And one more thing auntie, don't address me with courtesy, please. If you address me like a family member, I would love it."

"Is he that Subhashbhai who has once remained leader of congress party in the city?"

"Yes . . . he is the same. He is active in politics even today, auntie."

"Yes, when once he had come as a chief guest in our women organization function, I had seen him."

"Yes ... He might have come. At present, he is vice-president of Municipal Corporation too."

"Then I will have to meet him. He may be helpful to our organization."

"Certainly Auntie"

Till then Kajal brought snacks and cold-drink. Shilpa had it quickly and then hurried to leave. While leaving she said:

"It is dark now. I have to reach home before they worry for me, auntie. And Kajal I have to talk a lot with you. I want to have food of your hands, but some other day."

"Oh dear, it is your house now. Come whenever you wish. Come on a holiday so that we could get plenty of time to talk and have food."

Sushilaben now had begun to address her as a close relative. Kajal bid her farewell with a smile and said "do come next time."

As Aakash had no bike, so she brought her car next day too and took Aakash with her in the factory.

24

O n the Very next Sunday, without informing in advance Shilpa reached at Aakash's house at 9.0 clock in the morning by her car, she directly went to Aakash's mom and told:

'Auntie, you invited me heartily and therefore I have come."

'You did well, my dear. I really liked it. Now go having lunch too.

'Not only lunch, but I am going to have snacks and tea in noon and would leave in the evening, right Kajal.?'

"Yes, certainly, we would like too" Kajal spoke, looked at Aakash. Shilpa's arrival was surprising for Aakash too. He said 'Yes, it is completely right, will be enjoyable.

'Today I have come to relish food made by Kajal, listen to the story of Aakash—Kajal and to gossip with auntie."

'You mentioned everyone, but what about me?' Saying this Sureshbhai came out carrying a cup of tea in his hand.

"And I have come to meet you for the first time." recalled that Sureshbhai was not present in the house when she came last time. Kajal brought water till then. After drinking it, Shilpa went in the kitchen with Kajal instated of sitting. After some time Sushilaben too went in the kitchen within no time, sounds began to come out of gossip and language mostly; most of the sounds were from Sushilaben and Shilpa.

When they gathered to have lunch in noon at that time too she was behaving in such a way as if she knew this family for long and was a member of this family.

While having lunch she asked 'Aaksh how did you and Kajal fall in love?"

Aakash felt hesitant to discuss about personal matter on dining table, so he said 'It's a long matter, I will tell you about this in leisure some time."

"To talk in leisurely time, you and Kajal should come at my home. We will talk and have lunch together, we will watch movie and roam in Chandigarh, is it right, Kajal".

Kajal replied with smile "I aim at home, Akash has to free himself and manage his time."

'And is there no invitation to us? If Aaskh is your friend. So will you manage your relationship with a friend and his wife only? Now I have also a right upon you. Sushilaben interrupted.

'Certainly Auntie. It was only our friendly talk, you will have to come to meet. my parents, my father will be very happy to see your activities about women development. He will really feel nice to see you, tell me when will you come to have dinner?" directly said to decide the date of arrival.

"Oh dear if has been long to stay for a night in Chandigarh. It is not comfortable to stay at night. And we will have to stay if invited for dinner."

"Then please stay at our home. We have a guest room too, auntie"

That is right but if I happen to come sometime, we will surely meet all of you" Sushilaben concluded the matter saying this.

Till departure, she got all the information of her house and address from Shilpa.

After Shilpa's going, Sushilaben said, 'She is really a good girl, isn't she? she is amicable too. Her father has a status in politics too. Relationship must be maintained."

Before all could go to Chandigarh at Shilpa' house, Shilpa and Aakash had to go together somewhere. The matter happened just like this . . .

They had an important customer from Chennai. He was facing problems in his recently developed product and discussion regarding his die had been essential. Therefore, cmpany decided to call that customer of Chennai to Badi first. But the main tool room was in Puna. and the experienced engineers and managers had their sitting in Puna only. Even the customer was finding it far-flung to come Badi, so company decided to send of tool room engineer from Badi.

The company decided to send Shilpa to Puna and the company engineers in Chennai were asked to come in Puna where solution could be brought out after the discussion on mould and related mould problems. But Shilpa convinced to the management that one production engineer should accompany and one has to discuss the questions of moulding so that the solution of the problem can immediately and truly be achieved.

Therefore, company stated that Aakash would also go to Puna with shilpa.

Three days' program, was planned. There was a flight of 9.30 on Monday morning from Chandigarh to Puna. And the return was decided on Wednesday at 7.00 in the evening form Puna to Chandigarh flight. Akash was happy, with his reasons. And Shilpa was also happy with her reasons. But both were expressing form their faces that they have to go due to the responsibility of company otherwise they were not at all interested.

Monday in the morning Aakash reached at Shilpa's house on his Bike. From there they both were taken to airport by shilpa's car. It was first experience for Aakash to sit in flight. He had an experience of flying in the air but it was personal, alone and in the open air while today he had to sit with many passengers in the plane for the first time.

'Aakash, have you ever gone in flight anywhere before this?'

"No, I am sitting in the plane for the first time but you may have sat many time, haven't you ?"

'Yes . . . . every year we go to visit many places and mostly it is by flight specially form Delhi it is really amazing to travel by air".

Aakash kept quiet. He had also an experience of flight. It was only that he had no experience to go by plane.

"Shilpa, it was decided at first that only you have to go to Puna. Then how did they decide about me?"

"Oh dear . . . you know very well that I am really poor in technical knowledge. Therefore I persuaded management to take anybody from production and they got ready."

"If anybody was sent in my place, would you have liked it?"

"It is a job, I had to go." saying this she laughed. "But I persuaded them to take Akash so that problem solution could be perfect."

"But how did you suggest my name?"

"That's the matter! It is really strategic about all these plans Mr. Akash." Laughed saying this.

They got settled in plane. Shilpa allowed Aakash to sit near window so that he could happily enjoy plane journey.

Aakash didn't find plane journey much enjoyable. He was not able to enjoy watching the land form extreme height nor he could feel the touch of nature. And he used to fly in such a way so that he could profoundly experience the thrill of the atmosphere.

They directly went to hotel form Puna airport. Royal rooms were arranged for both of them. An arrangement of a car form company was made for them, they have to be ready at 2 o'clock, therefore, they had to get quickly ready and get fresh. They were hungry too, so they ordered light snacks sitting in one room only. After having snacks, both went to their respective rooms to get fresh and ready.

Aakash was just to go to take bath wrapping towel on his body and he got a call from company that "the party which was to come from Chennai today has not been able to come due to inevitable reasons. Now they will come tomorrow at 9 o'clock in the morning directly on factory. Therefore, you could enjoy sight-seeing in Puna today and get ready tomorrow at 8.00 a.m., company's car will pick you up."

Aakash become happy like anything. He got excited with the only thinking of roaming into Puna for the whole day with shilpa. He also wished to visit Osho commune, so there was a chance to get it fulfilled. He got excited with the thought of watching romantic movie with Shilpa in multiplex sitting together. Aakash rushed into Shilpa's room in towel only. Her room was just beside his room. Even he did not take care of knocking the door and he pushed the door after pushing its handle. The door got opened, he saw that Shilpa was also going to take both wearing bra on the upper portion and wrapping towel below. She covered both her hands on her breast watching Aakash. till then the hot image of Shilpa's beauty was imprinted on Aakash's mind. Akash got hesitated. Saying sorry, he went out but actually his mind remained inside only.

Going back into his room he dialled a number of Shilpa's room on intercom and told her the matter in detail.

He asked her to make a plan for going somewhere after sometime, Aakash got ready. He sat in her room but didn't dare to go to her room once again so kept waiting there. His door was knocked. When he opened the door he saw that she was there in a long frock with a mild and sweet but mysterious smile on her face. She asked removing Aakash's hesitation, "tell me, what is the program for today?"

"I think . . . ." saying this Aakash looked into the watch and said. "see, it is 12 o' clock now. We can watch a movie in multiplex in 12.30 show. Then we will see Osho commune at 4.00 o'clock in Koregaun park. In the evening we will visit any mall, have diner in a hotel and we will sleep after coming back.

"Ok, everything is alright but what is the need to visit Osho commune? Do you know, he is a notorious man. He is misleading people against their Sanatan Religion (Hindu Vedic Religion-coming down from ancient times), he speaks anything without considering others' respect. He was driven away form America just because of these reasons."

"Whatever it is, he is no more now. Everybody appreciates his ashram, so what is wrong in visiting his commune?"

"I have no problem in visiting the Ashram, but from when had you been interested in Osho?

"I have read a little about him. Sometimes, I have performed his meditations." He should have told this with a sense of proud, but he couldn't.

"Ok let us drop the lunch we will have something in theatre."

They watched 'Dil Chahta hai' in a multiplex situated near Koregaon park. At 4. o'clock, they reached at Koregaon Osho commune and joined into visitors tour. Aakash had a desire to visit Osho commune. He had heard about it from Baba and Arjun, and reading his books and also was interested in his meditation, so his wish was coming true today.

Osho commune was really beautiful. On one hand, there was Buddha hall covered with net and beautifully curving roads and on the other side, there was a book stall. Between two zigzag roads, there was a waterfall made from natural stones. The water rippled over the stones. All buildings were painted in black colour having greenish blue coloured window glass. There were huge bamboos spread around Buddha hall from which melodious music could be heard. All the followers, no matter men as women were in maroon attire. 20-25 visitors were moving around the commune, nobody was concerned about anyone, all the were in their own seventh heavens. Many followers were there, all were lost in their own enjoyment. Even Shilpa had to admit that this was really a unique and beautiful Ashram and is far better than other Ashrams. There was a sitting space in front of the book store where followers were sitting in their own joy. Among them there were more foreign-followers than Indian followers. All were sitting freely and expressing their feelings by touching and hugging each others. Somewhere they were kissing each others to which Shilpa whispered to Aakash:

"Oh shit . . . ! They should be ashamed of doing it in public."

"Then where should they do?" Aakash asked.

Shilpa scorned and replied, "Why, can't they do it home, is it to be done in public? How immodest people they are! They spoil the image of our nation and the society."

"But what if they want to kiss others wives or girl friends . . . they can't do it at home." Aakash joked.

"Why, are there no hotels available ? Why do they defame the Ashram? saying this expressed her disapproval.

After going round the Ashram and mall, they had some shopping and having good dinner in a restaurant they returned to hotel at 9.00 p.m. They placed their bags and sat in Shilpa's room and then Aakash told;

"I really find it right what you said in Osho commune."

"Which one?" Shilpa asked surprisingly.

"that . . ." saying this, he embraced Shilpa and kissed her strongly on her lips and said, "hotels should be utilised to kiss others wives or girlfriends."

"You . . . mischievous." saying this she pushed Aakash out of his room and closed the door.

From next day morning technical discussions began. Shilpa was behaving smartly taking care of her ignorance not being revealed. But Aakash was involved in the problems deeply. After a long discussion on many options and working solutions, he could bring solution of the questions acceptable to everyone. They had their dinner in the company on the day and then returned their hotel at 10.00 p.m. They were tired. Aakash would have gone beyond limit in his relationship with Shilpa but someone from inside controlled him. Perhaps, the ethical courage or his responsibilities torward Kajal, but he didn't cross his limit then.

Wednesday in the evening they returned to Chandigarh through flight. Shilpa's Car had come to take both of them. Taking his bike from shilpa's home Akash was began to leave for Kalka.

While leaving, Shilpa said, "Aakash, it was really enjoyable to spend these three days in Pune. I will always remember them."

"Same here . . . bye" saying this Aakash left.

All the routine work began in the company going in morning, having lunch in canteen with Shilpa and Arjun in noon and retuning in the evening there was only one difference and that was behaviour, she was behaving more affectionately with Aakash. It seemed that she was taking much care of Aakash. Arjun asked about this one day in the presence of Shilpa only.

"Aaakash, it seems that after coming back from Pune your relationship with Shilpa have become deeper."

"No .... there is nothing like that actually, we were in much contact of each other during these three days, so more communication took place betwween us so we became more familiar. Therefore, it seems like that, otherwise everything is formal." saying this Aaskh turned his eyes.

"It is alright if it is so. But please take care, Kajal is there only at your trust."

"Oh come on friend, how do you connect a common incident with Kajal's insecurity. Nobody can take place of Kajal."

Saying this Aakash concluded the matter but he was really trembled with fear regarding what Arjun's eyes had caught.

25

After coming back from Pune, Shilpa reached by car at Aakash's home at 10.00 a.m. in the morning on the third Sunday.

All greeted her with excitement epically Sushilaben and Aakash. Still nobody could ask her that how come she was here? But read the sense into the eyes of them which Shilpa read and said:

"Auntie, today I have specially come to have lunch made by Kajal and to talk to you and Kajal and lot. I have still to know the love story of Akash and Kajal."

"Dear! It is your house you can come whenever you wish." Sushilaben told.

"Auntie, papa was also appreciating you a lot. He was telling that Sushilaben will create her own prestigious identity in politics one day."

"Mummy, when did you meet Subhash uncle?" Akash asked surprisingly, Subhashbhai was Shilpa's father.

"Last time when Shilpa came here, in the next week, he had come to attend one of our meetings fortunately. There I could meet him. Where I talked to him about Shilpa, the acquaintance base became much deeper then. Subsequently he came as a chief guest in two functions of our organizations. And he donated Rs.50,000/- to a dalit women on my request. He is really a wonderful person, Shilpa." Saying this she looked at Shilpa with a smile.

"Now auntie, you equally owe a right, along with Akash to come to our home and have dinner." Shilpa said.

"But mummy you did not inform me that you met with Shilpa's father," Aakash told confused.

"What is the need to inform you about that?" Shushilaben scorned.

"Just for the sake of information. So that I can also know that how long my friendship with shilpa has been extended?"

"Ok, Akash leave that matter and tell me where the four of you are coming to have dinner at our home? Now both the families are known to each other." Shilpa said.

"It is difficult to say about dinner, we never had a halt at Chandigarh overnight." Shilpaben said.

"Why ? Dhara is there in Chandigarh, isn't she?" Shilpa mentioned Aakash's sister.

"Yes but as Kalka is near to Chandigarh. So we go to meet her in noon and come back in the evening. It has been 3 years staying at Chandigarh. Aakash was seriously ill then and admitted in the hospital, at that time we had a night halt." Sushilaben said.

"What had happened to Aakash?"

"Hepatitis-B—He was saved when I took vow of visiting Goddess Vaishnodevi."

"Not by your taking vow, but he was saved from Kajal's herbal roots." Sureshbhai interrupted.

"Oh come on, it is not possible to get cured with the treatment of such herbal roots where great doctors had failed. It was only the blending and vow of goddess Vaishnodevi which saved him."

"What others do is mockery and what you do is faith isn't it?" Sureshbhai said.

"What do you know about what is faith? leave it." Sushilaben scorned.

"You had ostentatiously taken the vow to visit Goddess Vaishnodevi, you should have visited by now, why didn't you yet?" Sureshbhai said.

"How can I go. The one who is cured with the blessings of Goddess, he doesn't get time from his company's work and Bank is more dear to you than me. Now only Kajal is there. The poor girl, instead of taking my care, I will have to take care of her." Sushilaben said.

At that time they heard the sounds revealing Kajal's nausea from the Kitchen.

Sushilaben was about to stand up but Shilpa stood quickly before her and ran into the kitchen asking her to sit.

After sometime she came out with Kajal and said suddenly; "Auntie, now you will have to go to worship Goddess Vaishnodevi, your daughter-in-law is about to become a mother."

"What!" everybody spoke out of happiness. Aakash looked at Kajal, She lowered her eyes down.

"Aunti, I will take you to the pilgrimage of Goddees Vaishnodevi. I will take leave on next Friday-Saturday. You, me and my mom will go by my car and will reach there in the evening. Next day, after praying to Goddess, we will stay over there during night and will return the third day morning.

"But dear, you need not take trouble for me when my close one's are not interested in fulfilling my vow." Saying this sushilaben looked at Aakash and Sureshbhai one by one.

"It's not like that Auntie, actually I and Mummy also wish to visit the temple Vishnovdevi so it will get fulfilled because of you."

Next Friday, Saturday and Sunday. Sushilaben went to Goddess Vaishnnodevi's temple with Shilpa and her mom. After coming back she was continuously praising Shilpa.

"She has taken care of me more than a son cares, it was really enjoyable. She is really a good, modest and virtuous girl." etc.

Aakash was happy with Shilpa as well as with Kajal. Shilpa had fulfilled his duty of taking his mom to Goddess Vaishnodevi and Kajal ahead conceived his child. It was next to impossible to find fault with Kajal's behaviour, love, service and nature. She took care of Aakash's all the requirements moment to moment. She had learnt to cook Aakash's favourite dishes. During night, if he takes fragment turn off or if he dashed his feet in sleep, she would start pressing his feet and she was looking continuously to him. Kajal's over-caring behaviour was becoming a psychological problem for Aakash. Kajal was always being ready to fulfil Aakash's wishes and needs whether they are physical or mental. No matter, whether she likes it or not. Because of this, there was no room for communication between them. There was no agreement and disagreement or displeasure and reconciliations between them to make life more interesting. There was only sweetness, no change in its taste, because of which Aakash was feeling a kind of boredom, otherwise they led a full and happy life.

The boredom which was developing in Aakash made him got sidetracked by Shilpa. Shilpa had affected graceful gestures, intelligence, appreciativeness, a style, a sweetness, a taste. She was a witty speaker and he was burning with the fire of separation created by the kissing incident at Pune. It was insatiable eroticism. His closeness was sharply noticed by Arjun. The way Shilpa waited for Aakash during lunch time, took care of him and the way Aakash got involved in

Shilpa's technical questions with interest indicated that their relation was proceeding in altogether a new direction.

One day Aakash and Arjun had to stay in the company till late night as the company was facing a problem in the running production and the company was in urgent need to that production. It was compulsory for both of them to stay in the factory till the technical question get solved and production work gets regular. They were sitting in the chairs nearby instructing the workers to work upon die. They had no others option but to sit there till the workers finish their work on die. And the work on die was about to take two hours. In between they had to supervise the work. Both started gossiping.

"Arjun, do you remember when I was ill, my mummy had taken vow for my good health to go to goddess Vaishnovdevi sitemap. This wish of my mom got fulfilled by shilpa before few days."

"But you were cured by Kajal's herbal roots, not because of taking vow? Anyway! that is alright but why did Shilpa take interest in fulfilling you mom's wish?

"It's because I have no time. Frankly speaking, I have no faith in all such things. I believe that I was cured with Kajal's herebal roats."

"It is good for you to always believe so, otherwise you may fall into some other disease with Shilpa's help."

"Don't crack a joke buddy. how can it be? Shlpa is just a friend."

"But it seems that she is being more than a friend for the last few days. Neither I nor Sunil, inspite of being your best friends, could not fulfil your mom's wish which Shilpa could do within a short time, why? there must be some closeness, right."

"No. It is not like that. My mother also knows Shilpa's father due to political common interest. The two families have become well-connected."

"See, Aakash, I am not interested in finding fault with anybody but I caution you to be aware from Shilpa just because of Kajal."

"Dear, you are taking the matter much seriously there is nothing like as you think of between us." Aakash said.

Arjun preceded the matter avoiding Akash's statement. "You don't know about it but I tell you that I and shilpa have studied in the same school in 11-12."

"Then why doesn't she know you? she has never mentioned that she knows you."

"She is right. I had come from Delhi to study 11-12 in Chandigarh. It was a huge school where we studied. There were 3 divisions of 11th standard and we were in different divisions."

Nevertheless, you must have met her sometimes. Though she was in other division you know her, accordingly she must have got to know you, isn't it so?

"There are two-three reasons behind it. when I joined that school in 11th standard she was there for many yeas. The second reason is that boys take care of girls more compared to girls. And the third and the last reason is that she was deeply in love with her classmate named Ajay. Their love story was very popular in the whole school being strong subject of discussion."

"There is no need to take the relationship of that age seriously. We should not consider any person inferiors due to his/her love chapter." Saying this Aakash reallocted Sandhya Yadav and Priya Pathak. Aakash continued, "It is the age when such mistakes are likely to happen." This time, Bheemo and Kajal passed through his eyes where he could see Bheemo forcing upon Kajal and Kajal was laying there silently without any resistance. It was painful memories for Aakash. Still he was generous enough to think about this incident with the perspective of philosophy.

"You are right, if anyone have relation only due to attraction, sentiment or immaturity it is worth forgetting. But here, the matter is somewhat different. Ajay Soni was very clever in studies and Shilpa was dull. Ajay Soni was helping Shilpa in studies even at the cost of his time, which Shilpa wanted. And truly speaking, Shilpa could secure 50% in 12th science just because of him only!"

"But how could you say this with guarantee that Shilpa pretended to love him to gain her selfish end?" Aakash argued.

"I could say this with assurance because Ajay Soni was really in love with her. After 12 science result, Shilpa began avoiding Ajay Soni. He requested Shilpa a lot, but she fell in love with Vikram Bhatiya, the son of his father's political opponent. Her father was also interested in this relation. Ajay could not tolerate Shilpa's relation with Vikram. He could not forget his love. As a result a bright boy who had the ability to be a doctor or engineer is only a clerk today after completing his B.Sc.

"How could you say so with assurance that what you are telling is the only truth?"

"Because I had also many friends is schools who knew Subhashbhai, Shilpa's father and her family closely. They were associated with his shop 'Women Paradise.'"

"But if Shilpa is in love with Vikram Bhatia today, why is he to not seen ever? Why does she not mention even his name?"

"It's because that relation is also broken. Vikram Bhatia and his father turned out to be more clever than

Subhashbhai. Shilpa's farther wanted to precede ahead taking the benefit of this relation but Vikram Bhatia left Shilpa and married with the daughter of a political leader richer than Subhashbhai who provided an opportunity to his father to precede ahead."

"But Shilpa's father is also a political leader. he has also a name and fame in the society."

"Yes, he is a political leader but of second category. Now remains the matter of prestige and respect, so he has sent Shilpa to Badi, away from Chandigarh intentionally so that people forget about this event easily. Otherwise, he is not at all interested in her ordinary job. Shilpa spends this much rupees in her car and clothes. If he wished he would have asked Shilpa to help in his business, but he thought that it was necessary for people to forget this event. Then only it was possible for him to find a groom for Shilpa."

Aakash was totally unaware of these. Though it was shocking, but still he was not ready to believe it. He decided mantally to confirm it and concluded the talk.

It was 3 a.m. by the time workers finished the task in the factory. Both left for home after keeping the production into running condition. Arjun stayed alone in Chandigarh, and they had to come back early next day, so Aakash said:

"Arjun, keep your bike here today and come with me my home. After having some rest and getting fresh, we will come back tomorrow together."

Arjun found Aakash's offer suitable. It was good for both of them to go together at this time Thinking that, he get ready to sit behind Aakah's bike.

Arjun asked sitting on the bike, "Aakash. did you inform Kajal about your being late today?"

"Oh ... buddy ... I just forgot to inform her due to work and gossip."

"Poor one, she might worry and would be waiting for you."

"No . . . no . . . she would have slept already."

"No . . . . I can tell you with assurance that she will be waiting for you keeping food on the kitchen platform."

"No . . . no . . . it's too late now, she might have waited till 10-11 and then went to bed."

They reached at Aakash's home while talking. Living room's light was on. The moment he stopped the bike, Kajal came out of the house immediately. "Today it's too late, isn't it?" she said with smile" is it you Arjun?

"I forgot to call you because of work" saying this Aakash and Arjun entered into the house he saw that a book was lying on sofa which was open and turned from back side.

Arjun said watching the book. "Oh Kajal have you learnt to read too?"

"I try a little bit. In our street, there lives a small boy named Kanho. I borrow books from him and learn."

"When?"

"Daily in the noon when Aakash and papa go to office in the morning and mummy go to attend her meetings in the noon.

"It's good." Arjun said.

"You both get fresh. I serve the food till then." Kajal said.

"But now there is no mood to have food, do you have Arjun?" Aakash said.

"You have come hungry after working long not had anything evening. When it will be served, you will find yourself hungery. First of all get fresh. When they came after getting fresh, food was served.

"Kajal did you eat?" Aakash asked.

"I will sleep after having dinner with you." Aakash and Arjun looked at each other. Aakash was surprised with

Arjun's guess. Kajal was waiting for him the same way as Arjun mentioned.

"Kajal, tomorrow we will have to go to factory at 10.00 a.m., so please wake us up at 8.00 a.m.

Next day getting ready and having full snacks, they both reached the factory.

26

After few days . . .

Aakash had just reached at his Badi-Plasto Tech factory before two hours and he got a call from his mother. She was a bit apprehensive in her tone.

"Aakash, come fast at home. There has been a great problem."

"What happened, mummy? You sound very fearful."

"Police has arrested Kajal. You immediately reach at the advocate Ashok Barot's office, we are coming there." It was really an insulting for a middle class family to have police arrival at their home. And if it comes with a charge of crime on the family member, it equals to the extremity of fear, sorrow, and harassment. And this was an Indian Police who is famous for taking advantage of helpless people, who is more interested in its execution of power than justice, who has an attitude of benifitting themselves under the pretext for punishment than complaint. Having police arrival with this psychology in the middle class family is like loss of prestige and chastity in the society. And in that Police today had arrived to arrest Kajal with a very serious accuse. Therefore, it was obvious for Sushilaben to get afraid of.

Without much discussion, Aakash left for Kalka seeking permission from his manager and informing the situation to Shilpa and Arjun in short. He directly reached at the advocate Ashok Barot's office. Before his parents came, Aakash called to Sunil.

Withion no time, Sushilaben and Sureshbhai reached there. They had come directly after meeting Kajal. Aakash asked them:

"What happened?"

"Come, let us go to directly to advocate's office, I will inform you there in detail." Saying this they entered Ashok Barot's office. Advocate Ashok Barot was very well acquintained with Sushilaben. They were familiar with each other too.

"Yes . . . Sushilaben, what brought you here?"

"Ashokbhai, police has arrested to our daughter-in-law."

"Tell me in detail, when, what and how did it happen?" Advocate Ashok asked.

"There lives a lady named Savita in our society, next to the street of our house. She had a young son whose name was Kanho. He was 8-9 years old. I and Savita were never in good terms. She is also a social activist like me. She is active in women organizations. I and she have always opposed each other. As a result, we have no communication or social contact with each other. If we meet by chance in someone's function, we try to avoid each other.

That Savita's son had been a child friend to our daughter-in-law for the last few days. When I was not present at home during noon time, he came to house without fail and played with Kajal. He also gave primary knowledge of reading and writing to Kajal as he studied in second or third standard. I was aware about Kajal and Kanho's meetings in my absence, but I had no much problem with that, although I didn't like it much.

That Kanho was not coming to our house, especially to meet Kajal during noon time for the last many days, so

Kajal became impatient to meet him. She really missed him. She could get to know from the other relatives of the society that Kanho is not able to come out of the house because of being seriously ill. Once she expressed a desire to meet Kanho, but I stopped her.

Yesterday in the evening, a neighbour of Savitaben came to meet Kajal who informed her about Kanho's situation being critically serious and told her that he continuously misses her. Kajal could not control herself. Today in the morning, When Aakash left for office, she told me to come back soon and reached Savitaben's house. She felt sympathy observing the situation of Kanho. She brought some roots of plants and leaves from outside and crushing and bringing liquid out of it, she asked Kanho to drink that liquid. After making him drink the liquid, she came back home and within an hour, Police came at home to arrest her.

When the reason of arresting was asked to the Police, they informed that due to the liquid given to Kanho, he has met with death after drinking it within 10 minutes. Therefore, his mother has claimed a charge of murder against Kajal who made him to drink the liquid."

Sushilaben preceded after taking a pause.

"In my opinion, Savita believes that I have used Kajal to take revenge on her and therefore with a vengeance, she has lodged this Police complaint."

"Mummy, where is Kajal at present?" Aakash asked.

"In Police custody, we have come here after meeting and getting the information from her only."

"Mummy, you know very well that Kajal is specialist of Ayurveda and plants. She had cured me too with this kind of liquid."

"If such wonders work some time, it cannot be accepted as a scientific treatment for ever and be not considered as a science at all." Sushilaben uttered scornfully.

"But her intention was to cure Kanho." Aakash spoke in favour of Kajal.

"But could she be able to cure? And before doing anything good to anybody, she should have thought well in advance to whom it is being done and what results it may bring! She must have known Kanho's mummy's nature. If she had asked me, I would have denied too. But without seeking my permission, she took this risk. And as a result she is now behind bars."

"Mummy, it is not the right time to discuss about what she should have done. It would be better if we think about to save her and get her out of the jail."

"Therefore, we have come to consult Ashokbhai." Sushilaben scornfully said.

"It is not possible to relieve Kajal until they get post-mortem report and that too in our favour." Advocate Ashok said.

"What should we do now? We must do something which relieves the situation and our tension." Aakash said.

"Let us hope to get the post-mortem report in our favour as early as possible." Saying this advocate Ashok explained the legal procedure of this case in detail.

By that time Sunil came. He had an apprehensive and fearful expressions on his face. Aakash briefed the whole matter to him. After then, they both went to meet Kajal in the Police custody. Kajal was locked in ladies lock up room. As she saw Aakash, she stood up suddenly and came running near him.

"Kajal, what has happened? Why did you try to cure someone?" Aakash asked anxiously.

"Why? What is wrong in curing someone?" Kajal asked a counter question.

Aakash had no answer yet he said:

"You must see the result of it now. Your world and this world is totally different. See, where have you reached today instead of being rewarded?"

"Let them do whatever they want. I have not done anything wrong. I need not worry for that. Whatever will happen, it will be completely fair."

Aakash was shocked to see her faith in existence in such a serious situation. He said.

"What more do you expect now to happen that you have maintained your faith in God? You have no complaint at all."

"No matter whatever the situation is, if you are with me, then I have no fear at all.'

Sunil got completely emotional with the innocent faith of Kajal.

Aakash said, "That is alright that I am with you. But you don't know this world, its people and its laws. Perhaps I will also not be able to prove you innocent and relieve you inspite of putting all the efforts." Aakash said in a disappointing tone.

"Then also I don't worry at all. I don't have any difficulty here. It is enough when you are with me." It was really sensible to see Kajal's innocence but the situation here was different. It was not proper time to respond to her love at present. It was a stressful situation and to think how to get out of the situation.

It was front page news and published in the next day newspapers. The supporters of Savitaben had spread the issue with all interesting spices. "An illegal ayurveda doctor took life of an innocent boy. Government must banish such self-proclaimed ayurveda doctors otherwise killings of innocent people would continue." "An innocent child died of an ignorant, illiterate treatment and unauthorised doctor's poisonous liquid." etc. There was only one demand that the criminal must be punished severely. This event was very huge for a small city like Kalka. The issue was spread like a storm upto Chandigarh.

In the afternoon, A post mortem report was presented in the court which was terribly shocking. It contained the statement that a child was died because of the poison getting spread in the sick body. Advocate Ashok tried but the court ordered Kajal be held in police custody in connection with the death of the child and announced the date of final judgement after three days.

Aakash became disappointed and sorrowful. Arjun and Sunil approached him. Aakash cried a lot putting his head on their shoulders. He was deeply worrying about what would happen now.

These three days passed in severe frustration. Media was greatly exaggerating the news. Organizations were aggressive. There was a mass who wanted to throw piles of questions. Aakash was completely disturbed. There was no hope to save Kajal. Sushilaben also tried to bring any solution meeting with Shilpa's father but the possibilities were highly pessimistic. During these three days, it was only Sunil who was with Aakash. There was no news of Arjun. Shilpa was only making sympathetic phone calls.

Aakash regularly went to meet Kajal in jail but there was no concern on her face. Her faith was permanent.

On the third day morning the newspapers were full with some other important matters. Today's case was not much emphasized. Therefore, it gave some relaxation. Aakash thought: It was good that newspapers were full with some different political disputes. Therefore, their news got less importance.

At 11:00 o' clock sharp, all reached the court. Court was full. Advocate Ashok was not visible anywhere. Aakash's eyes were looking for him. And suddenly he saw that Highcourt scholar advocate Madan Khurana advanced in the court to present Kajal's case. His name was very popular and his fees was high. All lawyers respected him. Aakash was dumbstruck.

Madan Khurana began with an argument "My lord . . ."

"First of all I would like to inform you that it was not an ayurvedic treatment. It was a domestic and safe remedy. It was almost like when you are suffering from headache and your wife serves you with mint tea. It was of the same kind the way aloevera liquid is applied to brighten your face. It was almost like to use emblic while suffering from the problem of indigestion." The opposite lawyer argued that it was not an ordinary plant but was poisonous.

Madan Khurana asked for the plant to bring in the court. And he presented a test report prepared by Dr. Parmeshwaram examined in Chandigarh Botonical Institute which clearly mentioned that this plant was innocently normal and ordinary.

Madan Khuran asked to crush the plant and prepare a liquid. Ant he invited anybody to drink it proclaiming that it was completely ordinary. All frightened but Arjun came and drank that liquid. After half an hour past, he was as normal and healthy as earlier.

Madan Khurana mentioned: The fact is that my lord if this plant had been given to the child earlier, he would have been saved. Child's death has occurred due to his illness. It has happened due to the spreading of feverish poison.

Kajal was proven innocent. Aakash bowed down before Madan Khurana and when he asked for his fees, he looked at Arjun and said "I have got my fees."

Aakash approached Arjun and asked "how did you do that?"

Arjun smiled and said, "I have not done anything great friend. On that day after your departure, I became nervous and tried to find you, made phone calls but I couldn't get you. Therefore I became more worried and in that I read the news in the newspapers next day. So I went to Kajal directly and got the information in detail and directly left for Delhi from there."

Why did you leave for Delhi? And how did you get its solution there?"

"See, I have never shared any private matter of my life but to tell you reality, I am an illegal son of a very potential political leader. Until he accepted me publically that I was his son, I did not want to go to him nor seek any help from him. Therefore, I came Chandigarh to study. I talked to him. He arranged to suppress the news of media. He played strategies to make the organizations inactive and sent Madan Khurana to fight this case.

"But what about Madan Khurana's fees?"

"He will pay for it."

"But friend, why did you compromise with your principles because of me?"

"Oh come on buddy, I have accepted Kajal as my sister, so I fulfilled the duty of a brother." Arjun said smiling.

Although Kajal came back home, questions of people, their rush and doubts were not getting over. Getting fed up one day from all these, Sushilaben told Aakash.

"Aakash, it would be better if you take Kajal in the Himalayan community for three-four months."

"But mummy, she is six months pregnant, what about her care?' Aakash uttered.

"If she stays here, all these people will not allow her, you or the family to live peacefully. Instead, she would be more safe and peaceful there, right Kajal?"

Kajal didn't say anything but Aakash said.

"But what about her health?"

"See, in community deliveries are done without the help of doctors and with naturopathy for years, right? Then what problem Kajal will have? She is also born and brought up there, am I right kajal?"

Kajal nodded.

Aakash said, "But the case is over now and there is no need to worry."

"But the members of society and relatives will create problems. If they see kajal, they will ask many questions, therefore, you must take her away from here."

Aakash agreed reluctantly.

They decided to leave next day morning.

Kajal got ready in the community attire and came on the terrace in the morning. Watching Kajal in the community attire, Aakash laughed and said with surprise.

"Dress is alright but what about the other luggage?"

"There I was living in the absense of luggage. There is no need of any luggage there. Nature is there. Here it was artificiality, therefore luggage was needed."

Aakash took time to comprehend her but there was a strong point in her statement. After sometime, they reached in community, to Baba.

Aakash informed everything of what happened in detail. And also informed about her stay there for sometime. He also consoled that he would continue coming in between. He also mentioned to take Kajal back for delivery if needed.

All the people of community became happy to see Kajal. Aakash also greeted them.

After meeting everybody in the evening, Aakash got ready to leave. Going at a distance, Aakash was trying to fly and Kajal came running to him. It was as if her eyes conveyed: "Take care of yourself. Don't worry about me and keep coming without fail."

Suddenly the atmosphere was filled with that familiar, mysterious charming fragrance. Aakash got intoxicated. He looked before Kajal with smile and then left.

27

akash returned home. From the next day, he began to go to company as per routine.

In the noon, Aakash, Shilpa and Arjun were sitting in the canteen to have lunch. Aakash and Shilpa had just opened their lunch boxes and Shilpa said:

"Did you leave Kajal at Himalaya, Aakash?"

"Yes" suddenly Aakash uttered out of surprise, "but how did you know that?"

Shilpa got little hesitant but suddenly became normal and said "looking at your face and lunch" Aakash would have thought more about that or uttered something, but Arjun said before that.

"Why did you leave Kajal there? Now there is no problem at all."

"I think that she was little frightened with this incident. And people were asking many questions to Kajal. Therefore we thought to bring Kajal back after everything getting peaceful."

"But she is pregnant, at least you should have taken care of her health." Arjun said.

"It is not like that Arjun! She is comfortable in the atmosphere of community and I will take her care and go there in case of need."

Days passed. In the days of job, Aakash's time was passing through but evening times and holidays began bringing a kind of solitude in Aakash's life. In the every corner of house, Kajal's presence was noticed by him. Though she was completely quiet. She was utterly silent. She was present everywhere, yet absent and because of that a kind of isolation created. Someone reminded of every work but there was nobody physically present to perform that work or help either. Someone woke him up at 5.00 in the morning. When he went out of the room, he sensed to be reminded of performing meditation by someone and he sat to perform it. When Kajal was there, she brought snacks and tea well prepared till Aakash got ready. But now he had to go downstairs and wait till her mother offer him tea and snacks. When he returned home in the evening, nobody seemed to wait for him. Nobody came immediately bringing honey and lemon juice. He drank water from the pot on his own and sat to watch TV. It was much difficult to spend the night. When he was single, he used to live in the room happily but now he was feeling an emptiness in the place beside. He got excited and this nervousness grew so extreme that he had to stand up and smell Kajal's night dress. In that he sensed Kajal's physical aroma. He could sense the same divine fragrance. Only after that, he could sleep. His nervousness was growing continuously. Observing him uneasy, her mother asked one day:

"Dear, are you alright? Why have been so nervous nowadays?"

"Mummy, Kajal's absence is disturbing."

"It is because you have got accustomed to her presence. After few days, everything would be normal." Mummy's statement sounded logical and true too.

He said 'but Mummy, I have got habituated to have food from her hands. What about the care which she took about my tea-snacks-food, clothes and cleaning?"

"It will also get set. If anybody else come and take care of your routine life, we will get habituated to her too. It all depends on our mindset and habit."

Mummy's statement was strong. Kajal's absence was noticed during leisurely moments only or else he didn't realize where his time passed in the company. In that, Shilpa was now taking his care more than earlier. She was not interested in cooking still she brought new dishes purchasing from Chandigarh's sweet and snacks' shops. Sometime she used to take interest in Aakash's matters to the extremity of irritation. Oneday, Aakash decided to take leave after lunch time. So she said:

"Why do you want to take leave? Do you plan to go somewhere?"

"Yes . . . I have to go to Chandigarh Leet College of Engineering in Chandigarh where we have studied.

"Why suddenly?" Shilpa continued inquiring.

"Actually, one of my friends Priya is in need of transfer certificate from the university. She has to submit that document in America for further studies." Aakash replied.

"But that can be done by her parents or brother-sister. Why do you need to go?" Shilpa continued asking questions without any right.

"Oh come on, you could ask this question to her when she comes here. Let me go now." Saying this Aakash left. He noticed that Shilpa's face was fouled with the attitude of Aakash.

Aakash thought that Shilpa would be angry for few days but she came his house on the very Sunday at 11.00 in her car. She took lunch with everybody and said after lunch being over.

"Auntie, I am taking Aakash with me to watch a movie. I will take him back in the evening after dinner. Do you have any problem?"

"Oh dear, what problem do I have? You and Aakash have to go. You both are mature. What problem can I have?" That day was spent well. Both watched movie together. They roamed in Rock garden, went to a good hotel and Shilpa dropped him home in the late evening. It was an enjoyable day.

Now Shilpa was paying more attention on Aakash. And this attention extended to mummy and house too, not limited upto Aakash only. One day, while leaving from the company in the evening, Shilpa handed a sweet box to Aakash and said, "This is Kajukatri. It is favourite to auntie, I have brought for her." Aakash accepted the box with a smile and sense of gratitude. In the evening, he handed the sweet box to his mother and said, "This is a sweet box which Shilpa brought for you specially."

"How nice girl she is, isn't she? Mummy said.

"Hmm . . ." Aakash nodded.

"She is educated and virtuous too. When we went to Vaishnodevi, at that time too, she took care of me a lot. Though she is educated and belongs to a rich family, she has no proud at all. She takes care of society, religion, friends and all."

"It is right." Aakash said.

"Daughter-in-law must be like her."

"Where ever she will go, they will be benefited."

"We could also get that benefit." Sushilaben exploded.

"Don't you know that I am married with Kajal?"

"I know that. I don't tell you to leave Kajal. Let Kajal stay in the community for ever and marry with Shilpa here. Kajal will be happy in community and we will be happy here with Shilpa."

"Why, is Kajal not happy here? Does she not give you happiness?"

"Kajal is certainly a girl of heart and good too. She takes care of me and your father a lot. But she is not capable to change herself to understand the society, people, rituals and arrangements of this world. The innocence which is important over there is considered as foolishness here in our world."

Aakash thought his mother's argument is true. It was not possible to argue with his mother's logic. And he had liked Shilpa too in the corner of his heart. Shilpa had a style, grace, strategy and modernity. She was able to live with the social customs. In addition, she belonged to a wealthy family. Aakash's life would become happy and wealthy if she comes in his life as his wife. It was also possible for his mother to satisfy the political determination. Still Aakash didn't give his permission nor show any willingness. He was only quiet. He came in his room without saying anything.

Again he missed the presence of Kajal. His heart was getting attached with Shilpa, still somewhere something was disturbing. A sense of deceiving badly to someone was giving a sting to him. A storm of dual thoughts continued harassing him. What should I do? Why should I do? Why shouldn't I do? What will happen if I do this and what will not happen? Thoughts quarreled and caused pain to Aakash. He would always think to go to Himalaya to get relieved on Sunday. He would think to go there in the community, meet Kajal and baba, but on each Saturday, Shilpa would make any plan to go with Aakash on Sunday. They would sometime go to watch movie, sometime to take dinner or sometime to visit to Pinjor garden or sometime to a river bank. Now Shilpa had also began to take liberties. In the movie, she would sit touching and holding his hand. In the emotional scenes, she would move his hands gently, while in the terror scenes, she would hold his hand tightly. She would lay on Aakash's shoulder in the moments of boredom. In the expressive scenes, she would pretend to cry and would invite Aakash to wipe her eyes. Aakash was also getting comfortable. He would kiss and hug her in loneliness too. But he didn't get more loneliness than this otherwise he would have gone ahead too. And Aakash had a sense of trust that Shilpa would have accompanied him.

Till he was in the company of Shilpa, he would remain involved in her beauty and in her cosmetic smell. But the moment he got lonely, he would get pain and suffering. He could not comprehend why was he getting so much pain?

One Saturday, he firmly decided to go to Himalayan community tomorrow where there was Kajal. Fortunately, that Saturday no plan was made by Shilpa for Sunday. He told his mother that evening "Mummy, I would go to meet Kajal tomorrow. Her delivery time is nearby, so I should go to see her health. And if necessary, I would bring her back with me."

"No problem son, but don't go tomorrow as we have to go to a private and familial party tomorrow evening. And it is essential to attend."

"At where is the party organized?"

"That is a suspense which would be disclosed tomorrow." Sushilaben smiled saying this.

Next day in the evening, when Subhashbhai sent a car to take them, Aakash realized that it was a party arranged at Shilpa's home and theefore she had not made any plan for the day.

When they reached there, Subhashbhai and his wife came to receive them at the gate. Taking them inside, they introduced them with their customer friends, political friends and with their family members. Aakash was amazed observing the results of political relationship developed by his mother. Subhashbhai had convinced her thoroughly. Within no time, Shilpa arrived in a white long frock. Shilpa was looking splendidly charming. She was looking so attractive to catch the eyes of all the party comers. When she came near, Subhashbhai spoke addressing everybody, "Friends, today is an event of happiness. I really feel pleasure to inform you that I announce my daughter Shilpa's engagement with Aakash." All cheered with a round of applause. Aakash could not understand what to say and do. He felt a deep pain. Before he gets comfortable, a plate of sweets and two rings were brought there. In the presence of everybody, they gave engagement rings to each other and got the acceptance of engagement.

Aakash was getting hurt extremely throughout the function. He was confused in the dual war of logic and argument, pain-happiness and true-false. Hardly they left late night after the party being over. As it was Subhashbhai's car and driver, it was not appropriate to say anything but he told to his mom going home:

"What did you do this? What was the need to hurry so much?"

"I have only done everything hurriedly, but not done anything wrong."

"You have done wrong too. You know very well that Kajal is going to be my child's mother. She is my legal wife."

"It is proper to consider her a wife only—not a legal wife. There is no proof of marriage. And these community people are not the legal citizens of India that they would come to fight here."

"Does it mean that we should do injustice? What about the future of my child?" Aakash asked.

"This is not injustice but a proper conduct into which both the parties would be happy. This world is not appropriate for Kajal. Kajal was not fit for your future. You should not stick to love only, love is not everything in life. You could be a businessman through Subhashbhai's reference and we can earn more prestige too in the society. And now remains the matter of the child. So the children of community are considered the whole community's children. They have no individual parents. So they will have one more child. And they will have mother, indeed." Sushilaben said.

"It was you who were appreciating this marriage of mine in your social meetings. It was you who had stated that my son has contributed in the development of tribal class marrying an illiterate girl of community."

"You will not understand. This is pure politics. And you need not understand this."

"Then what should I do?"

"Let the things happen the way I have planned. And you will be happy and wealthy. I am your mother so I would never intend anything wrong for you. So trust me."

"Just like me … See, I also try to be happy quietly, right?" Sureshbhai interjected.

"Just shut your mouth. Why do you interject when you have no idea about anything." Sushilaben scornfully uttered.

"Do you understand now Aakash that's why do I try to find happiness in my work?" Sureshbhai said. All kept quiet. Somewhere the sentence touched to Aakash.

Next day, Shilpa announced about her engagement with Aakash in the company. She distributed the sweets to everybody. All congratulated her. Only Arjun came and said, "Aakash, I didn't assume you to be like this." Aakash kept quiet.

Aakash's pain increased. Shilpa's feelings and domination were growing more now. One day, Aakash who had been intolerant in his pain said to his mother,

"Mummy, let me go and meet Kajal once. Let me see my child once. Then I will break that relation."

"Why can't you break now instead later on?"

"I don't know but I feel strongly that I deceive someone and play with someone's feelings. I am doing something wrong."

"Remove the sense from your mind that you are doing something wrong. You are only compromising with time. Once you remove this notion from mind, you will forget everything slowly and gradually. And you will get healthy when you forget the things."

"But let me go once."

"No . . . you don't have to go."

"You are denying now but what if my wings grow and carry me there? What will you do then?"

If wings were to grow, they would have grown long ago. It has been four months to Kajal's departure. How many times did you think to go there and visit Kajal? You are getting hurt still the wings have not grown yet. Now the wings also understand that you are right and they are with your decision. Nature has allowed you the power of taking decision on your own, and you have taken it up."

"The same nature is paining me to go there once. I want to meet Kajal and console her that we have taken this decision under certain circumstances. And she will understand. She will accept my this decision too, mummy."

Sushilaben had trust in that matter because Kajal had never expressed her desire. She was thoroughly dedicated.

"Ok . . . Go . . . But if you convey everything directly, in it there is a risk of your life too." Sushilaben said. Aakash recalled the scornfully furious face of Bheemo.

"Yes, it is posssible but I will talk about this at the appropriate time. I will talk about why I could not come.

I will inform her that the situation is not normal. I will promise her to frequently visit."

"And still if they don't permit, what will you do then?"

"Don't think much. I know these people closely. Baba favours freedom. They are not forceful people. I will talk about it if I find the situation proper, otherwise I will just return with a promise."

"Ok, but take care."

Aakash felt relieved after getting permission from his mother. But the pain continued. He was not prepared to lie for and before Kajal and his nature too was not such. He thought to say truth but how to say it, will decide after observing the situation only.

Next day morning, he got ready to go to Himalayan hills after so many days-months.

He wished and wings grew and he began flying in the sky. He floated in the air.

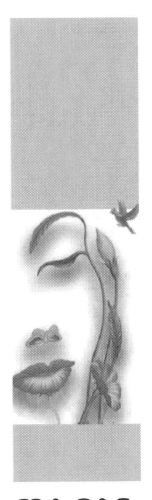

KAJAL

28

The same beautiful Himalayan mounts, valley, pine trees and streams were passed by, it was breezing slowly but today Aakash's attention was not there although his eyes were open. It was on the storm going on inside, on the strong movements of feelings. For some time, he would foresee a self-established factory helped by Subhashbhai, luxury, car and bungalow while sometime, he would foresee his unseen baby and innocent Kajal. Sometime, he would think of his mother's emotions and plans; while on the next moment, he would think of Bheemo's furious face and bitterly cursed sentences. Today he was passing through fear and courage simultaneously. He sensed courage inside him to talk about his engagement with Shilpa to the community people and simultaneously he sensed fear in the responsive anger of Bheemo.

In spite of these paradoxes and complexities, he didn't feel for a single moment to escape from the situation in the depth of his heart. He was only concerned on how to feel and how to manage the whole matter so that community Baba and Kajal get it with the least shock and understand his truth (the matter). He was being more fearful to face Kajal compared to Bheemo, still he was proceed to tell everything.

He could see now the same mountains, a narrow valley in the middle and a flat slope. He slowly got down in small ground near Baba's residence keeping all the thoughts aside, he moved ahead with a mental readiness to respond to whatever happens. At that moment Baba came out and uttered looking at him,

"Hello Aakash! How is everything going on?" Baba didn't ask to Aakash why he was not seen for a long time.

"Fine, everything is going well."

"Has everything got settled?" Baba asked this addressing to the event happened with Kajal.

"Yes, it is getting settled."

"So you have come to take Kajal back? Do you know you have been father of a darling daughter?"

"What do you say! When?"

"Before 10 days."

"How is Kajal, Baba?"

"She is fine. She is so well that she had just come to serve me the snacks. If you had come early, you would have been able to meet her." Aakash thought 'I have come late intentionally so that I don't have to face her.'

Aakash said, "Fine."

"Let's go to meet Kajal. She will be very happy to see you." Baba uttered and Aakash felt a deep pain in a corner of his heart."

"Before going there, I would like to talk to you on an important matter, Baba." Saying this he went on a stone and stood there when Baba came, they both sat there. Baba said "Now tell me, what the matter is?"

Aakash began slowly and logically talking about all the events after Kajal's departure from Kalka. He presented all the arguments with a maximum effort of satisfaction. He also informed him that Shilpa works together with him in his company. He also said that our world is tough and full of problems for Kajal. He also convinced that he is going to marry with Shilpa for the sake of his parents and taking his family, society, future and world into consideration.

Baba listened to everything quietly with closed eyes. When Aakash finished, he looked at him. Aakash lowered his eyes.

Baba uttered "Son no one knows what the fate of my Kajal will be. Let it happen what is desired by existence . . ."

"Baba I am very concerned about Kajal. I don't have any courage to talk to Kajal on this matter."

"I also sense the same trouble; but we should do one thing. Let us talk to Bapu and a few more people of community. I am sure that they will understand you."

"Even if they don't understand, I am ready to face any punishment given by them as I am also equally responsible in this fault. I should not have hurried to take Kajal in that world."

"It's alright. You stay here. I will go and bring them here. Baba left Aakash to stay there. After sometime, he returned with Bapu, Bheemo, one woman and a man. Bapu said immediately after coming.

"What happened, dear?" Bapu said lovingly, "What mistake was done by Kajal which caused you to take this step?"

"Bapu, it is not Kajal's fault. The fault lies with our world, its manners strategies, custom-rituals, society and behavior. I had to take this decision helplessly."

"If it is possible, would request you to think on this matter once again. Kajal will not disturb you. She will stay as you say. But she will be very upset if her heart is hurt." Bapu cried saying this.

"Bapu, you need not plead this way before him. I'll see how he is able to go out from here now. I wanted to kill him for the very first time but Baba interfered and saved him. Now Kajal will have to suffer as a result of his being rescued. I had told you that people of that world are utterly selfish, strategic and cheaters, but neither you nor Kajal believed me."

"Bheemo, please be quiet. If Aakash had been so down in his character, he would not have come to tell even this. There is something inside him which has forced him to come here. It is his honesty."

"Baba, don't say anything. Let Bheemo punish whatever he desires. I deserve his punishment. Bheemo, I don't have any problem." Saying this Aakash came forward.

"Bheemo, Kajal will not be happy if Aakash is either punished or killed. Whatever his destiny aspired has come before us. We have to accept it." Bapu said.

"But it is very difficult for me to forgive someone who is responsible for Kajal's present state. Keep your knowledge with you. I will not leave a man who has troubled and pained Kajal." Bheemo was fully passionate. He was furious enough to beat Aakash coming ahead but he stopped by Baba's words."

Baba said, "You are right. Aakash must be punished. But it is only Kajal's right to punish Aakash. If Kajal wishes, you can certainly kill him. We have no problem."

All decided to go to community together. All thought it right to convince Kajal. It was tough but inevitable too.

It was time for him to pass through that narrow track which was at the edge of mountain. Today, for the first time, Kajal was not with him. He had to take his own care. And to his surprise, he could pass through the path without committing any mistake. It was because he had to meet Kajal or existence was justifying his decision true.

Everybody reached where community people lived. Kajal looked Aakash from a distance. She was seating taking her daughter in her lap. As she saw Aakash, she ran toward him and said:

"Aakash, see, this is our daughter." Saying this, she offered her daughter to him and Aakash took her in his hug. He started kissing and fondling her.

"We have named her 'Rutu', did you like it?" Kajal said:

"Yes" Aakash was confused. He was in trouble on how to begin.

He could only say "Kajal!" Saying this he lowered his head and stood there. Baba and Bapu came near. They explained everything to Kajal in detail. Aakash has come to meet you for the last time. He has come to take a farewell. He is now going to settle in his world. They also told her that he is going to marry Shilpa now.

Kajal was stunned as if she was a stone. A woman came running and took baby from Aakash's hands. Aakash hardly said, "Kajal . . . Kajal . . . . It is the situation which has caused me to do this."

Kajal only said this much in response.

"It's ok Aakash, give Shilpa love on my behalf."

All were crying. All stood around. They were standing in the same way as they were during Kajal's marriage. On that day, the tears were out of happiness and departure. Whereas, today the tears were of pain and suffering. Nobody uttered a single word. All were passing through the same kind of pain and tears of last time. Bheemo was crying like anything.

Kajal's eyes were dry; they were full of terrible pain. Aakash felt suffocation in this heavy situation for which only he himself was the responsible person. He left taking permission of all. He looked into the eyes of everyone but he could not dare to look into the eyes of Kajal. He went to the open ground and slowly stood there. He looked towards the sky and bowed down. The wings grew. He was about to fly and he aspired to look at Kajal for once and for the last time. He looked at Kajal and into her eyes.

Kajal's eyes were filled with tears. There was immeasurable pain inside. They were deep. Tears were about to come out but that epiphany meeting of four eyes changed everything.

Actually they were only moments but in the moments of those four eyes meeting, Aakash saw that his body has been separated from him and he has leapt into the heart of Kajal. What remained was this huge universe which was consisted of whole Brahmand. It was an ocean of love only everywhere. He understood everything in that epiphany moment.

He understood everything what he was not able to in his life through words, arguments, thoughts and doubts.

There is an event of Krishna's life. One day Udhav asked to Krishna: "Dear God, I have heard that a man could see all his life lived by him in the last moments when he is on his death-bed. Is it true? Is it possible to see all the 70-80 years of life within few seconds only?"

Krishna said: "I will let you know this later on, let us go first and take a bath in river.".

Udhav and Krishna went to the river for bath. They went to the river to take bath and suddenly Krishna caught Udhav's neck and drowned in it into water. Udhav was scared. He tried to rescue him but could not escape from Krishna's strong trap. Now the death was definite. His whole life began passing through his eyes. After sometime Krishna lifted his hand and he came out of water.

Krishna said: "you were in water for a few moments only. Now tell me, did you come across your life?"

"Yes . . . Lord . . ." Saying this he bowed down to Krishna.

Aakash could also see everything. He understood everything.

He got the mystery of Devvani bird and its bite. It had brought Kajal's message of love. The mystery of his wings and flight was resolved. He used to come to Himalaya through wings neither for community nor for Baba but for Kajal only. Existence brought him here for Kajal's innate love.

Co-incidentally, he had purchased a garland for Kajal as a marriage sign which was in the customs of community. The mystery of how community people especially Kajal understood the language of silence, birds, trees and stones was resolved to Aakash now. It is because love has no language. He also understood Baba's insistence of meditation. It was because of meditation, he had been able to take part in the present event. He also experienced that he was alive today just because of Kajal. He realized that this life was for Kajal only. He also understood that whenever Kajal used the word 'existence', it meant only 'love'. It also became clear to him that Kajal had left this wonderful natural place the loving people of community and Baba and entered into his world just because of his love. He could also see that the fragrance from Kajal's body in the absence of any cosmetics was invitation on her part—it was pure love.

He could also see his mother's strategies. He could see Sandhya's physical love, Priya's mental love and Shilpa's socially calculative love. His mind which was accustomed to monetary and worldly objects could not even momentarily sense Kajal's in depth love in the same way as a fish could never see the ocean inspite of living into it.

Everything was clear now. His skepticism regarding Kajal and Bheemo's love vanished completely. What remained was only unbroken immeasurable and in-depth love, love and only love into which Kajal was visible everywhere.

He looked at Kajal once again. Her tear was about to get out of her eyes. He realized that if it fell down on the earth, it would destroy the whole world and bring complete destruction.

Aakash ran with his wings. He snatched a knife attached on the waist of one community man. He was about to cut his wings with a knife but before he does, his wings fell down naturally. He ran and caught Kajal in his hug before everybody. He drank her tears. He hugged Kajal hard and showered so many kisses on her face.

He understood that what he considered truth was not actually truth but love was the ultimate truth. He got the importance of meditation. He understood that he would not have been able to experience this sight and perception in the absence of meditation.

There was a huge change in the atmosphere. Tears of sadness in everybody's eyes turned into tears of happiness.

Baba looked above the sky and waving his two hands in the air said:

"Yes . . . God . . . Yes!

Discourse Narration

Years before, I had a chance to stay in a separate small resort in Nubraveli located in Lah—Ladakh. There was not an iota of population and modernity compared to the spaciousness of Nubraveli. It was a narrow valley on the two edges of which were straight and sloppy mountains between the two of which a so called river was flowing there. The scene was charming, mysterious and especially different to some extent. It seemed to leave a different print on the mind and heart. In the morning, when I was communicating with my friends' children, I recalled of Osho's story "Juho" and the present novel's seeds were deeply sown somewhere.

The story of "Juho" was somehow like this:

There was a girl who belonged to the mountain state. She was as innocent, beautiful and a girl of heart as the mountains. She was married to a boy residing in a city. The girl could not find proper co-ordination with the urban artificiality and became uncomfortable there. She was living by heart whereas the city and its people were living through mind and intellect as a result of which she became the victim of meaninglessness. Her heart grew impatient to go back to the mountains. Every morning, she would ask to her mother-in-law that 'mom, can I go to my village in the mountains?" and every time her mother in law would reply

"Juho" which means "tomorrow". Days passed. Whenever she asked to go to her village, she was replied "Juho". Finally her inner pain reached the extremity of impatience and she died.

It is believed that the dead girl is still flying in the mountains being a bird and saying "Juho . . . . Juho . . . Juho."

Osho was also reminded with this story. His trouble-free and exact sermons and meditation also brought to mind. The seed of this story continued developing with the inspiration of Osho and is present before you as a result of "Pankh: The Wings" today.

To develop the story, real life characters and their psychology was inevitable which widened from the existent life. Theatrical episodes were added to mention the essence and give a pace to its psychology.

Today people firmly assume that innocent and selfless love in contemporary times is next to impossible. But as per my experience, if one has the honesty to identify it and qualified psychology, it is possible to feel the essence and expression of such love. As the reader is preoccupied with his/her own assumptions and spectacles of experience, it was mandatory to create a personality who was born and brought up in a different geographic state and in a natural atmosphere to take him/her into trust. Therefore, a camp was created residing into Himalaya and living a natural life. Osho's story "Juho" and its character—an innocent girl was moving slowly and getting prepared in my eyes and thereby a Kajal was created.

Aakash is a character who resides in almost everybody to some extent. All determine higher values and yet live at an average rate. This also a reality. But Aakash lives with the consciousness of his sensibility toward higher values because he is honest from inside. His love toward nature is not so called but truly existent. Therefore, he is not just satisfied recalling the nature in his leisurely time but always puts efforts to get involved into planning for it. It is because of this reason; he is developed although beginning to live his life at a lower rate. He gets the messages of nature, of existence and this existence leads him in unknown places of Himalaya and introduces him with Kajal. Existence is mysterious, arbitrary and deep which leads the human being unconsciously into the direction of love.

Aakash too finds obstacles in accepting this situation and still develops with the support of nature, Kajal, Baba and Osho's sermons and meditation experiments. His sensibility and vision is enlarged due to all these. His inner self is extended to find, search and accept love and the story moves to its end.

Characters are real and their psychology is genuine. As a result of enlightenment, life reaches to its height which I have experienced with Osho's sermons and meditations. The story is crafted so that readers can perceive Osho in the models of life, human being and psychology.

Aakash and Sandhya's relationship had gender attraction, sex and body in its centre. Aakash and Priya had mind, intellect and logic in its centre. Aakash and Shilpa had societal norms, determination and calculations in its centre. Aakash and Kajal had existence and unconditional love in its centre.

The story would have met with an end if Aakash had not risen from the common human being. If his sensibility had not gone up from him, he would not have been able to identify the hint given from the existence. What if he had not put trust into unknown hands of existence!

It became possible in case of Aakash due to his meditation which was honestly and inevitably done and due to understanding ability of Osho's sermons, Baba and Arjun's preaching, Himalaya's nature and the existential acceptance of Kajal's innocent love.

This is a developmental story of psychology. This is an effort to widen the recessed psychology and not to pretend to look happy through external compromise.

I expect my message to be accepted.

—**Ramesh Patel**